J.D. RHOADES

A JACK KELLER NOVEL

DEVILS AND DUST

Copyright © 2015 by J.D. Rhoades

Cover design by 2Faced Design
Interior designed and formatted by Tianne Samson with E.M. Tippetts Book Designs

ISBN 978-1-940610-17-7
eISBN 978-1-940610-48-1

First hardcover edition February 2015 by Polis Books, LLC
60 West 23rd Street
New York, NY 10010
www.PolisBooks.com

POLIS BOOKS

To the memory of my father, Jerry Delano Rhoades, Sr. (1933-2014)

CHAPTER ONE

THE *JEFE* AFFECTIONATELY CALLED HIM *El Poeta* — the Poet. It had nothing to do with literary talent; in fact, the man driving the truck was almost completely illiterate. The nickname was in honor of the man's ability to curse. El Poeta was a virtuoso of invective. The *jefe* once said El Poeta could curse for twenty minutes and not repeat himself once.

The road he was driving gave him plenty of inspiration. The old truck bounced and rattled over the corrugated surface, abusing El Poeta's spine mercilessly.

"*Hijo de mil putas!*" He spat as the truck bottomed out on a particularly bad pothole. "*Me cago en la leche de tu puta madre!*" It was unclear if his rage was directed against the road, the truck, or the world in general.

Someone banged on the wall of the truck, behind El Poeta's head. "*Parate, pinche idiota!*" he shouted back. This close to the border was no place to stop for a piss break. That's what the buckets in the cargo area were for. If they sloshed a bit because of the bad road, that wasn't El

1

Poeta's problem. This was the road he knew the Border Patrol never watched. El Poeta didn't know if they just didn't know about it or if some palms had been greased to make them look the other way, and he didn't give a damn. His job was to drive the big truck to a deserted area just north of the border, hand each of the *pollos* in the back two bottles of water, point the way north, and get the hell out. It was up to them to figure it out from there. He slowed, stuck his head out the window, and squinted at the sky. It was still full dark, the stars glittering coldly above.

Suddenly, El Poeta saw headlights ahead. "*Mierda!*" he muttered. This road had always been clear before. As he drew closer, he saw two sets of lights, both belonging to large SUVs. They were side by side facing toward him, blocking the road.

Border Patrol. It could be no one else.

"*Me cago en Dios y los trescientos sesenta y cinco santos del año!*" El Poeta snarled in frustration as he pulled the truck to a stop. He briefly thought of bailing out and running for it, but he knew that would be idiotic. Even if he did manage to outrun the officers, he'd be stuck in the middle of the *pinche* scrubland with no *pinche* water and no *pinche* way home. No, he was fucked and he knew it. The headlights picked out a man dressed in a dark-green uniform and Smokey Bear hat striding toward the truck. El Poeta rolled down the window. He blinked as a flashlight was shined in his face.

The officer didn't speak for a moment. Then, "*Fuera del carro. Manos en el aire.*" The man's Spanish accent was terrible.

El Poeta obeyed and climbed out of the truck. He put his hands in the air, grinning in what he hoped was a placating manner.

"*En sus rodillas,*" the voice growled.

El Poeta was puzzled. This wasn't how it was supposed to go. Still, they had the guns. Slowly, he got down on his knees. Another uniformed man walked past him, to check out the back of the truck, El Poeta assumed. He couldn't see the faces of the men in the glare of the flashlight, but he did see a shotgun. A third man was climbing into the truck. El Poeta heard the engine fire back up. The driver dangled an arm out the window. El Poeta could see the network of tattoos covering the exposed flesh below the short sleeve. They looked like spider webs, wrapped around the man's forearm.

El Poeta's forehead wrinkled. "Hey," he said in English. "What the fuck…" it was the last thing he said before the man behind him blew off his head with the shotgun.

CHAPTER TWO

THE FRONT DOOR SWUNG OPEN. A harsh blast of sunlight lit up the cool dim interior of the bar. A young woman straightened up from where she had been placing bottles in the well behind the bar. She was short and broad-shouldered, her curves accentuated by her tight T-shirt and jeans. Her shoulder-length black hair was pulled back beneath a paisley scarf.

"We ain't open yet, hon," the young woman said to the figure who stood in the doorway.

That person stepped inside and closed the door. She was a slender woman in her mid-forties. Despite the desert heat outside, she was dressed in a long-sleeved white blouse and black denim jeans. She wore black gloves on her hands, one of which rested atop a gold-handled cane.

The woman brushed a lock of her long ash-blond hair out of her eyes with her free hand. "Mind if I wait inside?" she said softly.

The bartender looked her over. Her eyes narrowed at the sight of the gloves. It made her pretty face look hard. "Kind of hot to be wearing gloves, ain't it?" she said pointedly.

"I've got some scars on my hands," the woman said in the same mild tone. "I don't like people staring."

The look of suspicion on the bartender's face turned to embarrassment. "I'm sorry, hon. I didn't know. It's just that..."

The woman in the doorway waved it off. "No problem. Someone came into my place, wearing gloves in this heat—I'd get a little suspicious, too."

The bartender smiled. "C'mon in and have a seat. I reckon we can open early today." The woman took a seat on a barstool and leaned her cane against the bar. The bartender extended a hand. "I'm Jules. Short for Julianne, but nobody calls me that."

The other woman took the offered hand. "Angela."

There was a moment's hesitation, almost imperceptible, before Jules smiled again. "What can I get you?"

Angela scanned the beers lined up behind the bar. "Shiner Bock," she said. "And a glass of ice water, if you've got it."

"Comin' right up," she said.

Angela watched her as she fetched the beer and the water. She looked too young to be tending bar, especially in a rough-looking place like this, but she moved with perfect assurance, as if she were in her own home.

"Thanks," Angela said as the bartender put the beer in front of her. She handed over the money. "So, where's Henry?" She gestured at the sign above the bar. WELCOME TO HENRY'S, the sign proclaimed in faded red letters in an old-timey typeface.

Jules glanced at the sign. "Henry was my dad," she said. "He died last year. Liver cancer."

"I'm sorry," Angela said.

Jules shrugged, a gesture of resignation that looked too old for her. "Ain't nothin' for you to be sorry about."

"Still."

Jules smiled. "Thanks." She bent over again and went back to setting up the bar.

After a few minutes, Angela spoke up again. "I'm looking for Jack

Keller."

Jules froze, her hand halfway to putting a rocks glass on the shelf. She finished the movement, then stood up. Angela couldn't read the look on her face.

"So," Jules said in a small voice, "you're *that* Angela."

Angela took a sip of the water before replying. "He's mentioned me?"

Jules's mouth twisted. "Only in his sleep." She went back to work, but her motions now were angry, abrupt. "He ain't here."

"Is he working today?" Angela said.

Jules stood up. "What do you want with Jack?"

"Jack's a friend of mine," Angela replied, "and a friend of my husband."

The girl looked suspicious again. "Your husband know you're out here looking for Jack?"

Angela shook her head. "Doubtful. He disappeared about three weeks ago."

"So he run off," Jules said, her voice rising, "and you're looking up your old flames?"

"Jules," Angela's voice was low, but it cracked like a whip. It silenced the young woman's building tirade like shutting off a tap. "Jack's a friend, that's all. I'm not here to steal him away from you."

At that moment, the door swung open again, bringing in the light and the noise of a truck roaring by on the highway.

The man who stepped inside easily topped six feet. He had gotten leaner and darker since Angela had last seen him, and the desert sun had dried and toughened him like leather. The biggest shock, however, was his hair.

"You cut all your hair off," Angela said.

Jack Keller looked at her for a long moment, then shrugged. He ran a hand over the short stubble. "It gets pretty hot around here."

"I noticed." There was another long silence. "Can we talk?" Angela said finally.

Keller glanced at Jules, then back at Angela. "I have to get to work," he said. "But yeah. For a few minutes." He gestured toward a booth near the back. Angela walked over and took a seat. Keller followed. He sat across from her, hands folded on the table. His face gave nothing away. A moment later, Jules slid into the seat next to him. She slid an arm around his broad shoulders, her eyes daring Angela to say anything. Keller looked uncomfortable for a moment, then his face returned to its former impassivity. "How'd you find me?" he asked.

Angela looked amused. "After all those years in the bail bond business, you think I forgot how to run a skip trace? And you weren't even trying to cover your tracks, Keller."

"My question," Jules said, "is why?"

Angela glanced at Jules, then sighed. "Oscar's gone," she told Keller.

"That your husband?" Jules said, with a pointed look at Keller.

"Yes," Angela said. "My husband."

Keller looked down at his hands. "I'm sorry."

"He didn't die, Jack. And he didn't leave me. He disappeared."

Keller looked up. For the first time, a spark of interest flared in his eyes. "I'm sorry," he said again. "Where was he when you last…" The spark in his eyes died like an ember. He looked back down at his hands.

"He'd finally got enough money to bring his sons here from Colombia," Angela went on. "But they didn't show. He went to talk to the…to the people who were bringing them."

"Smugglers," Keller said.

"Well, he wasn't legal," Angela said, "so he couldn't very well do it any other way. But they couldn't tell him anything. Or wouldn't. I don't know. He was frantic. He said he was going to go find them. He told me not to worry." She barked a short, mirthless laugh. "Like *that* was going to happen."

Jules spoke up. "What does this have to do with Jack?" she demanded.

Angela didn't answer. She just looked at Keller. It was he who finally spoke. "She wants me to help find him."

"Why does she think…?"

"Because that's what I used to do for her. Track people down." He took a deep breath and blew it out slowly. Angela looked at him, unmoving. "And because Oscar Sanchez was my friend. I owe him." He looked at Angela. "And I owe you," he told her.

She shook her head. "You don't owe me anything, Jack," she said. "Any debt you ever owed me, you paid a long time ago."

"Yeah. Well," Jules said, "that's good to know."

Keller looked at her and his face softened. Angela felt a stab of jealousy. She quickly snuffed it out. *You took another road long ago,* she scolded herself, *and now you'll see it through. To the end.* "Actually," she said to Jules, "I don't know if I want Jack to help me with this. There's someone else I want him to talk to first."

Keller looked up. "Who?"

Angela slid out of the booth and stood up. "Lucas is with me. He's across the road."

"Who's Lucas?" Jules said.

"Another friend," Keller replied. He nudged Jules slightly with his hip. She got up slowly, her face expressionless. "So," she said in a flat voice, "you coming back?"

"Yeah," Keller said, "I am."

"You can come with us if you like," Angela said. "This affects you, too."

"You're goddamn right it—" Jules began, then she stopped. She looked at Angela. "I can?"

"Like I said, Jules," Angela said, "I'm here as a friend. On behalf of a friend. That's all."

Jules looked at her. Then she smiled slightly. "Okay," she said. "Look, I'm sorry—"

"Don't be," Angela said. "It's okay. You coming?"

Jules shook her head. "No. I got a business to run here." She looked at Keller. "And don't take all day," she said severely. "It's Friday, and this place is gonna fill up fast come five o'clock. I'm gonna need you."

Keller smiled. "I know. I'll be back."

The bright sunlight felt like a physical shock as they stepped out of the bar. A semi roared past on the two-lane desert highway in front of them, diminishing rapidly into the far distance, leaving only whirling dust and empty silence behind. There was no other traffic. A black

Cadillac CTS with a sticker from a car-rental company was parked across the highway, in front of one of the units of a worn-out looking motel. A sign in front announced it was the DES RT S NDS INN.

"Yeah," Angela said as they crunched across the gravel parking lot. "I bet the place really jumps."

"You'd be surprised," Keller said. "I don't know where they come from, but they start showing up right after five. The place fills up. The motel makes a few bucks giving them a place to sleep it off."

"Everybody wins," Angela said. They crossed the road. "Lucas said he'd be at the pool."

He was. Major Lucas Berry, U.S. Army Medical Corps (Ret.) sat at the edge of the postage-stamp-sized swimming pool behind the hotel, dangling his legs in the tepid water. He was dressed in a brightly colored pair of swimming trunks that provided a sharp contrast to his dark-brown skin. A cooler of iced Tecate beer sat on the edge of the pool beside him. When he saw Keller and Angela, he swung his legs out of the water and stood up. He was taller than Keller by a couple of inches, and broader. He extended his hand. "Sergeant," he said. His voice was a deep baritone that sounded like it should be coming from a burning bush.

Keller shook his hand. "Major," he smiled. Then the smile faded. "You here to see just how crazy I am?"

"Pretty much," Berry said. "Pull up a chair. Have a beer." Keller pulled up one of the plastic chairs that ringed the pool. He shook his head at the offered beer. Berry raised an eyebrow slightly at that, but made no comment.

"I'm going back in the room," Angela said. "This heat's too much for me."

As she walked away, Keller asked softly, "How's she been?"

Berry shrugged. "Worried sick about you, for starters."

Keller grimaced. "Sorry," he muttered and dropped his gaze to the floor. "When did she and Oscar get married?"

"About three months ago." Berry grinned. "Funny story, really. She asked *him*."

Keller looked up. "She did?"

"Yeah. He wasn't going to ask her, for fear she'd think it was just for the green card. But, good Catholic that he is, he was getting more and more conflicted about just shacking up. So she broke the logjam for him."

"Sound like you've all talked a lot."

"Yeah," Berry said. "Just as friends, though. Not professionally." He raised his sunglasses and looked directly at Keller. "But I'm not here to fill you in on Angela's life. She can do that herself. I'm here to talk about you."

Keller sighed. "I'm fine, Lucas."

"Uh-huh. That's why you got up out of a hospital bed, checked out against medical advice, and walked off without saying a word. And why you headed for, of all places, the desert."

Keller closed his eyes. It hadn't made any sense to him either. He had never had an easy life, but it was the Kuwaiti desert where things had really gone bad for him. He saw the burning Bradley fighting vehicle, heard his men screaming. *Burning, they're burning*…he took a quick, deep intake of breath and opened his eyes. Lucas was looking at him.

"I—we—spent years getting you out of that desert in your head," he said softly, "and yet you end up here. In the real one."

"Well," Keller said, "getting out of that desert meant starting to care about things again. About people. And that's what put me here." Lucas acknowledged the point with a nod of his head.

"And," Keller went on, "to tell you the truth, it's not bad here. I'm working. And I'm not wrecking myself doing it."

"You don't miss it?" Lucas said. "The hunt? The takedown? You used to say you lived for that. It was the only thing that got you up in the morning."

"And you used to tell me how fucked up that was."

Berry chuckled. "That I did." He fished another beer out of the cooler. "So you won't be coming back with us."

Keller looked at the water, shimmering in the blazing sun. "I didn't say that." He stood up. "How long are you staying?"

Berry gestured toward the nearly empty motel. "Well, much as I hate to leave this fine resort and its luxurious amenities, probably in the morning."

"I'll let you know then," Keller said. He walked off toward the bar.

CHAPTER THREE

AT LEAST THE TRUCK WASN'T bouncing as badly anymore. It was still stifling, and the smell from the toilet buckets was overwhelming. The last of the battery-powered lights was failing, so it would soon be pitch dark as well. The people crammed into the back of the truck sat shoulder to shoulder, hip to hip, knees drawn up, their misery wrapped around them.

"Why is this taking so long?" Edgar asked his older brother Ruben. "They said we'd only be in this truck a little while."

Ruben shrugged. He put his arm around his brother. Everything had taken longer than the *coyotes* said it would: the plane ride to Mexico, the bus ride to the little border town where they were taken to a warehouse, then packed like sardines into the truck, and now this. Ruben thought back to the moment a few hours ago when the truck had stopped. He was sure the sound he had heard was a gunshot. So were most of the other people, but they had stopped talking about it when the truck began moving again. Now, everything was silent except the roar of the engine and the whining of the wheels. It sounded like they were on an actual paved highway rather than the rough gravel roads they had traveled on for so long. *We must be north of the border. So why aren't they letting us out like they said?* The truck ground to a stop. The passengers stirred. There was a brief silence, then a loud creak, a banging noise, and the cargo compartment was flooded with bright light as the back door rattled up. Ruben tightened his grip around his brother's shoulder.

The people in the truck put their hands up, shielding their faces from the light. Two Anglo men were standing on either side of the entrance. They were holding weapons pointed at the people inside. A young girl near the entrance screamed. One of the men swiveled his weapon toward the sound. He had a shaved head and a scraggly beard. Ruben could see the tattoos on his arms beneath the sleeves of his black T-shirt. There were more tattoos on his neck. The tattooed man looked for a long moment at the girl who had cried out. She was barely into her teens, and pretty, her long black hair tied in a ponytail. She tried to back away, pushing up against the side of the truck in panic. The tattooed man stuck out his tongue and waggled it obscenely at her. The girl whimpered in fear, causing the tattooed man to laugh.

"Save it," the other man said in English. Ruben knew the language from school. Papa had written that he should study English for when he came to America.

The other armed man seemed younger. He had a full head of blond hair slicked back from his forehead and the coldest blue eyes Ruben had ever seen. Even in the stifling heat of the truck, Ruben shivered.

"The piss buckets," the blond man said. "Pass 'em out." No one moved.

"Goddamn it," the blond man said, "you people are going to have to learn English sometime. This is your first lesson." He gestured at one of the overflowing buckets with his weapon and looked at the old man sitting next to it. "You," he snapped, "bring it out." The old man didn't move. The blond man racked the slide on the shotgun. The old man scrambled to his feet so quickly that the tattooed guard giggled. He picked up the bucket. Awkwardly, he tried to get down off the tailgate with the bucket clutched in his hands. It sloshed a little, and some of the brownish-yellow sludge splashed on the ground. The blond man leaped back, but a few drops splashed on the legs of his khaki pants. The blond man screamed in outrage and grabbed the old man by the shirt. He hauled the old man from the truck and tossed him sprawling to the ground. He raised the shotgun to his shoulder and pointed it at the old man.

The old man rose to his knees, tears streaming down his face. "*Por favor,*" he croaked, "*por favor…*"

The other men in the truck stirred restlessly. Some began to get to their feet. The tattooed man raised his own weapon, grinning. "I wish you would," he said softly. "I wish you would."

The old man was still on his knees, begging for his life. A dark stain appeared at his crotch. The blond man laughed at that. Then he kicked the old man in the chest. The man screamed as he went over backward. The blond man advanced on him and kicked him again, this time in the balls. The old man's scream trailed off to a ragged croak and he doubled up from the pain, writhing in agony. The blond man reached to his belt and pulled something away from it. It was a stiff whip, about four feet long. The whip seemed to be made out of some kind of hide, rolled tightly, tapering from about an inch thick near the wrapped handle to a narrow point at the tip. The blond man swished the whip through the air, back and forth. It made a terrifying sound, like the beating of a demon's wings.

Suddenly, there was a third man there, striding purposefully around the side of the truck. He walked over to where the old man was squirming on the ground, pulled a black automatic from a holster on his belt, and shot the old man in the head. There was another chorus of screams from the truck and the man with the pistol looked up. Ruben had thought the blond man was a demon; this man was the devil himself. He was small, his shaved head barely coming up to the blond one's shoulders, but he gave off an air of tightly coiled and barely contained madness. His head was almost perfectly round like a cannonball, and his ears were small and lay flat against his skull. He looked over the people in the truck like a serpent regarding a boxful of white mice. There was no spark of humanity in his dead gray eyes, no pity or compassion. A couple of the women crossed themselves.

The man with the pistol turned to the blond. "We don't have time for games," he said. Despite his small size, his voice was powerful, the voice of a preacher or a politician. "Get the buckets emptied, get the water bottles in there, and get back on the road."

"What about him?" Blondie said, gesturing with his weapon at the body on the road. His face was sulky, like a child denied a favorite toy.

The man with the pistol didn't look down. "Leave him for the vultures," he snapped. He walked off.

"All right, you people," the tattooed man said. "Get that other bucket out."

This time there was no hesitation. The people moved slowly, as if they were in shock, but they moved. In a few moments, the other toilet bucket had been handed out to a young, bearded man who had been summoned from the inside of the truck to the road. His name, Ruben remembered, was Diego; he had been one of the few who had bothered to introduce themselves to Edgar and Ruben at the beginning of the trip. Diego took the bucket silently and stood by them, staring sullenly at the road.

"Good," the blond said. "You're already learning not to eyeball your betters." He gestured at the buckets, miming pouring something out of them. Diego picked up one bucket. Blondie pointed at the old man's body. "Empty it there."

Diego's back stiffened. Blondie pushed the shotgun up under his ear. "Do it," he said silkily, "or I'll fucking stick your head in it and drown you while Benny over there fucks you up the ass."

"Awww," the tattooed man said in a mock-whiny voice. "An' I was saving myself." He cut his eyes toward the girl he'd been ogling earlier. The girl started to cry.

Diego picked up first one bucket, then the other, and emptied them over the old man's body. He walked back to the truck, his head down, and climbed in. Benny threw the still-stinking buckets back into the truck. Blondie shoved a pallet of bottled water in and pulled the door down. It clanged shut like the gates of hell. They heard the truck start up again. Another woman began weeping. Ruben glanced over at

Diego. He was sitting with his head down, looking at the floor between his knees. Then the battery gave out on the light and they were in total darkness.

Ruben felt Edgar trembling beside him, then he began to shake with sobs. Ruben put his arm around his brother. He didn't know what to say or do. He knew that, at seventeen, it was his responsibility to look out for his fourteen-year-old brother. Still, he wished Papa were there to tell him how.

CHAPTER FOUR

"SO," ANGELA SAID, "IS HE…"

"Well, he's not rolling on the ground, tearing his clothes off, and howling like a dog," Lucas said. "That's something."

"You know what I mean," Angela snapped. She walked over and stood at the open window, looking out at the highway.

"And I know," Lucas said, his voice even, "that it doesn't make any difference if he's ready or not. He's coming with us. You know he is. You knew the moment you asked, Jack Keller would do anything at all to help Oscar. And to help you. Because you know that's the kind of man he is. He'll pick up the gun again. He'll go on the hunt again to save his friend. Even if it costs him his sanity."

She whirled to face him. "You think I don't care about that? About him?"

He didn't change expression. "On the contrary. I think you're still in love with him."

She laughed bitterly and brushed the back of her hand across her eyes. "Right. That's why I'm asking him to help me find my husband."

"Are you searching for Oscar out of love or out of duty?"

She didn't answer.

"Understand," he went on, "I'm not knocking duty. I spent twenty years in the Army. Despite all the bullshit, that word still makes me stand up a little straighter when I hear it. But you need to know why you're doing what you're doing."

She leaned her head on the glass. "Does it really matter that much?" she whispered.

"Yes," Lucas said. "It does." After a moment, he asked, "Do you love Oscar?"

She closed her eyes. "He's a good man. He's gentle and kind and he made me feel alive again."

"That's not what I asked."

"Lucas." She sounded weary enough to sleep a thousand years. "I don't know, okay? Can I just be alone for a little bit?"

He stood up. "Sure." He walked to the door. "I'll see you later." She didn't answer.

He stepped out into the light and the heat. He didn't feel like going back to his room. He saw a couple of cars had pulled up to the bar across the street. He decided to check it out.

The air-conditioning inside was cranked to nearly frigid. A couple of men in jeans and T-shirts were seated at the bar. Another pair was shooting pool at a table set in a tiny room off the bar. They stopped talking and looked at him as he walked in. Lucas took a seat at an empty stool. "Corona," he told the pretty, dark-haired girl behind the bar. There was a blank expression on her face as she put the beer in front of him, a wedge of lime stuck in the bottle's neck.

"Thanks," he said. He handed over the money and a dollar tip. He pushed the lime wedge down into the bottle, then extended a hand. "Lucas Berry."

"I know who you are," the girl said.

He raised an eyebrow. "Really?"

She nodded and really looked at him for the first time. "Jack said you'd probably be stopping by."

Lucas looked around. "Where is Jack, anyway?"

"I fired him," she said.

"Ah," Lucas replied. He took a sip of his beer.

"What does that mean? 'Ah'?" she demanded.

He smiled. "Sorry. I'm a psychiatrist. It's a habit." He scanned the bar. "Is there somewhere we can talk for a few minutes?"

"About Jack?" she said.

"Yeah." *I want to see what's got you so riled.* He thought he knew the answer.

She jerked her chin at the men at the bar. "I got customers. And now I'm shorthanded."

He took out his wallet. "Set 'em up a round," he said. "On me. That'll give you a few minutes."

She hesitated, then jerked the beers from the cooler. She set them in front of the men at the bar. Their faces lost the closed and suspicious look they had worn since he entered. "Thanks, pardner," the younger of the two said.

"No problem," Lucas said.

The girl carried the other two beers over to the men at the pool table, then came back, wiping her hands on a rag. "We can sit over here," she said, indicating a booth.

Lucas took his seat. "So," he said. "Looks like you've got the advantage of me."

"What?" she replied. "Oh. The name. Sorry." She stuck out a hand. "I'm Jules."

Lucas took it. "Nice to meet you," he said. "So, what's got you so pissed off at Jack Keller?"

"How's that your business?"

He shrugged. "Well, since he's my patient..."

Her expression changed to one of alarm. "Your...wait, has he got some sorta disease? Is he some kinda escaped mental case?"

He chuckled. "Nothing that bad." He eyed her shrewdly. "But I think you'd know if he was really dangerous."

She glanced down at the table. "He still having the nightmares?" Lucas asked casually.

She looked up. "How'd you know about—" She stopped, then

shook her head. "You got me," she said. "You're pretty good."

He grinned. "I get by."

The smile seemed to disarm her. "Yeah," she said. "He has them."

"Any odd behavior during the day? Times he seems to sort of go away?"

She nodded. "Once in a while."

He paused. "Violent outbursts?"

She shook her head. "He's never raised a hand to me," she said firmly.

Berry nodded. "And I don't expect he ever will. What about other people?"

She bit her lip. "Well..." she sighed. "Actually, that's kind of how we met."

"Go on."

"A couple of bikers were hassling me. Guys from away. Not regulars. A couple of the local guys tried to stand up for me. I grew up around here, and a lot of the regulars are like family. The bikers beat up Glen and Jeff. They tore the phone off the wall. Then they started getting real ugly. Talking about how they were gonna take me across the road and call all their buddies to break me in."

"And that," Berry said, "is probably where Keller stepped in."

She nodded. "Yeah. 'Til then he was just this guy who sat over in the corner. Never said much to anybody, just drank his two beers and left."

"But not then."

"No, not then. It was like he was a different person. He went flat berserk on those two. If a couple of the guys hadn't pulled him off, he mighta killed one of 'em. As it is, they both ended up in the hospital."

"They got lucky," Berry observed.

She went on as if she hadn't heard. "But then it was like turning off a switch. Next night, he was back, quiet as ever. He even paid for the chair he broke over the one guy's head."

"And you started seeing each other."

"Yeah," she said. "He started working here. I needed the help. He moved in with me after a few weeks." She lifted her chin defiantly. "I been alone since my daddy died and left me this place. I ain't apologizin' to nobody."

"I didn't ask you to."

Her defiant stance crumpled. "Sorry," she said. "It's just…"

"I know," Lucas said. "Small town, small minds."

"Yeah." She traced invisible lines on the table with her index finger. "He's really been through some shit, hasn't he?" she said quietly.

Berry nodded. "You can say that."

"And that lady across the street," she said, "is she about to put him through some more?"

"We don't really know what happened to our friend. It may be nothing."

Jules sighed. "But if he doesn't go and find out," she said bitterly, "I'm going to be seeing that damn look in his eyes until I get sick of it and throw him out anyway. That look like he wants to be somewhere else. That look of wondering what he could have done…well fuck that. He wants to go, he can go. What's the old saying…"

"If you love something set it free," Lucas quoted.

"And if it don't come back, then fuck it." Tears started in her eyes. "Goddamn it," she muttered. "I can't cry now. I got a business to run."

The door opened. Keller stepped in. There was a duffel bag slung over his shoulder. He spotted Jules and Lucas sitting together. He walked over.

"I'm ready," he said. "Just give me a couple of minutes."

"Okay." Lucas got up and walked to the door. He turned and glanced back. Keller was seated across from Jules, holding her hands in his. She was looking down at the table, but she was nodding her head. Lucas sighed and stepped out into the sunlight. He saw Angela across the road, throwing her bag into the backseat of the Cadillac. He waited for another truck roaring past before crossing the road.

"I'm leaving," she said. "You were right. This was a bad idea."

"I don't recall saying it was a bad idea," Lucas said.

She slammed the back door. "Well, it was."

"Wait a few," Lucas said. "Keller's on his way."

CHAPTER FIVE

"YOU WANT TO GO," JULES said, "then go. You don't owe me nothin'."

"I know, but I want to explain anyway." He took her hands in his.

"A few years ago," Keller said, "I was in a shitload of trouble." She looked up. He took a deep breath. "I killed a man. It was self-defense, but there was no one around to see that or tell anyone. Except Oscar Sanchez. He didn't know me from Adam, but he came forward and cleared me. And he took a lot of risks doing it. The brother of the guy I killed called me up and shot Oscar in the kneecap—while I listened—just to show how pissed at me he was." Keller closed his eyes. He could hear the pop of the gunshot, Oscar's scream over the phone.

"Anyway," Keller said. "I owe him. If he's in trouble…"

She sighed. "You have to go. I know." She smiled sadly. "If you didn't, you wouldn't be the man you are."

He took a deep breath. "There's more." He looked away from her. "A few months ago, I killed someone else. This time there was no way to call it self-defense. I had him on the ground, unarmed. But he'd tried to kill another friend of mine. And her little boy. I was afraid he'd try again. So I shot him. Then I shot him again. And again."

"So?" she said, but her voice shook a little at the look in his eyes. "He was going to kill a little kid? Sounds to me like the sumbitch needed killing."

"Probably. Definitely. But Jules, I *liked* it. I laughed while I was doing it." He stood up, then shouldered the duffel. "I'm not the man you think I am." He started walking toward the door.

"Jack," she called out. "I know you. You're not a bad man."

He stopped and looked back. He heard a voice in his head, a voice from a man he'd met back on a mountainside in Western North Carolina. A place where Keller had gone willingly into the dark.

You bring death, the man had said, *and hell follows with you.*

"Yeah," he said, "I am." He walked out.

THEY STOOD ON EITHER SIDE of the car, watching the door. After a few moments, Keller stepped out, his bag over his shoulder. He crossed the road, head down, watching the ground ahead like a soldier on a long march. He didn't look up until he got to the car. "Nice ride," he said.

"Thanks," Angela replied.

"Long ride from the airport to here," Lucas said. "Figured we might as well be comfortable." He tossed Keller the keys.

Keller caught them in the air. He opened the back door and threw his duffel inside. "Let's go."

CHAPTER SIX

I N THE DARKNESS, IT WAS impossible to tell how long the truck had been on the road. Hours. Maybe days. Ruben fell into a kind of trance, fear and exhaustion turning his mind blank. Finally, the humming of the tires on pavement stopped and the truck was bouncing and jolting over another rough road. Eventually, it stopped. The people crammed inside murmured and stirred. The back door was yanked upward again, and bright light streamed in.

"Okay, *muchachos,*" a voice drawled, "ever'body out. Time to see the judge."

Slowly, hesitantly, the people climbed out of the truck. Ruben and Edgar were the last ones out. Ruben looked around him, blinking in the bright sunlight.

They were on a flat space, pounded flat and worn down by multiple feet, in front of a row of long, low buildings that looked like barracks. Tall fences, topped with wicked-looking spirals of barbed wire, surrounded the area around the buildings. Beyond the wire, Ruben could see fields stretching out before the trees began again.

"Where is this place?" Edgar whispered. "Are we in prison?"

"No talking!" a voice barked. It was the blond man, still holding the shotgun trained on them. Other men with guns surrounded the group. "Form a line!" the blond man snapped. No one moved. The man raised the gun.

"Form a line!" Ruben shouted in Spanish. "Single file. Or he'll shoot us." They looked at him in surprise, but slowly shuffled into line.

The blond man was looking at Ruben appraisingly. "So," he said, "You speaka de English."

"A little," Ruben said. "I learned in school."

"Good. You're the translator. Tell these assholes to march." He gestured with his weapon toward a building down the row. The only tree inside the wire, a tall tree of a kind Ruben couldn't identify, grew in front of it. "Building Three. That's the Judicial Building." The blond man grinned nastily. "Pray it's the last time you have to see the inside of it."

"That building." Ruben pointed to the group. "Over there."

Surprise was turning to resentment, but they complied.

When they got to the building with the large number 3 painted on the front, they were herded through the door into a large room, empty except for a table along the back wall. A pair of flags, one the familiar American flag, the other one a kind Ruben could not identify, flanked the table. The man who sat behind the table was the same bald man they had seen shoot the old man by the side of the road. This time, however, he was dressed in a black robe. As the group shuffled to a stop in front of him, he picked up a large wooden gavel lying on the table before him and banged it twice.

"All of you stand accused of attempting to violate the sovereign and sacred borders of the United States of America. The court has seen the evidence against you, to wit, that you all were apprehended, without passport or other legal authorization, in a truck just north of the Texas Border. Do any of you wish to offer any defense?"

They looked at each other in confusion. Ruben's heart was in his mouth, but he had to speak.

"They don't know what you're saying," he said. The blond man moved toward him, but the bald man motioned him away.

"If they don't speak the language," he said with a deadly mildness, "they shouldn't be here."

"What court is this?" Ruben said. "I thought in America, you could get a lawyer. And a chance to speak."

"The courts," the man said, "have become too weak and corrupt to deal with the threats we face. It's up to the people to take justice back. To take their *country* back. And this…" he gestured with the gavel, "this is a court of the people, by the people, and for the people."

Ruben opened his mouth to speak again, but not quick enough. The bald man smacked his gavel against the wood with a sound like a gunshot.

"Very well then. No valid defense is presented. The sentence is life at hard labor."

"This is not right…" Ruben began. Pain exploded in the back of his head, driving him to his knees. He dimly heard someone screaming. A boot caught him in the stomach and doubled him over. Then another sudden shock of pain in his head, and everything went black.

CHAPTER SEVEN

"WHEN WAS THE LAST TIME you saw him?" Keller said.

Angela sat up, startled. She had been dozing in the backseat. It was the first time Keller had spoken more than a couple of words since they had pulled out of the hotel parking lot. They had been driving for hours in near silence, Angela staring at the back of Keller's head, wondering what to say, or when he would speak. Finally weariness had overcome her and she had closed her eyes.

"What?" she said, trying to collect her thoughts.

"Oscar," Keller said. "When was the last time you saw him?"

"Jack," Lucas said from the passenger seat. "Maybe we should talk about—"

"Later," Keller cut him off. "Right now I need to know just how cold the trail is."

Angela looked out the window. It was dark outside. All she could see was the shoulder of the road and the blacktop as far as the headlights reached. She had no idea where they were. *This was a mistake.* The thing that had made Keller such a successful hunter had always been his relentless focus. Once the hunt was on, there would be nothing else. It had been what defined him. It was also the thing that had nearly destroyed him.

Finally she spoke. "Three weeks ago."

"Where?"

"He was at home. But he was going to see somebody. Somebody who he thought might be able to help get his sons into the country."

"Did he give a name?"

She shook her head. "He said it was better that I didn't know." Keller didn't speak. "I tried to get it out of him."

Keller was drumming his fingers impatiently on the wheel. He took no apparent notice of her defensive tone. "How did he get the name?"

"We went and talked to an immigration lawyer," she said. "Some guy in Charlotte."

"The guy couldn't help him?"

"No. He told us that since Oscar was in the country illegally, and he had no relatives in the U.S., there was no way he could apply for visas for the boys. At least nothing that wouldn't take years. Then, as we were leaving, he called Oscar back in. Alone. When he came out, he was holding a piece of paper. It looked like there was a name and number on it. He wouldn't show it to me."

"How long was this before Oscar left?"

"A week. Maybe a week and a half."

"He didn't talk to anyone else?"

"Not that I know of."

"Okay then. That's where we start. The lawyer. You got a name?"

"Yeah. Delgado. Perry Delgado."

"You got a phone?" Keller asked.

"Yeah," Lucas said. He reached into the glove box. "I don't think he'll be in this late, though."

"I know. See if you can get us tickets to Charlotte. Closest airport to here is Phoenix."

"You don't want to go home first?" Lucas asked.

Keller's voice was tight with impatience. "The trail's three weeks old. It gets colder every second." He glanced in the rearview. "I'll need to pick some things up in Charlotte. Probably a car, too. Not a rental. You got the budget for that?"

"Sure," Angela said. "But why do you need another car?"

"If I get any good information from this Delgado character, Charlotte's where we part ways," Keller said. "You guys can go home while I follow —"

"No." Angela said. "I'm going with you."

"It doesn't work that way, Angela," Keller said. "I work alone."

"He's my husband. I go with you or the deal's off."

"Okay." Keller slowed the car down and began pulling to the side of the road.

"What are you doing?" Lucas asked.

"The deal's off. You go on home. I'll get out here and hitch. Maybe Jules'll give me my old job back."

"Damn you, Keller —" Angela said.

"You knew the way I worked when you dug me up, Angela." Keller's voice was hard. "We do this my way, or not at all." After he pulled the car to the shoulder, he threw it in park, and sat there with the engine running. He looked in the rearview again. "What's it going to be?" She didn't answer, just glared at him, her eyes locked on the reflection of his. "Fine," Keller said. He opened the door and got out.

He was reaching for his duffel in the back when Angela said in a low, furious voice, "Get back in the car, Jack." He didn't answer. He yanked the duffel out and turned away. Angela turned to Lucas. "Would you talk to him?"

"I think this is one you two are going to have to settle yourselves," Lucas said.

"He's not seriously going to get out here? In the middle of nowhere?"

Lucas looked out the back window. "Looks like that's exactly what he's doing."

"And you don't intend to do anything about it?"

"Nope."

"What the hell good are you, then?"

"Angela," Lucas said. "Whatever relationship you two are going to have, you're going to have to work it out if it's going to work at all."

"Damn it," she said. She snatched up her cane and slid over to the driver's side. With some difficulty, she got out the car door. They were on a four-lane highway, divided by a deep median. The empty land stretched out to the edge of sight, where it met the sky that arched overhead like an overturned bowl. The stars were hard, bright, and cold in the utter blackness of the desert night. Keller was walking toward the median, his duffel slung on his shoulder. She called after him.

"Can we at least talk about this after we talk to the lawyer? When we know if there's even anywhere to go?"

He stopped, turned around. His face was unreadable. Finally, he nodded. He started walking back.

"Okay," he said as he passed her. He tossed the duffel back in the backseat. He climbed into the back after it. "You drive for a while," he said. "We need to go straight through." She stared at him for a moment. He stretched out in the backseat and closed his eyes. She shook her head and got behind the wheel.

CHAPTER EIGHT

THE MATTRESS BENEATH RUBEN'S BACK was soft, lumpy, and smelled of mildew. His head pulsed with pain as he opened his eyes. The bottom of another mattress, crisscrossed with rusted wire supports above him, was all he could see. He tried to sit up, thinking the pain couldn't get worse. He was wrong. He lay back down.

"Easy, friend," a voice said in Spanish. Ruben turned his head, slowly. A man was sitting on the lower bunk of the bed next to him. It was Diego. "You took a bad shot to the head. One of those assholes hit you with his gun. From behind."

"My brother," Ruben whispered. His voice felt rusty. "Where's my brother?"

"He's here," Diego said. He raised his voice. "EDGAR!"

Ruben winced at the volume and looked around. He was in a long narrow room. There was a row of bunk beds against both walls. A long wooden bench ran down the center of the room, with posts rising to the ceiling every ten feet or so. The walls were wooden, rough, and unpainted. There were no windows, only slits high up in the walls, which let in a little light and less air. A few men lay on the bunks, with others gathered around one end of the bench, talking in low voices. Some were the men he'd been traveling with, but there were others he didn't recognize. *We aren't the first ones to be brought to this place.*

Edgar detached himself from the edge of the group and came over, worry etched on his face. He sat next to Diego. Ruben held out a hand. Edgar took it and squeezed. "I'm okay, little brother," Ruben said.

"Don't tell them he's your brother," Diego advised. "One of the guys who's been here a while says they separate everyone who's related. All the women and girls went one way. My sister was one of them. The men are here and in another house."

"What is this place?" Edgar said. "Why are we here?"

Ruben tried again to sit up. The pain was only slightly less, but he felt he could bear it. "Those men. The ones who brought us here. They said we broke the law."

Edgar looked frightened. "Are we in prison?"

Diego shook his head. "No. I was in jail in America before. The first time they threw me out. That was no real court. And they wouldn't put a boy this young in prison with older men."

"Then who are those guys?" Ruben asked.

"I don't know," Diego admitted. "But I think they're crazy."

"We have to get out of here," Edgar said. He was beginning to look panicked.

"How?" Ruben said. "They have guns."

"And the fence is electrified," Diego said. "They told me a man killed himself a couple of weeks ago. Ran and threw himself on the fence. This may not be a real prison, but they've sure set it up like one."

There was a commotion at the end of the room. Two men had come in, their machine guns held loosely at their sides. One of them was the blond man from the truck. The other was tall, skinny, and dark-complected, with what looked like a permanent five-o'clock shadow on his slack jaw and an unruly shock of dark hair shot through with streaks of gray that he didn't look old enough to have. He dangled a toothpick loosely in one corner of his mouth.

"Okay, *muchachos*," Blondie said. "Time to start earnin' your keep.

Line up."

Slowly, the men and boys shuffled into line. Blondie noticed Ruben. "Can you work?" he demanded.

Standing up had made Ruben feel shaky and nauseated, but there was something in the question that told him what his answer needed to be. He nodded.

"Good," Blondie said, "because we follow the Bible rule here. 'If any would not work, neither should he eat.' You may want to let the rest of your *amigos* know about that."

Ruben thought of asking what Bible verse covered hitting people in the back of the head with gun butts, but he held his tongue.

They were marched out of the barracks, down the dirt path in front of the buildings, and through a wire gate. The land outside was dead flat, with lines of trees forming a wall all around, at least a mile away. Fields began a hundred feet or so from the wire—beans close in, corn and tobacco farther away. Prodded by the voices of the guards, they trudged down the dirt road between the fields until they were ordered to stop. A large farm truck rumbled up then pulled to a stop in a cloud of dust, which made the men cough and wave their hands in an effort to keep the choking stuff out of their eyes and noses. "Get the baskets out of the truck," Blondie ordered. He gestured with his gun, and a couple of the men climbed up into the truck. The swarthy man with the toothpick still hadn't spoken. The men started tossing large wicker baskets out. "Everybody get one," Blondie ordered. The men on the ground looked at each other in confusion.

"Come on, damn it," Blondie fumed. "You wetbacks came here to pick beans, didn't you?" He bent down, picked up a basket, and thrust it at an older man in a flannel shirt. "Well, get your fucking basket and pick some fucking beans. It ain't fucking *siesta* time." The man took the basket, looking daggers at Blondie, who apparently didn't like the look. He grabbed the old man by the shoulder and shoved him toward the field. The man stumbled, turned as if to protest, and found himself looking down the barrel of Blondie's gun. "Go ahead," Blondie said. "Somebody always gets made the first example of. Might as well be you, *amigo*." The man turned back and walked into the field. Without looking at anyone, he bent down and began pulling the beans off the low stalks. Gradually, the others followed. Ruben and Edgar ended up side by side, next to the first man.

"I don't know what I'm doing," Edgar said. "I don't know how—"

"Look for the ones that are this color," the man said. He held up a fat seedpod, bright green. "Those are ripe. The others, leave for now."

"I said, get to fucking WORK!" Blondie bellowed.

Ruben and Edgar stooped and began to pick.

CHAPTER
NINE

THE LAWYER'S OFFICE WAS LOCATED on the fifteenth floor of a downtown office building. The paneling in the reception area was expensive, the lighting muted. Soft ambient music, which seemed to consist mostly of single notes gently struck and held for a long time, played in the background. The law firm's name—Daniels, Gower and Delgado—was hanging on the wall in flowing silver and gold script behind the flawlessly beautiful Latina receptionist. The whole effect was one of calm, tranquility, and elegance.

Jack Keller was spoiling that effect. He stood before the chrome and wood receptionist's desk, dressed in jeans and the same T-shirt he'd traveled in from Phoenix. It was late afternoon. Neither he nor Angela had slept, and they'd come straight from the airport. Keller had insisted. He'd felt the trail growing colder with each passing hour, and it was like an itch he couldn't scratch. Fatigue etched deep lines in Angela's face, but Keller felt as alert and energized as if he'd just come off eight hours' sleep.

"I'm sorry, sir," the receptionist said, "but if you don't have an appointment—"

"Tell him it's about Oscar Sanchez," Keller said.

"We were here a few weeks ago," Angela spoke up from behind him.

The receptionist gave her a professional smile. "Yes, Mrs. Sanchez, I do remember you." She turned back to Keller, the smile tightening. "But Mr. Delgado is very busy—"

"Tell him Jack Keller is here."

The smile vanished entirely. The receptionist looked at Angela, then at Keller, her face troubled. "Oh," she said in a small voice. "He said you might come." She stood up. "Please wait. Have...have a seat." She exited through a door behind her.

Keller turned to Angela. "Did you two talk to this guy about me?"

She shook her head. "No. At least not while I was there. But it was like I said. As we were leaving, Delgado called Oscar back in and closed the door. I wasn't real happy about that, but it was only a couple of minutes."

The receptionist came back out. The professional smile was back in place. "Mr. Delgado can give you a few minutes. This way."

Delgado stood up from behind his own huge desk as they entered. The desk was empty except for a gold-and-mahogany pen and pencil set and a single file folder. A picture window behind him gave a view of the buildings all around.

The lawyer looked to be in his early thirties, younger than Keller expected. He was a small, neat man, impeccably groomed, expensively dressed, and his demeanor was as calm and serene as the office. "Come in," he said, flashing them a brilliant smile. He extended a hand to Keller. "You must be Jack Keller. I'm Perry Delgado."

Keller took the hand. "Jack Keller."

Delgado turned to Angela. "And Mrs. Sanchez. So good to see you again." His eyes didn't look as happy as his words. She only nodded.

"Please," Delgado said, motioning to a pair of leather client chairs before the imposing desk, "have a seat." They sat.

"The lady outside said that you might have been expecting to see me," Keller said.

Delgado took his own seat. He clasped his hands on the table in front of him. "Don't take this the wrong way, Mr. Keller, but I had rather hoped I wouldn't. See you, that is."

"I get that a lot," Keller said.

"That's what I understand from Mr. Sanchez."

"What exactly did he tell you?"

"Mostly that if you showed up, it meant that he was in some kind of trouble. I assume that's what's happened?"

"He's disappeared," Angela said.

Delgado blew out a long breath. "Well," was all he said. He picked up the file folder and took a piece of paper out. "Mr. Sanchez signed this when he left. It's a release allowing me to give any information to you regarding him. If you came looking."

"So, you're covered. You won't get in any trouble," Keller said.

"Not with him, no."

"But maybe with some other people?"

Delgado put the paper down and looked at Keller. "Mr. Sanchez said you could be trusted. Completely. Those were his words. 'I trust Jack Keller completely. And you can as well.'"

Keller felt a tightening in his throat. His voice felt strangely hoarse as he said "I'm not a cop. I'm not Immigration. I don't care about whatever you might be up to. I just want to find my friend."

Delgado nodded. He stood up and faced the window. "I couldn't help him. Not like he wanted. Since he's married a citizen, maybe…and I stress maybe…I could have gotten him back in, if he'd left and gone back to Colombia to reapply. But that could take a year, maybe more."

"He was worried that the boys weren't safe," Keller said.

"Yeah," said Delgado. "I get that. There's been an uptick in violence. Kidnappings. Drive-bys with innocent bystanders killed. He was worried, and I don't blame him. But getting them here, as fast as he wanted? There was no way."

"Not legally," Keller said.

Delgado turned away from the window. He was smiling. "Surely you're not suggesting that I would do something illegal. Even to help a man as nice as Mr. Sanchez and," he inclined his head to where Angela was sitting, "his lovely wife. And his sons who he felt were in so much danger in Colombia."

"Surely not," Keller said. "But."

Delgado sighed. "But." He looked down at the desk for a moment, tapping his fingers absently. In the silence, they could hear the muted sounds of traffic in the streets below. He looked up. "Leave me a number," he said. "I have to talk to some people first. Tell them what Mr. Sanchez said about talking to you. I'll encourage them to do that."

"I need the information now," Keller said.

Delgado looked at him steadily. "I can't give it to you now. Not without permission."

Keller stood up and started toward him. "Jack," Angela said.

Delgado didn't back away. The window left him no place to go. "Mr. Keller," he said, "all I can do is give you my word that I will do everything in my power to help you. But some of this is out of my hands."

Keller stopped. "If I don't hear from you, I'll be back."

Delgado shrugged. "And maybe you will beat the names out of me, and maybe you won't. But if you do, they still won't talk to you. And they will not take kindly to it. These are people, Mr. Keller, who it is better to have as friends than as enemies."

Keller stood there, feeling his heart pounding in his chest, the blood pulsing in his temples. He felt his hands curling into fists. He remembered the relaxation exercises Lucas had taught him. He took a deep breath, then another, deliberately uncurling the fingers.

"How long before you know?" Angela's voice seemed to come to him from far away.

"Tomorrow," Delgado said. "At the latest."

She stood up and handed him a card. "Please call at this number," she said. "It's my cell."

Delgado bowed slightly. "I promise," he said, "I'll get back with you as soon as I hear. Now if you'll excuse me?"

"Come on, Jack," she said, "Let's go."

A S THEY WAITED FOR THE elevator, Angela stole furtive glances at Keller. He seemed outwardly calm, in contrast to how he'd looked when the lawyer had implied he might not be able or willing to help them. She'd seen the tightening of his jaw, the narrowing of his eyes, the telltale signs of the rage in him fighting its way to the surface. For a moment, she'd been afraid he was actually going to try and beat the information he'd wanted out of Delgado. Then he'd brought it under control. But she wondered if he'd be able to do it the next time. She wondered what she'd awakened when she'd brought him out of the desert.

The elevator arrived, and they stepped in together. "So," she said, trying to sound casual, "it may be tomorrow before we know anything from Delgado. We should probably get some rest."

"Yeah," Keller said. "But I need to make a stop first." He glanced at her, then gave her a longer look. His voice softened. "You're exhausted."

"I'm fine," she said, but she felt the weight of the long and sleepless hours on her. Her legs ached, and her eyes felt raw, red, and full of sand.

"Lucas should have found us a hotel by now," Keller said. "Call him. Then you go rest."

"What are you going to do?" she said.

"I may need some things," he said.

"Like guns."

"You heard Delgado," Keller said. "We may be dealing with some pretty sketchy people soon. I want to be…" He stopped as he saw the look on her face. "What?"

She shook her head. Her shoulders sagged. "I want you to go home, Jack. Back to that bar, and that job, and that nice girl who's falling in love with you. Go be boring. And be happy."

The elevator had reached the ground floor. The doors opened onto the lobby, all glass and concrete and well-tended plants. Neither of them moved. "What the hell brought that on?"

"The way you reacted when that lawyer looked like he was trying to stonewall us. The look on your face when you talked about arming yourself so you could go deal with, as you put it, 'sketchy people.'"

"And how was that?"

The door started to close. Angela stepped out, with Keller following. They stood in the lobby of the office building, the flow of people parting around them in their way to the elevators. "Jack, tell me how you feel. Right now."

He smiled. "Now you sound like Lucas."

"I'm serious. Tell me."

"I feel fine, Angela."

"Just fine?" His brow furrowed for a moment. *He's so beautiful.* The sudden feeling pierced Angela like a dart.

"I feel good," he said. "I feel...great."

"You're as alive as I've seen you since you walked into that bar," she said wearily, "because you're hunting again."

"Yeah. So?"

"So that's not the path you need to be taking. You took that way out of the desert once, and it nearly destroyed you. I feel like if you go that way again...I'm afraid of what might happen to you. You're an addict, and I'm giving you the needle again."

"Look," Keller said, his voice rising. "*You* looked *me* up, okay? *You* came to *me.* If you didn't want me to—"

"Hey," a voice said. They turned to see Lucas Berry walking their way. He stopped and regarded them for a moment. "Am I interrupting something?"

"No," Keller said. "I was just telling Angela she needed to get some rest."

"We all could stand a good night's sleep," Lucas said. "I for one am jet-lagged to hell and back. What did the lawyer tell you?"

"He apparently sent Oscar on to some other people," Keller said. "Not exactly legal."

Lucas nodded. "Smugglers? *Coyotes,* I think they're called."

"Yeah," Keller said. "And he's going to see if they'll talk to us."

"In the meantime," Angela said, "Jack wants guns."

"Ah," Lucas said.

Keller sighed. "I know what that 'ah' means."

Lucas shook his head. "You always read too much into it. Whatever.

I suggest we table the issue of guns, have an early dinner, and get our heads down for a few hours of sleep. We've got a lot of miles to go." He saw the look on Keller's face. "You have to eat, Jack," he said. "And sleep. Tired men make stupid mistakes."

Keller sighed. "Okay," he said. "But after dinner—"

"Sleep," Lucas said firmly.

DELGADO WAS STANDING AT THE window, talking into the Bluetooth headset that allowed him to move freely while talking on the phone. "A man was here," his voice was steady; only the way he drummed his fingers on the window betrayed his agitation, "looking for Sanchez. Or whatever the hell his name was." He listened for a moment. "Yes. Keller. That was it. So Sanchez told you about him, too?" Another pause as he listened. "What the hell happened out there?" Delgado demanded.

CHAPTER TEN

THE MOUNTAIN WAS BURNING.

The acrid smoke filled Keller's eyes and nose, choking him. It was redolent with the sweet aromas of pines and fir, but underneath was the ever-present reek of burning flesh. He looked up into a sky with no sun, no stars, only the smoke flowing and writhing above him as if it were a living thing. Black birds whirled and dipped through the clouds, cawing in harsh rusty voices. He looked down to see a group of figures surrounding him, each with a hand raised and a finger pointing accusingly. They were burning as well, their flesh blackening and melting away as the flame wrapped around them. He saw Marie, the woman he'd loved, her son Ben clutching his mother's leg as the fire devoured them both. He saw DeGroot, the man he'd shot in cold blood, kneeling a few feet to her right. On his face was a mocking grin that slowly dissolved, the fat sizzling and popping as the flesh melted, revealing the equally mocking grin of the skull beneath. He saw Lisa, the young Hmong girl who'd tried to help him. She was looking at him with the same expression of shock she'd worn when the sniper's bullet

47

had taken her. Behind her was the man who'd killed her. He was the only one not burning. His face was covered with the camo mask that was all Keller had ever seen of him. He stepped forward, seeming to pass through Lisa's body as she fell apart into ash and blackened bone.

You bring death, the man said, *and hell follows with you.*

"That was wrong," Keller thought. It had been Harland, Lisa's adoptive father, who'd made that accusation. It didn't make it any less true. "I know," he whispered.

"KNOW," one of the birds above him called down in its derisive, croaking voice. The others took up the call. "KNOW. KNOW. KNOW."

"Jack," a voice said.

"No," Keller moaned. "No. No."

"JACK!"

Keller's eyes opened. Lucas Berry was bending over him. "Jack," he said again. "Wake up. You're having a nightmare."

Keller sat up slowly. "I'm…" he said, then took a deep breath."I'm awake." He looked around to get his bearings. He was in a hotel room. He was lying in one of the beds.

The other was unmade, and Lucas sat down on it. He was clad only in a pair of plaid boxer shorts. "Bad dream," he said.

Keller ran his hands over his face. "Yeah."

"Tell me about it."

Keller laughed weakly. "You always do psychoanalysis in your underwear?"

"It's a new technique. I'm thinking of writing an article on it. Now talk to me."

Keller swung his legs off the bed. "Can I take a piss first?"

When he returned, Lucas had pulled out a ragged blue terrycloth robe that looked as big as a tent and wrapped it around him. "Better?" he said.

"Much." Keller sat on the edge of his bed and pulled on his jeans.

"So what was the dream?" Lucas said.

"I don't remember."

"Bullshit," Lucas said.

Keller sighed. "Okay. I was on the mountain."

"The mountain?"

"Where it happened. Where I shot DeGroot."

"Let's start by reframing that. The mountain is where you saved Marie's life. And her son's. And your own. She told me all about it."

"Did she tell you that I shot DeGroot when he was on his knees? Unarmed? Helpless? Did she tell you I shot him again and again, until the gun clicked empty? Did she tell you I was laughing like a goddamn lunatic while I did it?"

"Yes," Lucas said softly. "She did. And she told me why. She told me DeGroot had some sort of juice. Someone high up looking after him. He was going to get out. He'd told her was going to come back after her. And her boy. He was going to torture them to death because that's what he did. And he'd get away with it, because that's also what he did. He had that juice. So he had to die. She also told me that you took the gun from her to keep her from shooting DeGroot in front of her son. You did it so she wouldn't have to."

Keller looked down at the floor. "Angela says she's afraid of what this will do to me."

"Are you?"

Keller thought for a moment. "A little."

"So don't do it," Lucas said. "We'll find Oscar some other way."

"No," Keller said. "This is something I have to do. Oscar's my friend. I owe him."

"You've said that. But is that the only thing that's going on here, Jack? Just duty? A sense of obligation?" Keller didn't answer. "Back in Arizona," Lucas said after a few moments. "How was your life?"

"It was fine," Keller said.

"Looked like it. You had a job. A place to stay. That girl Jules…she seemed nice."

"She was. I mean, she is."

"So why leave?"

"I told you—"

"Yeah, yeah, you owe Oscar. But I couldn't help but notice how much more engaged you seem now than you did back there. Your eyes are brighter. There's a spring in your step that wasn't there before. Face it, Jack, you're enjoying being on the hunt again."

"Angela says the same thing," Keller said. "But so what? Are you saying that's a bad thing?"

"No," Lucas answered. "Not at all. But you need to recognize that about yourself. You're a hunter. A warrior. Not a killer. Embrace it. Don't try and run from it. You tried to run back to the desert. And it didn't work for you. If it had you wouldn't have come back."

"Embrace it?" Keller said, his voice rising. "I killed a man, Lucas. *And I liked it.*"

"Not the first man you've killed," Lucas observed. "Maybe not the last. But as far as I can tell, you never killed anyone that didn't try to kill you first. Maybe that's why you enjoyed it so much. How does the song go? 'It ain't no sin to be glad you're alive'? It doesn't make you the monster you apparently think you are. You did what you did to protect what you love." He looked at the clock and sighed. "It's almost six thirty. I'm going to grab a shower and try to find some breakfast around here. How about you?"

"Yeah," Keller said. "Breakfast sounds good."

There was a knock at the door. Lucas got up and answered. Angela stood there, holding a cell phone. "I just got a text…from Delgado."

"He gets up early."

"His contact will talk to us. And she's seen Oscar."

"She?" Keller said.

She held out the phone. "Rosita Miron. She's Delgado's aunt. And she lives a few miles from Fayetteville."

CHAPTER ELEVEN

THEY HAD STARTED OUT AS ten men and five women; now there were only eight men. The women were kept separate, in another one of the long, narrow barracks. The men rarely saw them, but they knew what was going on in that sealed building. They saw guards going in and out, heard the crude comments and jokes they made. It was making them all crazy, but none dared make a move against their captors. Not after what had happened to Diego.

They worked every day from just after dawn until just before sunset, in the blazing heat of summer. Some worked the fields, some were marched to the forest at the back of the compound to cut down trees and clear-cut land. A sawmill built at the edge of the cleared area turned the usable trees into lumber. Every morning, they'd be rousted from their beds by one or the other of their guards banging a metal ladle on a galvanized bucket, which he'd then leave inside the door. The bucket held their meager breakfast, usually thin oatmeal, occasionally a white corn porridge, similar to the *mazamorra* they'd grown up eating. Diego, who'd been north before, told them the dish was called "grits."

That was before he was executed.

They'd been working the field three days after their arrival, always under the watchful eyes of two men with guns, radios, and belts hung with equipment that Ruben couldn't identify. The guards varied, but the most common one was the blond man who'd been among the group that had first taken them prisoner. He liked to walk up and down the rows, weapon loose in his hands, and carry on a conversation with his fellow guards about what he'd done the night before, inside the women's barracks. He always pitched his voice loud enough for the workers to hear. Most of them didn't speak English, so the words meant nothing to them, but Blondie's hand gestures and the kissing and slurping noises he made with his thick, wet lips were enough to get the message across. Ruben understood most of it, but he kept his head down. The guards also carried stiff hide whips like the one Blondie had wielded the night they were taken. The whips were used to "smarten up" anyone who lagged in their picking or "eyeballed" a guard, which was the word for anyone daring to look them in the eye. He'd heard Blondie refer to the crop as a *sjambok*, and he claimed it was made of rhino hide from South Africa. Whatever it was made of, it left nasty painful welts with even the lightest stroke. No one wanted to feel what it could do with real force behind it.

Ruben had been picking in the row next to Diego, his mind far away. He'd quickly learned the trick of letting his thoughts drift, going elsewhere. Going home. He thought about breakfasts with his aunt and uncle, who'd been raising him since Papa left. They told him Papa would come for him, would take him to America, away from the violence and the threats of kidnapping that still hung over the cities. He didn't think of this place as America. America was the country of basketball and fast cars and pretty women. This place...he didn't know what this was. Sometimes he wondered if the truck had crashed and he was in hell. But he didn't see how that could be. He'd gone to Mass, made his confessions, said all the words and been granted absolution by Father Enrique. He looked up and saw Diego. The look on the older man's face startled him out of his reverie. He heard Blondie coming up the row, chattering as usual.

"I tell you, bro," he said, "I had that pretty lil' *chica*, the one with the ponytail, an' I was doin' her from the back. I had that ponytail in one hand." He demonstrated with a clenched fist. "An' I was slappin' her ass with the other. She starts goin'," his voice went to a high, girlish falsetto "Ay, Papi. Ay, Papi..."

Diego roared with rage. He stood up and charged Blondie. The man was so surprised, he didn't see the blow coming until it had connected with his chin. His head snapped back and Diego hit him again, this time in the nose. The other guard, a pudgy little moon-faced man with a camo boonie hat shading his fat, sweating face, was running toward them, yelling into his radio.

Time seemed to slow down for Ruben. He saw Blondie step back and bring his gun to bear. He saw and heard Diego screaming at him, as if daring him to fire. He saw Boonie Hat yank a black device from his belt and point it at Diego. Diego's entire body went rigid, and he began to convulse. His eyes rolled back in his head and he fell to the ground shivering like a man in a fever. Blondie turned his gun on the other men, who'd stopped picking and stood up, faces blank with shock. There was blood around his mouth and his eyes were insane with rage. "BACK THE FUCK UP!" he screamed, although no one had made a move toward him. He stood there, breathing heavily, and then spoke to Boonie Hat. "Secure that bastard," he said. Boonie Hat took something off his belt and bent over. Ruben saw the glint of handcuffs in the hot sunlight. Blondie raised his voice again. "LINE UP!" he shouted. "BY THE ROAD!" He glanced at Ruben, who was standing slack-jawed, goggling at where Diego lay twitching on the ground. "Boy," he snapped, "tell them to line up. By the road."

Ruben looked up, unable to speak. He looked at his brother. Edgar was crying.

"DO IT!" Blondie screamed. "Or I swear to Christ, I'll kill every one of them. You bastards can be replaced. Easily."

In a shaky voice, Ruben told them what to do. They complied, walking like shell-shocked troops stumbling off a battlefield. Ruben took his place in the line, on the other end from Edgar. He knew if he stood next to him, his brother would expect comfort. But he also knew

Blondie's cruelty firsthand. If the guard realized that Edgar was his little brother, who knew the sick ways he'd find to use that knowledge to torment him?

When they were in line, Blondie turned to Boonie Hat. "Cover them," he said. He walked over to where Diego lay on the ground, cuffed and helpless. He pulled the sjambok off his belt and lashed it back and forth. It made that familiar chilling whistle as it cut through the air.

"*Muchacho*," he said. "You just bought yourself an all-expense paid tour of hell. And I'm gonna enjoy being your tour guide." He kicked Diego in the stomach. The man doubled up, gagging and retching, robbed even of the air it would take to scream. Blondie raised the sjambok over his head and brought it down against Diego's side with all his might. The blow split Diego's shirt and cut into the skin beneath. This time Diego did scream, a raw, terrible sound of animal torment.

"Oh," Blondie said, with exaggerated concern, "did that hurt?" He raised the whip again. Diego whined like a dog and tried to squirm away. Blood soaked his shirt where the sjambok had sliced open fabric and skin. Blondie followed him relentlessly and brought the whip down. Diego shrieked again, so loudly that some of the men put their hands over their ears. Ruben stole a look at Boonie Hat. The man's eyes flicked back and forth between the line of trembling men and the torture going on a few feet away. He looked as if he was going to be sick.

"Please," Ruben whispered to him. "Please. Make him stop."

Boonie Hat turned back to him. His piggy little eyes narrowed. "Shut up," he said, "unless you want to take his place." Another whistle, another wet sound of splitting flesh, another scream. Boonie Hat flinched, but he made no other move. Ruben closed his eyes.

From behind him, he heard the sound of an engine. He turned slightly to see a large black pickup truck speeding down the dirt road toward them. The truck braked to a stop, kicking up a cloud of dust that blew up around the line of standing men. Blondie stopped his beating and turned to watch.

The truck just sat there, the only sounds the rumble of the engine and Diego's sobs and whimpers. The windows of the truck so heavily tinted there was no way to see inside. Ruben felt a shiver of dread, an atavistic impulse to flee whatever was behind that darkness. The door opened and a man stepped out of the driver's side. It was the hairless man that had been there when they were taken, the man who had served as the judge at their mock trial. Another man holding a shotgun climbed out of the passenger seat. The bald man walked past the line of men as if he didn't notice them, over to where Blondie stood over Diego.

"Sergeant," he said. "Report."

Blondie gestured with the sjambok. "Son of a bitch attacked me, General."

"Language, Sergeant Kinney," the man said.

"Sorry, sir."

The bald man bent over to look at Diego. He stood up and looked at the blood on Blondie's mouth. "Corporal Bender," he said over his shoulder. "Is this true?"

"Yes sir," Boonie Hat replied. "Guy went crazy. Charged at Caleb—I mean, Sergeant Kinney—and busted him in the mouth."

"Very well," the bald man said. "Put him in the back of the truck. We're taking him to Building Three."

Blondie bent over and grabbed the back of Diego's shirt. "On your feet," he ordered. He was smiling like a child who'd just gotten everything he wanted for Christmas.

"The trial will commence immediately. Sentence will be carried out at sunset. No rations tonight." From down the line, Ruben heard a man groan. Dinner was no better than breakfast, usually just some sort of stew with a little bit of meat in it and some bread, but it was all they had. Ruben felt his own stomach cramp with disappointed hunger. The General pointed at the man who'd groaned. "And none for that one tomorrow. Now, back to work." Blondie had pulled Diego to his feet and was dragging him stumbling over to the bed of the truck.

"You heard the General," Bender shouted. "Back to work!" Slowly, the men shuffled back toward the field, their heads down. Ruben noted how skinny they were getting. He'd begun seeing his own ribs visible beneath the flesh, and his brother's. *They're working us to death. They mean to kill us all.*

CHAPTER TWELVE

THE BIG WHITE WOOD-FRAME HOUSE was situated on a huge lot, in the countryside of northern Moore County. The long dirt driveway ended at a parking area full of pickup trucks and battered used cars. A huge oak tree shaded half the front yard, under which a group of Latino men in jeans and work shirts were gathered around a large grill constructed from an oil drum cut in half. They were drinking beer and laughing at some joke. There was a basketball goal off to one side where younger men were playing what looked like a hotly contested game. Young women, with babies in their arms and toddlers running and shouting nearby, sat at a picnic table. A radio set on a picnic table was playing a bouncy song with Spanish lyrics that was heavy on guitars and accordion. As Keller and Angela pulled their rented sedan to a stop behind a new-looking Ford pickup, the basketball game and the joking around the grill stopped. Everyone but the young children stopped what they were doing and watched them get out of the car. The only sound was the shrieking of the younger ones as they played on, oblivious. The smell of grilling meat reached

Keller as he walked toward the house, Angela beside him with her cane. It was making his mouth water. He glanced over at the basketball players. They were watching him with stony faces. The tallest one, who looked to be the oldest, held the ball under his arm. Keller gave that one a nod. He didn't respond.

A man with a single streak of gray in his dark hair detached himself from the group at the cooker and intercepted them halfway to the porch. "May I help you folks?" he said, with only a trace of accent and no trace of a smile.

"Yes, sir," Angela said. "We're here to see Mrs. Miron." She held out her hand. "Angela Sanchez."

The man took it and looked at Keller. "And you are?"

"Jack Keller." Keller extended his own hand. The man released Angela's hand and shook Keller's. His grip was firm. "Frank Flores," he said. "Does Mrs. Miron now you're coming?"

"Yes, sir," Keller said. "We called ahead."

"It's all right, Frank," a woman called from the porch. "They can come in." She said something in Spanish that Keller couldn't catch. But the man seemed to relax.

"Okay," he called back, then he smiled. "You want something to eat?" he said. "We got plenty. A beer, maybe?"

"Thanks," Keller said. "Maybe later."

"Get Maggie to fix them a plate, Frank," the woman said. She'd come down off the porch to meet them. She was short and plump with a broad, strong face. She looked to be in her early fifties, but her hair was still mostly jet-black, with only a few strands of gray. She was clad in a bright red dress and matching heels. Keller noted the diamond ring she had on one hand, as well as the large gold earrings in her ears. Her eyes looked them both up and down appraisingly as well.

"Okay," Frank said. He may have been the oldest one present, but it was clear that the woman was in charge.

She held out a hand to Angela. "So," she said. "You haven't heard from Oscar?"

"No," Angela said as she took the hand. "Have you?"

"Come inside," Miron said. She looked at Keller. "You'd be Jack

Keller, then."

"Yes, ma'am," Keller said. "I'm a friend of Oscar's."

"So he said. Well, you might as well come in, too." They followed her up the steps and into the house. There were more people inside, mostly women of varying ages and their children. There was a loud conversation going on in the kitchen. Two children were arguing over a toy in the hallway. Miron barked something at them in Spanish and they quieted down. "CONSUELA!" she yelled toward the kitchen. "Come do something with these two!" She turned back to them. "Sometimes I can't hear myself think in this place," she grumbled. "This way." She led them into a bedroom, which had been converted into an office and closed the door. "There," she said, taking a seat in an old leather chair behind a large antique desk. "That's better."

"Sorry to disturb your party," Keller said. He took a seat in a large armchair in one corner as Angela sat down in the other. "What's the occasion?"

She smiled at him indulgently. "This isn't a special occasion, Mr. Keller. This is how it always is here on the weekends. Latinos don't need a special occasion to spend time with family."

There was a knock at the door. "Come in," Miron called. A pretty, dark-haired teenaged girl came in, balancing a tray in one hand and carrying a couple of bottled beers by their necks in the other. The smell of roasted meat, peppers, and limes came in with her. She stopped when she saw Keller and her eyes lit up. "Well, hi," she said.

"Just put the tray down on the desk, Magdalena," Miron said. "And close the door behind you."

"Yes ma'am," the girl said, abashed. But she gave Keller a flirtatious look as she left.

Miron sighed. "Pardon my niece," she said. "She's at that age."

"Oh, don't worry," Angela said. "He gets that a lot."

"Thanks," Keller said.

"Please," Miron said, "eat. No one goes away from my house hungry."

Keller was chafing to get down to business, and he could tell Angela was about ready to jump out of her skin with impatience. But

Miron was so emphatic, it felt rude to turn her offer down. Besides, his stomach had been growling since he got out of the car. "Smells great."

The meal — *carne asada* with rice on the side — was juicy and flavorful, the peppers and spices exploding in the mouth with a hint of lime to moderate the heat. They washed it down with ice-cold Sol beer while Miron chatted about her family. When they were done, their plates were both clean. The woman nodded as if they'd passed some sort of test. "Now," she said, "Let's talk about Oscar." She looked at Angela. "First," she said, "I don't know where he is. Not exactly."

Angela seemed to deflate a little in her chair. "What can you tell me?"

Miron looked back and forth between Angela and Keller for what seemed like an eternity. "Ma'am," Keller said finally, "I know that you're worried. You don't know us. But we're not the cops. We're not Immigration. We don't care what you do."

"I wouldn't have to do it if your country was even a little more realistic about its immigration policy," the woman said.

"I don't care about politics, either," Keller said. "I just need to find my friend. If he's in trouble, I need to help him. He did it for me."

"I help people, too," Miron said. "I help them find better lives."

And it looks like you get paid pretty well for it. "Yes, ma'am," he said.

She took a deep breath. "Okay. My nephew occasionally sends people to me. People who, for one reason or another, need help getting into the country. Or who have family members they need to get in, but who can't get in legally."

"Like Oscar," Angela said.

Miron nodded. "I put him in touch with some other people. In Mexico. They made the arrangements."

"What arrangements?" Angela asked.

"I don't know exactly," Miron admitted. "He had people that were going to get him to where people left Mexico to cross the border. And he was going to meet them on the other side. In the U.S."

"Where were these places?"

"Again, I don't know exactly. I don't handle the arrangement. I just make the introductions. But…"

"But what?"

"Something went wrong. One of the trucks was lost."

"Lost," Angela said. She looked stricken.

Miron nodded. "It turned up in the desert. Empty. And there's been another since then."

"Which was the one that Oscar's boys were on?" Keller asked.

Miron looked away. "The second one."

"So you knew," Angela said. "You knew there'd been trouble. And you took Oscar's money, and you arranged for his sons to be put on a truck, and…" She rose to her feet. Her face was red with growing rage.

Miron didn't stand, nor did she meet Angela's eyes. "I thought maybe it was an accident. It had only happened once."

"So what happened when the second truck went missing?" Keller asked.

"The one with Oscar's sons on it," Angela added bitterly.

"He said he was going down there," Miron said. "To the entry point. And he was going to find out what had happened. He was going to find the boys."

"So where is this place?" Keller asked. "This entry point."

Miron shook her head. "That, I can't tell you." She held up a hand as Angela began to speak. "Because I don't know. All I have is a phone number. And an e-mail address."

Keller tried not to grit his teeth in frustration. "So who are these people? Sounds like they're the ones we need to talk to."

Miron shook her head again. "I can call them. See if they'll agree to meet with you. But I can't make any promises."

"Can you call them now?" Angela said. "Please." She said the last word as if she hated it.

Only then, did Miron look up and meet her eyes. "Yes," she said softly. "I'll try. But you'll need to wait outside."

"Okay." Keller stood up. "Come on, Angela."

She stood up as well. Angela took a card out of the pocket of her blouse and laid it on the edge of the desk. Miron made no move to pick it up. "This is where I can be reached," she said. Keller followed her out the door.

Outside in the hallway, Angela leaned her head against the wall. "She knew," she whispered. "*They* knew. They knew something was wrong. That it might not be safe. And they put people on the truck anyway. *Children.*"

"I know," Keller said. He put a hand on her shoulder. "But we have to work with them. At least for now."

Angela reached up and put her hand over his for a moment. Then she straightened up. "I need to use the restroom," she said. "I'll be back."

"I'm going to step outside and get some air," Keller said. "Come get me." She nodded.

Keller passed the kitchen and went out on the porch. He took a seat on the top step. The men had moved over to the picnic table and were wolfing down the food. The basketball game was still going on.

He agreed with Angela. Putting those people, including children, in danger was unconscionable. But they needed the information only Miron could give them. Without it, they were at a dead end.

"Hey," he heard someone said. He turned to see the teenager, Magdalena, taking a seat on the step next to him. She was smiling broadly.

"Hey," Keller said, as noncommittally as he could. *This I absolutely do not need.*

If the girl noticed his chilly tone, she gave no sign of it. "What's your name?" she asked.

"Jack," he said.

"Nice to meet you, Jack. I'm Maggie." She stuck out a hand.

Keller took it. "Short for Magdalena, right?"

She wrinkled her nose. "I hate that name. It's so...*old* sounding."

"It's not so bad," Keller said. She was still holding on to his hand. He pulled away.

"So that lady you're with," she said, "is she your wife?"

"No," Keller said. "Just a friend."

"Maggie," a male voice said. Keller looked up. The tall young man from the basketball game was standing at the foot of the steps. He didn't look happy.

Maggie sighed theatrically. "What is it, Cesar?"

He said something to her in Spanish, low and fast. Keller didn't catch all of it, but he thought he heard the word *puta,* and that gave him the gist. He saw her jaw clench. She replied to him, also in Spanish, practically spitting the words back at him. The other young men had begun to gather, and Keller heard one of them snicker. *Goddamn it.*

Cesar bent over and tried to grab the girl's wrist. She yanked it away. "You keep your hands off me!" she said. Cesar reached again.

"Hey," Keller said quietly, "knock it off."

Cesar straightened up, eyes narrowed in rage. "Stand up, asshole."

Keller stayed put, looking up at him. "Really?" he said. "You're really going to do this?"

"I said get up," the young man yelled. "You fucking *pussy!*"

Keller sighed and stood up. "I'm not going to fight you, kid." He noticed that the group of older men had left the picnic table and were hurrying toward them. He hoped they would get there in time to short-circuit the confrontation the kid seemed determined to have.

Cesar nodded. "Yeah," he sneered. "That's what I figured." He started to turn, as if to walk away, then came back, fast, throwing a hard right at Keller's jaw. He was quick, and fired up, but the feint was so obvious, the kid might as well have sent Keller a postcard. Keller threw a cross block that directed the punch past him, the kid's momentum spinning him around and leaving him off-balance and sideways to Keller, his ribs exposed. Keller fought down the reflex to step forward and break those ribs with a short jab to the torso. Instead, he grabbed the young man by the shoulders from behind, turned him the rest of the way around, and shoved him hard. As Cesar stumbled, trying to get his footing back, Keller raised his leg and gave him a shove in the ass with his boot. Cesar went sprawling on his face in the dirt. The girl screamed. Cesar rolled to a sitting position, glaring at Keller with hate in his eyes. He started to get up.

"Kid," Keller said, "if you stand up, it better be to shake hands. Because if I have to put you on the ground again, you're not getting up. At least not on your own."

"Son of a bitch," the young man said. He struggled to his feet and crouched as if ready to charge.

"CESAR!" a voice barked from behind him. Keller didn't take his eyes off the kid. He sidled to his right to put the speaker in his field of vision. It was Rosita Miron. She spoke to the kid rapidly in Spanish, her voice a scourge of anger and outrage. He tried to answer her, but she overrode him, the words and the tone lacerating the young man until he stood, head down and sullen. One of the older men, the one who'd spoken to him earlier, came up and put a hand on his shoulder. Cesar shrugged off the hand and stalked away.

Keller looked around. The group of men, young and old, stood in a rough semicircle, staring at Keller, their faces hard and unfriendly.

"Sorry," Keller said. "A little misunderstanding." He turned to Miron. He didn't see any friendliness there, either.

"I think you should leave," she said.

"I agree," Keller said. "But what about the information we need?" He saw Angela come out on the porch behind Miron. "The information *she* needs," he pointed at Angela "to help find her husband?"

Miron shook her head. "I can't help you," she said. "My contacts don't want to talk to you."

"That's not acceptable," Keller said.

"Not..." Miron's dark face grew even darker with anger. "How dare you come to *my* house, and tell *me* what's *acceptable*? You people... you think you own everything." She pointed at the cars in the lot. "Get out," she said in a hard, angry voice. "Now."

"Jack," Angela said, "let's just go."

He turned to her. "We can't..."

"Jack," she said quietly. "Please." She came down off the porch. "Come on." She led the way, moving with slow dignity behind her cane. The circle of men parted to let her through.

He could feel the blood pounding in his temples, feel the rush of adrenaline ramping up, but he followed her to the parking lot. "Look," he said, "stay here. I'll go back and try to talk to her again."

"No," Angela said. "We need to go. Now."

"But if we do that," Keller said, "we're stuck. We're at a dead end."

"Not exactly," Angela said.

"What does that mean, 'not exactly'?"

"It means that while she was running outside to see about the commotion, I stole her cell phone," Angela said. "We can look at the last number called. And it may have the numbers and the addresses of the people she does business with."

"Okay," said Keller. "I see your point. Let's go." They got in the car. When they were almost at the end of the driveway, Keller said, "She's really not going to be happy when she finds out you've got her phone."

Angela looked back. "I think she just did."

Keller looked in the rearview mirror. The big Ford truck was barreling down the driveway after them.

CHAPTER THIRTEEN

"SHIT," KELLER SAID. HE PUNCHED the gas and the tires on the rental squealed as they hit pavement. The car fishtailed for a few heart-stopping seconds before Keller got it back under control. He headed down the two-lane road that cut through the rolling countryside.

"He's gaining," Angela said. The rental was comfortable, but underpowered. Keller saw the big truck growing larger in the rearview mirror. He gritted his teeth and pressed the gas pedal down all the way. They only pulled ahead a little before the truck accelerated and began gaining again. Keller looked down at the speedometer—85...90...95. The rental's engine was beginning to strain.

"What do they think they're doing?" Angela said as the truck drew within inches of their back bumper. Then she yelped as the truck sped up and rammed them. The car shuddered from the impact, but Keller held it under control.

"Guess they really want that phone back," he said.

"What are you going to..." the truck hit them again, causing them to swerve slightly.

"Guess we're going to have to give it to them," he said. He saw a sign up ahead and put on his signal.

"Jack," Angela said.

"Listen," he said. "We don't have much time." As he began slowing, he told her what to do. They reached a wide spot in the road where an abandoned gas station stood. The front plate glass windows were long gone and boarded up and rusted stumps of piping stuck up through a crumbling concrete island where the pumps used to be. Keller pulled to a stop on the time-shattered concrete slab of the parking area. Weeds grew up between the cracks, brushing against the bottom of the car as they stopped. The truck pulled in right on their tail. Keller took the phone from Angela and got out. Three men got out of the truck. One was Frank, the older man who'd greeted Keller when they'd first arrived. The other was a squat ugly man with acne scars on his face and muscles bulging against his tight T-shirt. The third one was Cesar. He was grinning and holding an L-shaped tire iron.

"Howdy," Keller said. "How can I help you fellows?"

"Your friend took something that didn't belong to her," Frank said. "And we need it back."

Keller held up the phone. "You mean this?"

The man nodded. "Yes. That."

"And if I give it back," Keller said, "We can go on our way?"

Frank shook his head in apparently sincere sorrow. "I'm afraid not," he said.

Cesar broke in. "We're going to fuck you up, bitch." He slapped the tire iron into his palm for emphasis. Acne Scars had come up to stand on the other side of him.

"Cesar," Frank said impatiently. He turned back to Keller. "Tia Rosita says you need to be taught a lesson. And warned to stay away." He nodded at the car. "Your lady friend will not be harmed."

"She's too messed up to fuck, anyway," Cesar said nastily.

"Oh," Keller said. "Well, that's a relief. I guess. Still, I'm not sure I can give you what you want."

"Then," Frank said, "we'll have to take it. Cesar. Mateo." The two men advanced on Keller, grinning.

"Oh, all right," Keller said when they were a couple of feet away. "Here." He tossed the phone underhanded at Cesar's face. Startled, the young man stepped back and instinctively swung the tire iron as if he was trying to bat the phone away. He missed, the wild swing almost catching Mateo in the chest. Keller stepped forward, seized the iron with his left hand, and punched Mateo in the face with his right. Mateo's head snapped back, but he recovered from the blow quickly. He swung at Keller, who was twisting to his right, grabbing the iron with both hands now and using Cesar's grip to pull him sideways into Mateo and throw off the aim of the punch. In the tangle that followed, Cesar loosened his grip on the tire iron and Keller ripped it out of his hands. He used the momentum to spin around, drop to one knee in front of Cesar, and smash the iron into the younger man's knee as the counterpunch went over his head. Cesar screamed and fell to the ground, clutching the shattered knee in both hands. Keller stood up, reversing his grip on the iron, and jammed it into the gut of Mateo, who was charging forward, arms outstretched to wrap Keller up and bear him to the ground. Mateo grunted in pain and doubled over. Keller raised the iron above his head, ready to bring it down in a blow that would have crushed Mateo's skull. He checked himself at the last second, tossed the iron aside, and waited for Mateo to try to straighten up. When he did, slowly, Keller finished him with a short, chopping right to the jaw that dropped him to the ground next to Cesar, who was still writhing on the ground, holding his knee and keening in a high, thin voice.

"I tried to tell you, kid," Keller said to Cesar. He looked over at Frank. "He's going to need to go to the hospital for that knee."

"You don't know what kind of trouble you've brought down on yourself," Frank said.

"I think I do." Keller looked at the pieces of the cell phone scattered on the concrete. "Tell Mrs. Miron I'm sorry about the phone. But tell her, and whoever she works with that I have the SIM card."

Frank looked confused. "The what?"

Angela was out of the car, standing beside it. "It's the little computer card that has the phone's information on it," she said, "including the contacts."

"Tell her for me, I meant it when I said I don't care about how she makes her money," Keller said. "I don't care about getting any of her friends in trouble. All I care about is finding my friend. That's it. And to do that, I need to talk to the people he talked to. That's all I want. If I don't get it, though, I know some people who'd probably like to have the information I have. About Delgado, and Miron, and what's on that SIM card. Think about it." He turned and walked back to the car.

"I'll tell her," Frank called. "But these people you want to talk to... they do more than just move immigrants. You've made some very bad enemies."

Keller turned as he opened the car door. "Well," he said, "it won't be the first time." He and Angela climbed in and drove off.

CHAPTER FOURTEEN

"**W**ELL," ANGELA SAID, "THAT WAS...INTERESTING."

"That's one word for it," Keller said. "You do have the card, right?"

"Yeah."

"Okay. We get another phone that uses the same kind of card. See what we can pull off the contact list."

"You think that'll give us anything?"

Keller glanced in the rearview mirror to confirm they weren't being followed. "Probably not."

"They're most likely using burners," Angela said, referring to the prepaid cell phones meant to be used a few times, then discarded so they couldn't be traced.

"Most likely," Keller said.

"Which is why you were provoking them. You want them to come after you."

Keller just nodded. "Yeah."

She shook her head. "You're enjoying this."

They were entering a small town. "Yeah," he said. "I am." He took a right at the town's lone stoplight. "You got a problem with that?"

"Actually, no. You want to know why?"

"Sure," he said. "We've got a long drive ahead of us. We might as well make conversation."

She sighed, "Okay. I know I've been fretting over you like a mother hen. But I care about you, Jack. And I know how close to the edge you walk sometimes. It scares me."

Keller didn't answer. He took another left, out of town, headed for the highway that would take them back to Angela's home in Wilmington. The place where Keller had once lived. The place where he'd found a way out of the desert in his head, before he'd had to do things that sent him right back there.

"It scares me sometimes, too," he said quietly.

She nodded. "But back there, at that fight...you had the chance to kill someone. I could see it. You had that tire iron raised, ready to smash that guy's skull...and you didn't do it."

He replayed the incident in his mind. Certainly there'd been a savage and primal part of him, in the back of his mind, screaming for him to bring the iron down, to feel the shiver run upon his arm and into that bloodthirsty place in his head, to hear the crunch of metal crushing flesh and bone. But he'd pulled back. "I didn't need to," he said.

She smiled. "Exactly." She leaned back in the seat and closed her eyes. "I'm going to take a nap. Wake me when you want to change drivers."

He drove on in silence, through small towns, then bigger ones, then back out into the country again before reaching the main east-west highway that led to the coast.

He looked over at Angela. Time and care had etched a couple more lines on her face than he remembered, but there was still the same strength in her face that had brought him out of the numbness he'd been living in since the war, the same beauty that had made him think that living again might be something he'd be interested in doing. She'd given him a job chasing bail skips that gave him the jolt of adrenaline he needed to shock him awake again. That had taken him into even darker places, but he'd felt alive for the first time since that night in the Kuwaiti desert when a stray American missile had killed his entire squad, sparing him only by chance.

He'd loved her then. She'd turned him down, still suffering the physical and emotional effects of her own near-death at the hands of her abusive husband who'd left her scarred and damaged, but not broken.

Then had come Marie. He'd fallen in love with her, and that had helped him get past how he felt about Angela. But then, the things he'd done to protect her and her son had exposed his own dark side and the brutality and violence he was capable of. He'd recoiled from that, just as Marie had. He'd retreated again, back into a different desert. Back to the devils and the dust.

And now, Angela had brought him back again. He wondered what he'd have to do this time. He wondered what it might do to him. *You're a warrior, not a killer*, Lucas had said. *Embrace it. It doesn't make you the monster you think you are.* He hoped that was true.

Keller shook his head as if to clear out the cobwebs. *Enough of this. I've got a job to do. Someone to find. And a friend who needs help.* As he rolled through the flat fertile lands of the coastal plain, he began to smile. By the time he crossed the Cape Fear River Bridge into Wilmington, he was whistling.

CHAPTER FIFTEEN

BENDER AND THE OTHER GUARD, a skinny, cadaverous-looking man who never spoke around the toothpick in his mouth, had marched them back to the camp as the sun had started to sink behind the trees. They didn't go back to the barracks, however. They were lined up outside Building Three, between the end of the building and the lone tree that stood nearby. They stood there, slumped with exhaustion and trembling with fear, until the door opened. Kinney walked out, one end of a thick rope hanging in coils on one shoulder. Diego was on the other end of it, hands still cuffed behind him, the rope knotted into a noose around his neck. His face showed the unmistakable signs of a beating. One eye was completely swollen shut, the other looked straight ahead with the glassy stare of one already dead. His shirt was gone, his body crisscrossed with raised welts and lacerations. There were patches of dried blood caked on his chest and back.

The General came next, dressed in his black judge's robe. As Kinney, still smiling, led Diego past the line, he stopped in front of the queue of men and crossed his arms. "A trial has been held," he intoned, "and verdict announced. This man has been found guilty of assault on a lawful authority and attempting to escape lawful punishment. As an example to you all, the sentence is death." Ruben heard a sob from down the line. He prayed it wasn't Edgar, but kept his own face stony. The last thing he wanted to do was attract the attention of any of these madmen, this so-called General especially.

"Turn and face the tree," the General said, "and do not close your eyes if you want to keep them in your heads." Some of the men seemed confused. The General turned to Ruben. "Tell them."

"He says we have to watch," Ruben told them in Spanish, "or we'll be punished."

Slowly, they turned. More than one man was crying now. *Shut up, you idiots,* Ruben raged inside, but the General took no notice. Or maybe tears were what he wanted.

Kinney stood beneath the tree and unspooled the rope. It took him a couple of tries to toss the free end over a high branch. When it finally went over and dangled down within reach, Kinney grabbed it and pulled it tight, causing Diego to rise up on his tiptoes. Kinney gestured with one hand to Bender, who slung his gun and joined him on the end of the rope. The thin man kept his gun trained on them.

"Does the condemned man have any last words?" the General asked.

Diego's one open eye showed a last glimmer of defiance. "Yeah," he croaked in a dry, ruined voice. "*Cuando llegue al infierno, voy a coger a tu puta madre por el culo.*"

The General looked puzzled. He turned to Ruben. "What did he say?"

Ruben hesitated.

"Well?" the General asked.

Ruben cleared his throat. "He said, 'When I get to hell, I'm going to fuck your whore mother in the ass.'"

The General's face darkened with rage. He motioned to Kinney and Bender. They began to step backward, pulling on the rope. Diego was hauled into the air. His face turned red, then purple. He began to kick. His struggles grew wilder, more desperate, as they hauled him higher.

His eyes bulged and horrible strangled sounds came from this throat as his lungs tried desperately to draw air through a windpipe shut by the pressure of the rope. The crotch of his pants darkened and liquid dribbled from the one leg of his pants. Kinney was laughing in a high, hysterical giggle. Bender just looked determined. The General stood expressionless, his hands behind his back. All of the other men were sobbing, but Ruben kept his face like stone. Like the General's. "They want to see us suffer," he thought. "I won't let them."

It took Diego almost five minutes to die. When he finally hung limp, tongue bulging, eyes seeming to start out of his head, the General turned to them. "Back to your barracks," he said. "And back to work tomorrow."

THE GENERAL SAT IN THE dark, behind his empty desk, and sent up a prayer. Not a petition for the soul of the man he'd just sent to hell, but a prayer of thanksgiving to his God for being allowed to do His holy work. "Thank you, Lord," he breathed, "thanks be to You, O Elohim, You for making me your General. Your Sword Arm."

In his former life, Martin Walker, the man who now called himself General, had only risen to the rank of Staff Sergeant in the American Army. Twice. After the second time he'd been found drunk on duty, he'd been given a bad-conduct discharge, booted out of the Army with loss of all pay and allowances.

He'd been a different man then. He'd even had a different name. When he'd found Jesus, or more accurately, when Jesus had found him, he'd left all that behind—the drink, the fornication, the gluttony, and weakness of the flesh. He'd held onto one thing: his hatred of the lower races, the ones whom God had marked as inferior but that Satan had been raising to power, diluting and poisoning the greatness of America, God's true Promised Land. He still remembered the smirk on the dark black face of the JAG Captain who'd thrown him into exile. Satan had won that day, and Satan had continued to hold sway over him until the Church of Elohim had found him and taught him the nature of his true tormentors. They had put him back together, given him new purpose, and a new name.

Satan had had his victories since: that nigger-loving prosecutor in Ohio, for example, made a martyr of Father Elihu, the man who'd founded the Church of Elohim. Even now, the man who'd given Walker his life back was rotting in a cold prison cell in the Midwest, in the belly of the beast, surrounded by the devil's dark servants and protected by only a very few sworn disciples. It had been Father Elihu who'd given Martin this task: take the money they'd made from selling the black devils the powders and pills that were their own destruction, come to this place, and make a new Israel, where the faithful would make a place for themselves and live according to God's natural order. "You aren't a foot soldier any longer," Father Elihu had said to him on the last day they'd met. He'd been thinner, almost gaunt, and his beard had been shot through with gray, but the fire of God's truth still burned in those brilliant blue eyes. "You are the General. The Sword Arm of the Lord. Lead the people of God." He'd placed his hand against the glass of the visitation room, his eyes locked on Walker's. "Like Moses, I won't see the Promised Land. But you will be my Joshua." Walker had placed his own hand on the opposite side of the glass, unable to speak, so great was the upwelling of pure love he'd felt for Father Elihu.

Since then, he'd conducted his war against the minions of Satan from the shadows, playing the animals off against one another, using their moral weakness and the greed and lust for power of their leaders to bring their downfall. God had made their efforts prosper. It wouldn't be long before the border erupted in another vicious power struggle. Both sides secretly encouraged to slaughter each other and supplied with the tools of war by the Sword Arm of the Lord, in exchange for the drugs he was using to kill more of them on the streets of America. It was the only way to keep their numbers manageable in light of their insane breeding rate. Men's own weakness and sin was the General's greatest weapon in doing the great work of the Lord.

A sudden feeling came over him. A light pulsated at the edge of his vision, a bright curtain that slowly moved down across his eyes until he saw the world through a vibrating veil of light. He'd seen that light before, and he knew what to do. He fell to his knees beside the desk.

"I'm here, Lord," he said, his lips pulled back in a horrible rictus that made a mockery of the word *smile*. As the feeling came over him, he sank to the floor beside the desk.

He awoke, staring at the ceiling, unsure for a moment of where he was. Despite that, he felt a great sense of peace, as he did after all of his ecstasies. He'd read the word in a book on the lives of the saints, and he knew right away that was what he was experiencing. The spirit of the Lord came upon him and told him of great mysteries.

He'd seen a city rising from this fertile earth, a city as white as alabaster, where God's chosen race could live free from the machinations of Satan and the inferior races he'd bent to his evil will. That city would be built by the labor of those minions, as their penance for serving evil. Their chastisement would be severe, as it was today, but necessary. When it was built, God's chosen would come to him and he would lead the white race—the true Children of Israel now that the Jews had refused God's Messiah—to a new and glorious millennium.

The vision faded, leaving him weak and trembling. Someday, he'd see, not through a glass darkly, but face-to-face. For now, he took the ecstasies as God's sign that he was on the right path. They'd been happening more and more recently, which he took as a sign. Sooner or later, one of them would happen in front of the men. He'd have to explain it then, but he had faith that they'd understand.

He got to his feet, a little unsteadily. After a moment, he straightened up and adjusted his clothing. "God is great," he whispered. "Blessed be the name of the Lord."

CHAPTER SIXTEEN

AFTER ALL THIS TIME, IT felt strange to be back in the office where he'd once worked. H & H Bail Bonds was in the same Wilmington storefront, a few blocks from the courthouse. He sat behind his old desk, a few feet away from Angela's. Paperwork was spread out across it. He noticed a couple of FTA notices, sent to the bonding company when a client failed to show. They'd have one hundred eighty days to bring them back to jail or forfeit the money they'd put up.

"So who you got working skips?" Keller asked.

She shrugged, looking oddly embarrassed. "Couple of freelancers," she said. "One of them's a new guy, just back from Afghanistan." She turned back to her computer. The phone they'd picked up at a Walmart, the twin to the one she'd taken from Rosita Miron, was set on the desk next to it. She was researching the numbers on the SIM card. She sat back. "I've got the last couple of numbers she dialed. I figured one of them would be the contact in Mexico."

"And?"

"Like I thought. No information. Even when I ping the sources I'm not supposed to have."

Keller grimaced. "Damn."

"You going to drop the card off with the local Feds?"

He shook his head. "It'll get Miron and whoever she's dealing with in trouble. But that won't do us any good. The only value that card has is the threat that we might use it. If we do, the threat goes away, and so does our leverage."

The phone rang. Angela picked it up. "H & H Bail Bonds." She listened for a moment, then sank slowly into the chair. "Yes," she said, "this is Angela Sanchez." She looked at Keller. "Yes, Mr. Keller is here, too. I'll put him on." She nodded to the extension on Keller's desk. Keller walked over and picked it up. "Jack Keller," he said.

The voice on the other end was deep, smooth, with a trace of Spanish accent. "Mr. Keller. I understand you wish to speak with us."

"Depends," Keller said. "Who are you?"

"I'm the person Oscar Sanchez came to see about his problem," the man said.

"Ah," Keller said. "You're Mrs. Miron's friend."

A pause. "Yes."

"And your name is…?" Keller said.

"My name is not important."

"It kind of is," Keller said. "I mean, if we're going to sit down and meet and all, I like to know the name of the person I'm speaking to."

"I'm afraid the meeting you suggest is not possible."

"You'd be amazed what's possible if you're properly motivated," Keller said. "How much would it motivate you to keep that SIM card with your contact information on it out of the hands of the Immigration people? Or, say, the DEA?"

The man chuckled. "Are you threatening me, Mr. Keller?" Keller started to answer but the man cut him off. "Never mind," he said. "I represent a man named Auguste Mandujano. Do you know the name?"

"Can't say I do," Keller said.

"Perhaps you should research it." the voice said. "Of course, much of what you'll find is exaggerated. Tabloid nonsense. But some of it is true."

"Which part?" Keller said.

"Enough to make you a little more respectful. A little less flippant."

"Sorry," Keller said. "It's a failing of mine. The flippancy, I mean. Also, my psychiatrist tells me I have problems with impulse control. When I get angry, I tend to do reckless things."

"Things like releasing information off SIM cards to the authorities?"

"Yeah. Like that."

"You overestimate the effect that would have."

"I don't think so," Keller said, "or else you wouldn't have called."

"I can tell you this much," the voice said. "Oscar Sanchez came to see us. He was concerned about his sons. But we sent him away."

"He'd paid you to get his sons across the border," Keller said. "Were they in one of the groups who went missing?"

There was no answer.

"How does that happen?" Keller persisted. "How do you lose a truck full of people? Much less two?"

More silence. Then, "Some people have been talking more than they should."

"People open up to me," Keller said. "So let's just assume I know a lot. Tell me what happened with Oscar Sanchez."

"As I said. We sent him away. We had no information for him."

"And he just walked away?" Keller said. "'Oh thanks, so my sons are missing, I'll just be moving along, and by the way, just keep the money I paid you'? I'm assuming you didn't give him a refund."

"He wasn't happy," the voice said. "But there are always risks in this sort of venture."

"Like the risk of disappearing off the face of the earth? I'm sure you tell your customers that, right up front."

"This conversation is becoming pointless," the voice said. "I've told you what you asked."

"No, you've told me a bunch of evasive bullshit," Keller said. "I think I need to come see Mr. Mandujano personally."

"That would not be wise."

"Like I said, poor impulse control," Keller said. "See you real soon now." He broke the connection and looked over at Angela. She had put the phone down and was typing something into the laptop computer on her desk. She sat back and studied the screen, then turned it around without expression. Keller walked over and looked.

"So," he said. "This Mandujano fellow's not one to keep a low profile."

"Drugs," she said. "Weapons. Prostitution. Human trafficking."

"And yet," he said, "Mexico doesn't want to let our folks have a word with him."

"So he's connected."

"Looks like it." Keller bent over. "Jesus," he said. "Is this supposed to be his house? I can't read it because the website's in Spanish."

She turned the computer back around, read the captions. "Yeah. The guy's practically a rock star in Mexico."

"Well," Keller said, "that'll make it easier to find him."

"You can't be thinking of going there," she said.

"This guy, or his people, was the last ones we know of who saw Oscar—" He stopped himself.

She finished the sentence for him. "The last ones to see him alive."

"Yeah."

"You think they killed him."

"There's no evidence of that," Keller said.

"Just this guy's reputation."

He shrugged. "He said that most of that was 'tabloid nonsense.' But yeah, Angela, it's a possibility. These are people who aren't fond of people who ask too many questions."

"And you want to go down there and do just that."

"I don't know any other way to find Oscar. Or find out what happened to him."

"If he's alive, he'll come home," she said. "If he's dead…" she closed her eyes and said, "then we have to find out who and why, don't we?"

"Partly right," Keller said. "Except not 'we.' I'm going alone."

She opened her eyes. "Like hell."

"You said yourself. It's dangerous."

"I'm not some wilting flower, Jack. You know better than to think I'm going to sit back here and wait for news."

He tried another tack. "Don't you have a business to run?" he said.
"Yeah. So we better make this quick." She stood up. "I'll go pack."

THE MAN ON THE PHONE stared at it in disbelief. Keller had hung up on him. No one hung up on him.

"Well?" Auguste Mandujano said. "Are we done with this, Andreas?"

Andreas Zavalo put the phone down on the glass table next to his lounge chair. He was a fat man, dressed in a loud Hawaiian shirt and cargo pants. His brown skin glistened with sweat and suntan lotion. "He says he's coming to see us."

Mandujano stared at the brilliant blue water in the pool for a moment. Then he sat up. The girl in the chair next to him sat up as well, watching, alert to see if he required anything. She was blond, beautiful, and no more than eighteen. Mandujano didn't look at her, Zavalo noticed. "What about this Sanchez?" he said. "Has he been back?"

Zavalo hesitated. "He's been asking around," he said. "In the bars. The church. Some of the shops. I think he's trying to find the warehouse."

Mandujano turned to look at him. His eyes were invisible behind the dark sunglasses. His mouth was a tight line.

"I was getting ready to send a couple of men to persuade him to stop," Zavalo said weakly.

"No," Mandujano said. "Bring him here. I want to find out what he knows about this Keller."

"What do we do when he tells us?" Zavalo asked. He had no doubt that he could make Sanchez tell him whatever he wanted to know.

"I'll decide that when the time comes," Mandujano said. He stood up. The girl was still looking at him. Mandujano didn't acknowledge her presence. "I'm going to go take a nap," he said. He walked off. The girl stared after him. She looked at Zavalo, her wide, lovely blue eyes asking what she should do.

"Go to your own room," he said, as kindly as he could. "He'll send for you if he wants you." Mutely, she got up and walked toward the house. Zavalo sighed. With all the other shit he had to attend to on Mandujano's behalf, he now had this nosy American, Keller, to deal with. And he had to find his boss a new playmate. Obviously this one was starting to bore him. She'd become too compliant, too thoroughly broken. The boss liked it when they fought.

First things first. He picked the phone back up and started to dial. Then he stopped himself. Like the girl, this phone had reached the end of its usefulness. Groaning with the effort, he stood up, and went inside to find another phone.

CHAPTER SEVENTEEN

THE BARRACKS WERE SILENT, THE men numb with the shock of watching Diego's murder. Most of them lay on their bunks, staring. Ruben sat on the edge of his, leaning across to where his bothers sat. Edgar had stopped crying, but his eyes were still red. Ruben was holding his brother's hands in his. He struggled to find some words of comfort, but nothing came. His stomach growled.

There was a commotion at the door of the barracks. Ruben let go of Edgar's hands and sat back. Kinney, the blond-haired guard, had entered. He didn't have his submachine gun with him, but he had a pistol in an unsnapped holster on his waist and the sjambok in one hand. His nose was swollen and discolored from where Diego had hit him.

Some of the men sat up, glaring at Kinney. He looked back at one of them. "The fuck you looking at, *amigo*?" he said in a soft, threatening voice. The man didn't answer. He lay back down, staring at the ceiling.

Ruben felt apprehension twisting in his belly along with the hunger. The guards rarely came all the way into the barracks anymore. In the mornings, they stood outside, shouting and pounding on the flimsy wooden walls to wake everyone up, then to order them outside after their breakfast. His fear grew worse when Kinney came and stood at the foot of his bed. He didn't dare look at Edgar. *Don't let them know you're related*, Diego had said.

Kinney pointed at Ruben with the sjambok. "You," he said. "General wants to see you."

"No," he heard Edgar whisper.

"Shhh," Ruben said, and stood up. "What for?" he said in English.

Kinney raised the sjambok. "You need a reminder of what your place is here, boy?"

"No," Ruben said.

"Good. Now git."

Ruben walked toward the door, Kinney following behind. He felt the eyes of the other men on him. His knees were shaking so badly he almost stumbled and fell. He wondered if the blond man was taking him to be hanged next to Diego. He wondered if they'd beat him first with one of those terrible whips. He tried to remember his prayers, but his brain seemed frozen.

Outside, the air was hot and sticky. Harsh white lights burned at intervals along the fence surrounding the compound, throwing inky black shadows across the open spaces. He could see a shadowy figure in the guard tower nearest the gate.

"That way," Kinney pointed with the sjambok toward Building Three.

"Wh-what did I do?" Ruben asked. The only response was a shove with the end of the leather whip. They walked where Diego still hung from the tree. His neck was stretched grotesquely. As they got closer, Ruben saw that someone had removed Diego's pants. A slight breeze stirred his hanging body, and Ruben saw what they'd done. Someone had castrated him, and they hadn't been careful or precise about it.

"Guess he won't be fucking anyone in the ass, huh?" Kinney laughed.

Ruben collapsed. He fell to his knees retching, but all his empty stomach could bring up was bile. That seemed to amuse Kinney even more, and his laughter rang in Ruben's ears like the mocking cackle of demons. *We really are in hell,* he though dazedly. Suddenly, Kinney seemed to tire of the joke. He grabbed Ruben by the hair and yanked him up. Ruben cried out in pain as he staggered to his feet.

"C'mon, Pancho," the man sneered. "Can't keep the General waiting."

Inside, the room was the same as when Ruben and the others were first brought there: the flags, the table, the bald man sitting behind it. The only difference was, the man wasn't wearing a robe. Instead, he was dressed in military-style fatigues. He was reading from a sheaf of papers held in one hand. As Ruben and Kinney entered the room, he looked up.

"Ah," he said, and his voice was almost friendly. "Come here, boy. I have some questions for you."

Ruben walked forward, shuffling like a sleepwalker. When he stood before the table, the General looked him up and down. "So," he said, "You seem to have an excellent command of English."

Ruben didn't answer. Kinney smacked him in the back of the head. "Answer the General when he speaks to you."

"Yes," Ruben managed to croak. That earned him another smack in the head.

"Yes, *sir*," Kinney said.

"Yes, sir," Ruben said.

"Are you educated?" the General asked. "Have you been to school?"

"Yes, sir," Ruben said.

"You can read and write?"

"Yes, sir."

The General chuckled. "A bit like teaching monkeys to do sums. But it has its uses." He set the papers down. "From now on," he said, "you're going to be my...let's call it a liaison...to your fellow prisoners. You'll make my instructions known to them. I will expect you to keep me informed on their activities as well. In return, you'll have lighter duties. I may find something administrative for you to do. The important thing is, I'd like to avoid any more trouble like we just had. Trouble should be nipped in the bud before it has time to turn into a situation where I have to do what I just did."

Ruben couldn't believe what he was hearing. You…you want me to inform on the others?"

The General rubbed his eyes. "It may surprise you to know, young man, that what happened today gives me no pleasure. It could have been avoided had I known of that man's attitude problem."

"He didn't have an attitude problem," Ruben said. "He had a problem with this guy…" he gestured at Kinney, "raping his sister and bragging about it in front of him."

The General's voice turned to ice. "Sergeant Kinney's lapses in judgment will be dealt with as I see fit," he said. "But you need to learn your place, young man. It is your people's destiny to serve."

"My…" Ruben was dumbfounded. He shook his head in disbelief.

"You don't believe that?" the General said. "You've already been judged by history. Did you not study history in whatever squalid little hole of a schoolhouse you came from?" his voice rose and his eyes took on a messianic gleam. "You lost half your country to a superior people, with superior weapons and intellect. Now, what's left of your country is a cesspool of corruption and violence. You cannot govern yourselves. That's why so many of you want to come here and take from us by force of numbers what you can't by fair competition. You want to drown us in a brown tide. Well, some of us see what's happening. We see the inability of our so-called leaders to stop the invasion of our homeland. And that's just what it is, boy. An invasion. An act of war. And in that war, there is treason at the highest levels. In that event, patriots need to do what they need to do."

"I'm not even from Mexico," Ruben said. "I'm Colombian." He raised a hand to cut off the response. He felt weary enough to sink through the floor. "Whatever," he said. "I won't do it. I won't be an informer."

"Then at dawn tomorrow," the General said, "your little brother will take your late friend's place in the tree." Ruben's shock must have showed on his face, because the General chuckled again. "I have more sources of information than you know, boy. Now what will it be?"

Ruben's mind was racing. "Okay," he said. "I'll do it. But only if you get those people some food. They've been working all day. They're starving."

The General continued to look amused. "Now you presume to bargain with me?"

"No," Ruben said, "but..."

"No *sir*," Kinney spoke up.

"No sir," Ruben said, "but you need them to work, right? They can't work as hard if you don't feed them. Some of them are already getting sick."

The bald man seemed to ponder for a moment. Then he nodded. "All right," he said. "Sergeant Kinney, have the mess hall prepare them the usual ration. But," he looked at Ruben, "I expect you to get them to work hard tomorrow. I'll be watching their output. If they fall behind..." He shrugged.

"They won't," Ruben said, "if you feed them."

"Very well," the General said.

"One more thing," Ruben said.

The General had been turning to leave. Now he turned back, an amazed expression on his face. "My," he said, "You are a bold little monkey, aren't you?"

Ruben ignored the insult. "That man," he said. "The one you hanged. Cut him down. Don't leave him there. Not like that."

The General shook his head. "He needs to serve as an example to the others."

"You made your example. Cut him down and let us bury him."

The General looked at him. Ruben couldn't read what was in those cold dead eyes. Finally he said, "All right. But you can cut him down yourself. Sergeant Kinney, get him a tarp to wrap the body in."

"Yes, sir," Kinney said. He didn't sound pleased.

"You and one man, a man you pick, will be the burial detail, boy," the General said. "After that, it's back to work."

"Yes sir," Ruben said. The next words were the hardest he'd ever said in his life, but he knew they might buy him some leeway next time.

"Thank you, sir," he said.

CHAPTER EIGHTEEN

THE HOTEL WAS SMALL, NOT fancy, but clean, and the front desk guy spoke passable English. Its main attractions were that it was only a short drive from the bridge that led across the Rio Grande to the Texas side, and you could check in without a credit card. Keller had liked that when he saw this place on the website where he'd searched for cheap hotels. It may have been unjustified paranoia, but he was about to start stirring things up. The fewer ways people had to trace him, the better he liked it.

Jack Keller had been outside of the borders of the United States only one time before, when he deployed to Kuwait. His path had taken him via Paris and Cairo, courtesy of the U.S. Army. He hadn't had any chance to see either of those places, or much of Kuwait, either, before he was dropped into a hot, dusty, and boring forward base to await further orders. Then there was the war and all that came after. He hadn't felt much like leaving the country again after that. He wasn't that far from the border now, and couldn't go too much farther on just his tourist card, but driving across that river, from Texas to this small, dusty town at the ass end of nowhere felt like crossing a line in his head as well as on the map.

The town was called Ciudad de Piedras, and it had been little more than a wide spot in the road south of the Rio Grande until the 1990s. That was when the explosion in small assembly factories called *maquiladoras* brought thousands from the countryside to find work putting together everything from cheap blenders to aircraft components. Seemingly overnight, the place was a boom town. Boom towns brought money, and money brought people like Auguste Mandujano.

Keller stood on the inner balcony of the hotel, resting his elbows on the railing, looking out over the pool. The harsh white summer sun was going down, the buildings casting long shadows into the courtyard. Darkness was coming, and that darkness was where the hunter in him lived and thrived.

The hotel was built in a U-shape, with the open end of the U facing a crowded noisy street. The office and restaurant sat across the ends of the "arms" of the U, narrowing the gap into the courtyard. Keller's room was at the bottom of the U, with Angela's next to it.

He had no idea if Mandujano was even in town. The man had houses all over Mexico, Central America, and the Caribbean. Keller had been a little shocked to see how easy it was to find the places online. Mandujano apparently felt secure enough this side of the border to be brazen about flaunting his wealth. Magazines and news websites, mostly Mexican, had reported (some breathlessly, some with evident disgust) on the "narco-palaces," as one website (a disgusted one) put it.

But only one of those houses was this close to the U.S. Border. It was as good as any place to start trying to find out about human smuggling. Besides, Keller had the feeling that when he started asking questions, Mandujano's people, maybe even the man himself, would come to him.

He heard a door open behind him. Angela came to stand next to him, leaning on the balcony rail. "Getting dark," she said. "Hope it cools down some."

"It will," Keller said.

"So what's the plan?"

He shrugged. "Find the places where the locals hang out. Show

Oscar's picture around. Ask if anyone knows Mandujano."

"And wait for someone to try and stop you."

"Be positive. Maybe they'll invite us up to the house for cocktails."

"Stop trying to be funny. This is dangerous, Jack."

"Which is why I didn't want you to come. And I don't want you to come with me tonight."

"You don't think I can handle myself?"

"I think I'll work better if I don't have to be worrying about you."

"Then don't," she said.

"It's not something I can help."

"Well, I worry about you, too. I can't help that, either." She sighed and turned toward him. "We might as well get it out in the open, Jack."

"Get what out in the open?" he said, even though he knew what she meant.

"This is stirring up a lot of old emotions. At least it is for me."

He didn't answer at first, just kept looking out over the pool. She closed her eyes and shook her head. "Great," she said, "leave me hanging."

"I feel the same way," he said quietly. "But that kind of complicates the fact that we're looking for your husband."

"A little bit, yeah," she said.

"I'm not going to stop," he said.

"I know. Neither one of us would ever forgive ourselves if we stopped looking now. But what are we going to do when we find him?"

If, he said to himself. "I don't know. We'll figure that out when it happens." He shoved himself away from the railing. "And it's not going to happen if I don't get to work." He turned to her. "Angela, stay here. Please."

"You've forgotten something," she said. "You don't speak Spanish. I do. Who are you going to get to translate?"

"I'll think of something," he said. "I'll find someone."

She shook her head. "We need to get going."

He sighed. "Jesus, you're stubborn."

"Pot, meet kettle."

He had to laugh at that. "Okay," he said. "You win. Let's go."

IT WAS THE SORT OF place you found in any town that grew too fast. A neon-lit strip of shabby bars, shops with iron grates on the windows to protect their inventory after hours, populated with scatterings of people who slouched watchfully in doorways, conducted conversations with heads held close together, and drifted in and out of the shadows. A narrow, hard-to-navigate street made even trickier by parked cars and the occasional stumbling aimless pedestrian who had apparently lost the concept of crossing at the light sometime earlier in the evening.

Keller had the window down. The tinny blare of music from the bars mixed with the rumble and clatter of vehicles whose pistons and mufflers had seen better days, punctuated from time to time by bursts of laughter and shouted Spanish.

"So," Angela said, "Where do we start?"

Keller spotted a vehicle that looked out of place, a shiny back diesel Mercedes. There was a parking place across the street. "Here seems as good a place as any." He maneuvered the old Jeep, which they'd bought for cash in El Paso, into the space between an ancient station wagon — with cardboard where one window should be — and a bright yellow Volkswagen Bug that looked as if someone had tried to repair the finish with a can of spray paint. The battered old Jeep fit right in.

They got out and Keller locked the vehicle. A young man sauntered up to them. He wore knee-length red shorts and a San Diego Padres jersey that hung on his skinny frame like a tent. He looked no older than twelve or thirteen. "Hey," he said.

Keller straightened up. "Let me guess," he said. "You'll watch my car and make sure nothing happens to it. For five bucks."

"Shit no, man," the kid said. He grinned. "Fifteen."

"Sounds like a lot," Keller said.

The kid shrugged. "Bad neighborhood." He looked at Angela, who'd gotten out and come over to stand by Keller. "Not the sort of place a guy normally brings his lady, you know?"

"I know," Keller said. "We're looking for someone."

The kid tilted his head back and looked at them with narrowed eyes. "Yeah, well, I don't know nobody. I'm, like, a stranger here myself."

Angela smiled. "We're not cops."

The kid didn't look convinced. "Uh-huh."

Angela took a photograph out of her back pocket. "We're looking for this man." She held the photo out. The kid backed away a little, then came forward and took it. He cocked his head to one side, as if considering. "He owe you money or something?"

"He's my husband," Angela said. "He came down here looking for someone, too. But then he disappeared."

The kid looked up. The hard, cocky facade was gone. He looked young again. "That happens around here," he said in a small voice. "A lot." He handed the picture back. "Sorry, lady," he said, and he actually sounded like he meant it. "I never saw this guy."

"Okay," Keller said. "So, tell you what. You watch the car."

"Fifteen bucks," the kid said.

Keller gestured across to the Mercedes. "How much you charge that guy to watch *his* car?"

The kid looked, then barked out a short laugh. "Funny."

"What's funny?"

The kid rolled his eyes as if Keller had asked the stupidest question in the world. "That guy don't need no one to watch his car. No one messes with him."

"Maybe he's the guy we need to be talking to," Keller said.

"Yeah," the kid said. "You do that, homes. Let me know how it works out for you."

"Ten bucks," Keller said. "Five now, five when we get back."

"American?"

"Yeah," Keller said, getting out his billfold, "American." It was full of cash. Keller had figured he might need to spread some around to pay for information. He held out the fiver. The kid took it.

"You talk to that guy," the kid said, "you better hope he likes what you have to say."

"Or what?"

"Or else I'm out my second five bucks."

CHAPTER NINETEEN

THE BAR WAS TINY, JUST a guy behind a wooden counter with a few stools in front of it and bottles lined along wooden shelves behind. A slow, sad ballad in Spanish blared from a jukebox near the door.

There was a narrow aisle between the stools and a row of tables along the outside wall. The clientele seated on the stools seemed mostly male, men with suspicious eyes that looked them over, then turned back to studying the bar top. They were dressed in blue jeans and work shirts. A couple wore trucker hats; one had a white cowboy hat sitting on the bar in front of him.

All of the tables were empty...save one. The man seated at that one stood out in much the same way as the Mercedes stood out on the street. He wore black slacks and a matching black shirt with an ornate silver tracery across the chest and shoulders. A woman was seated across from him, a young brunette in a skirt and white blouse. She held a piece of fabric that she twisted nervously between her hands. She was saying something, but her head was down. She wasn't looking at the man in black. The man looked over at them, turned back to the woman, then did a double take and stared at Keller and Angela as they walked to the bar. The woman started to say something, but the man in black shushed her with one raised finger.

"*Buenas tardes,*" Angela said to the bartender, a stocky, fortyish man with thick dark hair, and a nose that looked like it had been broken more than once.

He nodded. "*¿Qué le gustaría ordenar?*"

"*Agua, por favor,*" Angela said.

"*Cerveza,*" Keller said. He looked behind the bar for something he recognized. "Tecate." The bartender nodded and pulled the beer and a bottled water out of the cooler. Angela started talking to the bartender, pulling the picture of Oscar out of her back pocket. Keller tuned her out and watched the man in black. Seated, Keller couldn't tell how tall he was, but he was powerfully built, with broad shoulders and large, thick-fingered hands. His hair was thinning, but slicked back and sprayed with something that made it look hard and shiny, like shellac. His eyes were small and set close together. Those eyes never left Keller. The woman said something else. The man's response was short and apparently so sharp, it made the woman visibly flinch. She got up from the table, her face hardening with anger. She was beautiful, Keller saw, with sculpted cheekbones, full lips, and wide dark eyes. Her full breasts strained against the tight blouse. She shook out the piece of fabric and began tying it around her waist. An apron. She obviously worked there. She raised her head and caught Keller looking at her. She straightened up and smoothed the apron down, smiling at him. He took the beer and raised it to his lips. She walked toward him, her eyes on his. She didn't speak as she sidled past him, close enough that her hip brushed his. Keller looked over at the man in black. He looked angry enough to chew nails.

Angela turned to him. "The bartender says he hasn't seen Oscar." Then she saw the expression on Keller's face. "What?"

"Give me the picture," Keller said.

"Okay." She handed it over. The man in black was rising from his chair, his face set and hard. "Oh, boy," Angela said.

"Just translate for me." He shoved himself back from the bar.

As the man in black strode down the narrow aisle between the bar and the tables, Keller advanced to meet him, plastering a big friendly smile on his face. As they drew closer together, Keller stuck out a hand. "Hey, pal!" he said in a hearty voice. "You look like a guy who might be able to help us out."

The man stopped, his eyes narrowed and his brow furrowing with confusion. He didn't take the offered hand. Keller heard Angela's rapid-fire translation next to him. Out of the corner of his eye, he could see the men at the bar turning to watch the show. Keller held out the picture of Oscar, keeping his other hand extended for a friendly shake.

"We're looking for a friend of ours," Keller went on in that same slightly too loud voice. "Came down here not long ago. His name's Oscar Sanchez." Keller waited a beat. "I'm Jack Keller." He waited for the reaction. If this guy, as he suspected, was some kind of soldier in the Mandujano Organization, he might have been told to keep an ear out for those two names.

He was disappointed. Neither name seemed to register. The guy still looked confused, but the confusion was wearing off and turning to suspicion. The guy had been temporarily disarmed by Keller's dumb-*turista* approach, but it wouldn't be long before he turned back toward his default state of anger and arrogance. Keller wondered if he should just coldcock the guy right now and get them the hell out of there.

Angela said something else. Keller caught a word he recognized. *Marido.* Husband.

The man looked back and forth, between Keller and Angela. Then he reached out and took the photo from Keller in his fat stubby fingers. He studied it for a moment. Keller dropped his hands back to his sides. The song on the jukebox finished. There was no sound for a long moment. Everyone was watching the three of them. Then as the opening chords of Van Halen's "Runnin' with the Devil" blasted out of the cheap jukebox speakers, the guy shook his head and handed the photo back. He said something to Angela, then turned and gave Keller a hard look. He took out a billfold and dropped a couple of bills on the bar. With another look at Keller, he walked out. The men at the bar turned back to their contemplation of the woodwork.

"Was it something I said?" Keller asked.

"Come on." Angela led him back outside.

They stood under the sign, which simply said BAR in large neon script. The sign buzzed and popped as if it was going to explode into a shower of sparks any moment.

"What was that all about?" Angela said.

"I figured that guy might be part of Mandujano's local crew," Keller said. "I figured if we were going to ask anyone, it ought to be him."

"So you wanted to piss him off by making eyes at his girlfriend?"

"What? No. That wasn't..."

"Whatever, Keller," she said. "Let's move on." She walked off without looking back. He followed her, baffled by the ice in her tone.

They didn't have any better luck in the dozen or so bars, cheap restaurants, and small convenience stores where they stopped to show the picture and ask questions. They were greeted mostly with suspicion and silence. No one would admit to having seen Oscar, and the mention of Mandujano's name seemed to make people forget not only what little English they had, but most of their Spanish as well. Finally, exhausted, they began the long trudge back to where they'd parked the Jeep. It was at least two in the morning, but the streets were still busy. The shouts and laughter had become more ragged, maybe even slightly desperate, but the party went on.

"Think that kid's still watching the car?" Angela said. Fatigue was making her limp slightly, the pain of her old injuries flaring up.

"Nah," Keller answered. "He's taken the money and run by now."

"Hope the car's still there," she said. "At least enough of it to get us back to the hotel."

It was. True to Keller's prediction, the boy had gone. In his place, slouching against the hood of the Jeep, was the girl from the restaurant. She'd changed out of the skirt into blue jeans that hugged her lush hips, but she was still wearing the white blouse. "Hey," she said as they drew near. She sounded like she was greeting friends she saw every day.

"Hey," Angela said as they slowed.

The girl stood up. "I hear you looking for your husband," she said, her English thickly accented.

"That's right," Angela said.

"You still got that picture?"

Mutely, Angela handed it over. She looked at it for a minute. "Yeah," she said. "I seen him."

"When?" Keller said.

She shrugged. "Couple, three days ago."

"Uh-huh," Keller said. Something about her demeanor was too elaborately nonchalant. It seemed artificial. She was trying to work some sort of con, he figured. He expected to be hit up for money next. Then he noticed that she kept looking back at the car.

"So," he said, "where was he? What was he doing?"

"Asking around," she said. "You know?"

"Do you know where he went?" Angela said.

She shrugged again, glancing to the car, and then back at them. "Not really, but he said he'd be back. Maybe tomorrow night."

"Okay," Keller said. "We'll be back tomorrow night. *Gracias.*"

"*De nada.*" The girl sauntered away, hips swinging.

"She's lying," Angela said in a low voice.

"Yep, hope she's better at waitressing than she is at lying." He walked over to the Jeep and bent over. He slid a hand up into the wheel well nearest where the girl had been leaning against the car.

"What are you doing?" Angela asked.

His fingers traced along the rough, grime-encrusted inside of the fender. He encountered something that felt as if it was made of plastic. He tugged at it. There was a slight resistance, then the object came free. He pulled it out. It was a flat black plastic box with a pair of black buttons on its face. The back was a magnet to hold it fast to the metal of the car.

"Is that what I think it is?" she said.

"Yep," he said. "GPS tracker."

"These guys are high tech," she said.

"Not really," he said. "You can buy these at Walmart now. Worried moms use them to track their teenagers. Suspicious wives use them to figure out if hubby's going to a motel."

"Or vice versa," she said. He could tell she was shaken, even as she tried to keep her voice light.

"Yeah."

"So they know we're here," she said.

"Pretty much," he said. "Just not exactly where."

"So what are you going to do?"

"Depends," he said. "Are you going to head back north and let me handle this?"

She shook her head. "No."

"Okay, then," he said. He reared back and threw the device as hard as he could up onto the metal awning of a closed and shuttered pharmacy.

"What was that for?" she said.

"As long as you're here, I don't want them to find us."

"And if you're here alone," she said, "you're okay with that."

"Yeah. Pretty much."

"And what do you think would happen then?"

"Well, I hope we'd be able to have a civilized conversation about where Oscar might be," Keller said.

"Yeah, because these drug lords and smugglers have such a great track record for civilized conversation."

Keller shook his head, giving her an exaggerated look of disappointment. "That's a little bigoted, don't you think?" he said.

"Don't joke about this, Jack. These people are killers."

"So am I."

"Are we back to that again?" she said.

"No," he said, "we're back to the hotel. We need to get some sleep."

"And what about tomorrow?"

"We do the same thing again," Keller said. "Ask around. See if anyone's seen him."

"And poke Mandujano in the nose some more."

"That, too. Hey, you got a better idea?"

She sighed. "No. Not right now. I'm exhausted."

"So let's go."

They made the drive back to the hotel in silence. Keller kept checking the rearview mirror to see if they were being followed. A part of him was disappointed that he saw nothing. He could feel the rush building up, the feeling he always got when he was hunting. He felt they were getting close. He wasn't sure why, but it was a feeling he'd learned to trust.

He pulled into the courtyard and parked. They trudged up the stairs in silence. Keller was unlocking the door to his room when Angela put her hand on his shoulder. He turned around.

"Jack," she said softly, "let's both just go home tomorrow."

"What about Oscar?" he said.

"I don't think we're going to find him," she said.

"You're just tired. Get some sleep."

"What if he's —" She stopped.

"Dead?" Keller finished. "If he is, I want to know how it happened. I want to know why. And if someone did it, they're going to answer for it."

"I don't want you to get hurt," she said. She put her arms around him. He hesitated slightly, but then hugged her back. She felt good against him. He ran a hand through her hair. She made a small sound, deep in her throat, then gently pushed him away. Her eyes were glistening. "Go," she said, then turned and walked back into her room.

Keller went back into his own room. He took off his boots and lay back on the bed, staring at the ceiling. He knew Angela was probably right. Oscar was probably dead, buried out in the desert somewhere. But he couldn't stop the hunt. The relentlessness that had made him so good as a bounty hunter was too ingrained. He could no more stop now than he could stop breathing. But what if Oscar was alive, and Keller found him? What then? He still had feelings for Angela. She clearly had the same feelings for him. But Oscar was his friend.

Keller lay there, those same thoughts running round and around in his head. He lay there, aching to get up and go knock on Angela's door. He strained his ears, waiting and hoping for her knock on his. But there was only silence. *Jesus, could this get any more fucked up?* Finally, he drifted off into a fitful sleep.

In the morning, Angela was gone.

CHAPTER
TWENTY

I T WAS HARD FOR RUBEN to decide. For a moment, he considered just cutting Diego down and burying him by himself. He didn't think he could bring himself to ask someone else to face that grotesque, dangling thing that was once a man. A friend. He didn't even know if he could get any of the older men to help him, and he knew he wasn't going to ask his little brother. But he knew that it would take him all night, if not longer, to do the job alone. He hesitated outside the door of the barracks.

"Well," Bender said, "get on in there, and get you some help. I ain't got all fuckin' night."

Moving like a man in a dream, Ruben opened the door and went in. The men looked up from their bunks. Some of them were startled, as if they hadn't expected him to return.

He looked at the man on the closest bed to him. His name was Dante. He didn't say much, but Ruben recalled that he'd said he hoped to make enough money in America to bring his fiancée north as well. All of that seemed so far away now. Dante was watching him curiously, as if puzzled by the look on his face.

"*Que pasa, ese?*" he said softly. "You don't look so good."

"I need your help, Dante," Ruben said. "We have to bury Diego."

"Bury…" Dante looked around, as if searching for someone else to do the job.

"Please," Ruben said. "We can't just let him hang there all night."

Dante closed his eyes, then nodded. "Okay," he said. "I'll help."

Ruben heard the bang and rattle of buckets outside. The men sat up, eyes widening in fear. "They're bringing food," Ruben said. "Dante and I have to go do something." He saw the dubious looks on some faces, the beginnings of grins on others. He realized how that must have sounded. "They're going to let us bury Diego." He gestured toward Dante. "Dante and I. Will you save us some food? For when we get back?"

The pudgy guard named Bender entered. He was carrying one of the big galvanized buckets their food came in. Ruben could smell the stew that they typically got for dinner. It was a thin broth, with only a few chunks of meat and some shriveled carrots and potatoes, but at that moment, it was enough to make Ruben's stomach growl. "Please," he said, "we won't be long." The men wouldn't look at him. Finally, Edgar's voice piped up from the back of the room. "I'll save you some food," he said. "Don't worry. Hurry back."

"Come ON, Goddamn it," he heard Bender shout from outside. Ruben turned and walked out, Dante trailing in his wake.

Someone had left a tattered blanket laid out on the ground next to Diego's dangling body. A pair of shovels rested on it. Kinney slouched a few feet away, in the shadows, his submachine gun held loosely in his hands. "About damn time," he grumbled. "*Vamanos, muchachos.* We got shit to do." His glance in the direction of the women's barracks left no doubt as to what that was.

Dante looked up at Diego's corpse and crossed himself. Ruben could hear him whispering something under his breath, "*El Senor es mi pastor,*" he murmured, "*nada mi falta.*" The Lord is my shepherd, I shall not want…

"How are we supposed to get him down?" Ruben asked Kinney

Kinney shook his head in disgust. He drew a long knife from his belt and walked to where he'd tied the end of the rope around the tree. With short, impatient strokes, he sawed at the rope.

"Quick," Ruben said to Dante, "spread the blanket out. Under him."

Dante hesitated. "Hurry," Ruben urged as he rushed to grab the rope. He didn't expect Kinney was going to lower Diego gently to the ground. He was right. When the rope parted, Ruben gasped as he tried to take the total weight of Diego's body, then cried out as the rope began to slip through his fingers, abrading the skin from his palms. Dante looked up from where he was spreading the blanket, a look of horror on his face at the ghastly sight of Diego's body descending almost on top of him. The rope was a line of fire between Ruben's palms. He sobbed as he let go. Diego's body collapsed to the ground, almost on top of Dante, who screamed like a woman and jumped back. The body crumpled like a puppet with its strings cut. As it collapsed, a long, piteous groan escaped the slack lips.

"*Dios mio!*" Dante cried. "He's alive!"

Kinney laughed nastily. "No, you dumbass monkey," he said. "That's just air leaving the body. Now get to work."

Ruben walked over and tried to straighten Diego's body onto the spread-out blanket. He grunted with the effort, but it was like trying to move a bag of wet cement. "Come on," he panted to Dante. "Help me." The man shook his head, the whites of his eyes showing like a spooked horse.

Kinney ratcheted the charging lever on his machine gun. "He said *help him*, monkey."

With a low moan of horror, Dante began to help. It took a few minutes to get Diego arranged on the blanket, after which Ruben wrapped the sides over Diego, obscuring his bloated and ruined face.

"I'll say this for you, *muchacho*," Kinney said to Ruben. "You got more balls than this other *pendejo*." Dante didn't react to the insult. He stayed on his knees, head bowed, whispering his prayer. Ruben put a hand on his shoulder. "Where can we bury him?" he said wearily to Kinney.

"This way," Kinney said. He started off across the compound.

"Come on, Dante," Ruben said. "Please."

Dante got to his feet. He'd stopped praying. He didn't look at Ruben as he picked up one side of the blanket. Without a word, the two men carried the dead weight of a man once known as Diego, sometimes dragging him, but mostly managing to get him an inch or two off the ground. They followed Kinney across the compound, moving from harsh white light to black shadow, until they reached the back fence, on the opposite side of the compound from the fields. There was a gate, just wide and high enough for a man to go through, locked with a large padlock. Ruben could make out the outlines of a long, open-sided, shed-like building beyond the fence.

"That's the sawmill," Dante whispered. "Do you think they mean for us to cut him…"

"No talking," Kinney barked. He took a key from a ring on his belt and unlocked it. They carried Diego's body through the gate and toward the mill. There were none of the floodlights that lit the central compound here; the waning moon, interrupted by the clouds that blew across it at irregular intervals, provided the only illumination. In the dim light, Ruben could make out the shapes of machinery inside the shed. Kinney stopped for a moment by one of the machines. They lowered Diego's body to the concrete shed floor, panting with the effort. "Keep going," Kinney said as he straightened up. He was carrying something in the hand not holding the gun. They picked up Diego's body with an audible groan, carrying their burden through the covered area and out into the open land beyond.

The moonlight revealed a scene like something from a war zone. All the trees were gone, only a few ragged stumps remaining like shredded bones poking from the ends of hacked-off limbs. Kinney led them into this ravaged landscape, under the uncertain and wavering moonlight. Finally, he stopped. "Here," he said.

Ruben looked. His stomach turned to ice. There were at least twenty places where the earth had been disturbed, laid out neatly in two rows of ten rectangular plots each. Diego would not be the first person buried here. Ruben knew he wouldn't be the last. There had been others before them. "All of us will end up here," he thought numbly. "They'll work us to death, starve us, execute us if we try to fight." A feeling of black despair washed over him. *Papa, I need you here.* But his father was nowhere to be found. Ruben had no idea where he was. There was no way he was coming to save them.

"Here's your shovels," Kinney said. He tossed a couple of short-handled spades on the ground. "Get digging."

Ruben looked at him. The black despair began to take on a dark fringe of red rage around its edges. He almost charged Kinney right then, blind with the need to wipe that smirk off the blond man's face. The thought of the dead man at his feet stopped him. He looked over at Dante. There'd be no help from that quarter. All that would happen would be that Ruben would be lying dead from Kinney's gun next to Diego. That was if he was lucky. If he wasn't, he'd face the same agonizing death and humiliation as Diego had. And Edgar would be alone. *One more day,* he decided. *Maybe if I live one more day, something will happen.*

"Come on," he told Dante. "Let's get to work."

They began to dig, the short-handled shovels making the job more difficult. Kinney paced back and forth, watching them, occasionally glancing up to where the clouds scudded across the moon. They'd been digging for at least fifteen minutes before Kinney began to talk, as if their silence disturbed him. "This shit takes too long," he said. "We need to come up with a better way of disposing of waste. That's what you are, you know. Waste. I read about how one of your drug lords used to get rid of bodies. He had a guy called the 'soup maker.' Used to dissolve bodies in acid. The guy said he learned the formula from the Israelis. That figures, doesn't it? The Mexicans learning from the Jews. Maybe we should make up a big old stew pot out here. Save some space."

Dante stopped digging and looked up at Kinney. "Why don't you..."

"Shhhh," Ruben said. He knew what Dante was about to say would end up with him dead, and maybe Ruben as well. Dante just gave him a disgusted look and turned back to his digging.

Kinney hadn't noticed the near interruption. While Dante was talking, another guard walked up. He and Kinney conferred for a moment in low tones. Finally, Kinney nodded. "Good news, *muchachos*," he said in his horrible parody of a Mexican accent. "Corporal Colton here says another load's coming north. That means some more of your people will be coming to keep you company." He grinned. "We seem to be using them up pretty quick."

Ruben didn't answer. He just put his head down and kept digging.

CHAPTER TWENTY-ONE

THE DOOR TO THE ROOM was slightly ajar. Keller felt a sense of foreboding as he pushed it open. The room was empty. When he looked around, her bags were gone. It was as if she'd never been there. He stood in the center of the room, feeling a cold twisting in his gut. He walked out to the balcony. The Jeep was still in the parking lot. If she'd left on her own, it hadn't been in the only vehicle they had. It was logical to conclude, then, that she hadn't left on her own. He didn't know how, he didn't know where she'd gone, but he had to assume Mandujano's people had found them some other way. The bottom seemed to drop out of his stomach as the realization hit him. He'd failed her. He'd failed to keep her safe. He felt his fists clenching, as if of their own accord. The rage was building in him, turning the icy fear to a roiling ball of pure heat. He caught a glimpse of himself in the small mirror above the dresser. Before he knew what was happening, he advanced on it and tore it from the wall. He was raising it over his head to smash it against the floor when he heard a soft knocking. He lowered the mirror.

The knock came again. "*Senor* Keller?" a familiar, timid voice said.

Keller laid the mirror on the top of the dresser. He covered the distance to the door in two quick strides and yanked it open.

The young man who'd been working the front desk when they checked in was standing there. He flinched slightly at the look on Keller's face. "Where is she?" Keller demanded.

The clerk swallowed nervously, his prominent Adam's apple bobbing as he did. He held out a manila envelope. "I...I was told to give you this."

Keller took the envelope. "By who?"

The clerk looked away. "A man. A man who came to the desk."

"The lady who was staying in this room," Keller said, "where is she?"

The clerk shrugged. He still wouldn't look at Keller. "She left."

"No shit. How did she leave?"

"She left with a couple of men. One of them was the one who said to give you this."

"What did they look like?" Keller said.

Another shrug. "Just men. Well-dressed. Nice suits."

"What were they driving?"

"Nice car."

"A black Mercedes diesel, maybe?"

The clerk nodded, a sick look on his face.

"You know who they are," Keller said, and he put a hand on the young clerk's shoulder, turning the man to face him. "And you're going to tell me."

"Please," the clerk said, his voice breaking as his eyes met Keller's, "just open the package. Your answers will be in there."

Keller let go. The man was clearly terrified, either of Keller or of the people who'd left the package. *Probably both.* He opened the envelope and looked inside. The envelope held only a small cell phone and a white card, the size and shape of a business card. Keller took the cell phone out, then the card. There was a number written on it.

"I need to get back to the front desk," the clerk said, his eyes pleading.

"Go ahead," Keller said. "I may have some questions later. Stick around." The man nodded once, then fled.

Keller sat down on the edge of the bed. He looked at the phone, then the number. He dialed.

The call was answered on the first ring. "*Senor* Keller," a voice said. It was a different voice than the one he and Angela had talked to earlier. The accent was the same, perhaps a little thicker, but the voice was higher.

"Where's Angela Sanchez?" Keller said.

"She is with me," the voice said. "And she is quite safe."

"She'd better be," Keller said. "And she better stay that way."

"*Senor* Keller," the voice said, "it is just that sort of aggressive attitude that made me invite *Senora* Sanchez to breakfast this morning."

"Let me talk to her."

"Certainly. In a moment. And she will, I hope, persuade you that your usual tactic of kicking down doors and shooting people will be unnecessary in this instance."

"Put. Her. On," Keller said through clenched teeth.

The man sighed. "Very well."

Keller heard a muted conversation that he couldn't make out.

In a moment, Angela's voice came on the line. "I'm okay, Jack."

Keller felt relief flooding through him. "Really?"

"Really. They didn't hurt me, and they didn't force me to come."

"Then why did you?"

There was a rustling noise on the other end and the first voice came back on. "Now. Are you satisfied that *Senora* Sanchez is not being harmed? Or coerced?"

"Let's just say I'm cautiously optimistic. For the moment. What do you want?"

"I want to have a meeting."

"So do I."

"Yes," the voice said, "but I want to have it without any unpleasantness. You have a reputation, Mr. Keller, as being something of a hothead. A violent man."

"Now who would say a thing like that?"

"Oscar Sanchez, for one."

"So you have talked to Oscar."

"I have. And he assures me that you are a dangerous adversary to have."

"Oscar may have been exaggerating."

"Perhaps. But I did not get where I am by taking unnecessary risks. Or by getting into unnecessary wars, even ones I am certain to win." The voice sharpened. "You see, *Senor* Keller, I am also a dangerous adversary to have. And in this situation, I am an adversary with more men, and more guns. And you are, let us not forget, in my country. On my home ground." The voice softened. "But I am also willing to make peace where peace can be made. To do business in a businesslike manner, where that can be done. That is why I am still standing, while many of my competitors are not."

"Okay," Keller said, "you've sold me, Mr. Mandujano."

"Good," the voice said. "I believe you know the location of my house. The young man at the front desk will have a paper with the exact directions on it. I'll be expecting you. Alone, unarmed, and willing to talk business like a reasonable man."

"Sure," Keller said. "But I'd be a lot more reasonable if you'd let the lady go."

"I have no guarantee that that's true," Mandujano said. "And I have every reason to believe you'll be more reasonable if she stays. But in any case, I believe she wishes to stay and to be part of the meeting as well, since Mr. Sanchez will also be in attendance."

"Oscar's there?" Keller said.

"He is on his way," Mandujano said. "And so, I assume, are you."

"Count on it," Keller said.

"*Hasta pronto, Senor* Keller. We will save some breakfast for you."

CHAPTER
TWENTY-TWO

THE HOUSE WAS A MILE or so outside the town, beyond where the crowded streets trailed off into a collection of crude tar-papered shacks and old rusted house trailers, then to the familiar empty scrubland where only a few gnarled and stunted bushes grew.

Keller spotted the high wall that surrounded the house as soon as he got off the main road, following the directions on the GPS device the nervous desk clerk had handed him. As Keller drew nearer, he saw where even the sparse vegetation had been cleared away within a quarter-mile of the walls, leaving only parched earth. There would be no way to sneak up on the house, or to get away from it without being seen. It was perfectly designed to keep people in as well as out.

Keller pulled up in front of the gate, a massive structure of heavy timbers strapped together with iron. It stayed closed. "Come on," Keller muttered. "I know you know I'm here. Quit playing games." As if in answer, the gate began to open slowly. Keller pulled forward, but stopped as two men came out. They were dressed in identical BDU pants, with tight black T-shirts showing off the muscles beneath, but it was the H & K submachine guns they carried that made Keller stop. Both wore sunglasses. One of the men stopped a few feet away, while the other advanced on the Jeep. He was a dark-skinned black man, short, but compactly built, with a shaved head. Keller's foot tensed on the brake. As promised, he'd come unarmed, but if either of the men raised their weapons, he'd run right over them. If they both fired, he knew he'd be dead, but maybe he could take at least one of the goons with him. He relaxed slightly as the man approaching slung his weapon on his shoulder. He stopped a few feet away and made a circular motion with his hand. *Roll the window down.* Keller did.

"Out of the car," the man said. He had a distinctly American accent. "Engine off. Leave the keys." Keller turned the engine off and slowly got out. "Hands on the fender," the man said. "I need to search you." The tone was businesslike rather than aggressive. A professional. Most likely ex-military. The clipped way he gave orders was the giveaway.

"I was invited here," Keller said, but he assumed the position anyway.

The man did a quick but thorough frisk, then stepped away. "Okay," he said. "Through the gate."

"What about the car?" Keller said.

"You'll get the car back," the man said.

"Think I could get it washed in the meantime?" Keller said.

"Funny," the man said. "Now move."

Keller moved, walking ahead of the guard. Just inside the gate, he stepped into an oasis. In stark contrast to the sere landscape outside, the grounds inside the wall were richly landscaped, with hedges and beds of brightly blooming flowers. He walked along a path of flagstones set into a manicured green lawn. "This place must cost a mint to irrigate," Keller said to the man behind him. The man didn't answer. Keller caught sight of something and stopped dead. "Jesus. Is that a *lion*?"

The beast was lying down, but his head was up, watching them behind the thick iron bars of a cage set up against a wall of the house. A bright blue awning provided shade over the cage. His great golden eyes regarded them impassively. He was panting in the heat, the broad pink tongue hanging out.

"They let it out at night," the guard said, "to patrol the grounds. Keep moving." Keller shook his head and resumed his march.

The house itself was set on a slight rise. It was a sprawling, flat-roofed stucco edifice with only a few small windows. It reminded Keller of some of the homes he'd seen in Saudi Arabia. The path led up to a front door that opened as they approached. A fat man with a steel-gray brush cut was standing there, dressed in a suit. His clothes fit better and looked more expensive than the guard's. It wasn't physical power he was trying to show off. He didn't look pleased to see Keller.

"Mr. Keller," he said. Keller recognized the voice as the one from the first phone call, back in Wilmington

Keller put out his hand. "We've talked on the phone," he said, "but I never got your name."

"No," the man said. "You didn't. Follow me." He turned and walked back into the dimness of the house.

Keller dropped his hand to his side and turned to the guard. "Doesn't anyone in this country shake hands?"

"Go on in," the guard said. He looked amused. "The last guy that kept Mr. Mandujano waiting got fed to the lion."

Keller figured the man was bullshitting, but went into the house anyway. He was in a small foyer. The door on the other side led into a large room paneled in what looked like redwood. The far side of the room was a series of tall glass windows overlooking a wide patio floored with gray stones. Another series of terraces beyond the patio led down to a large pool. The fat man stood impatiently by a glass door to the pool area. He turned, opened the door, and walked out. Keller followed.

A group of people sat around the pool in lounge chairs. One of them was Angela. She stood up as he approached. He took a step toward her. He wanted to break into a run, to grab her, to take her in his arms. Then he saw someone else standing up, smiling at him. Keller stopped. "Oscar," he said.

Oscar Sanchez walked over. He looked thinner than when Keller had last seen him, and he'd shaved off his mustache. The combination made him look younger than the man Keller remembered. There was a bruise on one side of his face, but he was smiling. "Jack," he said, and embraced Keller. "My good friend. I knew you would come."

Keller hugged him back, looking over Oscar's shoulder at Angela. She wouldn't meet his eyes. Keller broke the hug and held Oscar by the shoulders. "Of course I did, buddy. I owe you. Big time."

Another man was rising from the farthest lounge chair. He was short and balding. The skin on his scalp was peeling slightly from the sun. He had a slight paunch over the top of his swim trunks. His eyes were invisible behind dark glasses, but Keller thought he looked like an accountant on vacation. He held out his hand. "Mr. Keller," he said. "I am Auguste Mandujano."

Keller took the hand. "Jack Keller."

"Please," Mandujano said, indicating a nearby table shaded by an umbrella. "Sit. We have much to discuss."

CHAPTER TWENTY-THREE

RUBEN HADN'T SLEPT THE ENTIRE night before. His hands had been toughened somewhat by the farm work, but digging Diego's grave had still raised blisters on his unprotected hands that pained him all night. He was also hungry. When he'd gotten back, Edgar had tearfully told him that he'd tried to get the other men to save him some food, but they hadn't listened. Ruben looked around the room. The other men wouldn't look at him. *I got that food for you*, he wanted to shout at them. *I got them to let us give Diego a decent burial.* But it didn't matter. To them, he was a collaborator. And he was just too tired to do anything but try and comfort his brother. "It's all right," he said. "Did you get anything to eat?" Edgar nodded, eyes still glistening. "Okay," Ruben said, relieved. If they'd taken his brother's portion, he'd have to do something about it. He collapsed on his bed. For a long time, he just lay there and looked up at the upper bunk. His hands hurt, his empty stomach tormented him, but it was the memory of what he'd just done that really kept him awake. He remembered the thump of Diego's body falling into the grave he'd just dug, the sting of sweat and tears in his eyes, the rich smell of the newly turned dirt combined with the cloying, sickening smell of the dead man's body. He'd paused to mumble a few words over Diego's body, stumbling through what he could remember of the service for the dead. Dante had just stood there, looking down. Neither of them had spoken to the other since.

It took forever for morning to come. Ruben didn't know how he was going to get through the day of work, as exhausted and sore as he was, but he got up with the other men. He made sure that both he and Edgar got their morning ration before they were lined up for the walk to work. As they stood there, waiting the command to move, Ruben saw the gates opening and a white van drive through. His heart sped up as he saw what was following. It looked like one of the military armored trucks he'd seen in the streets of Bogota, only larger. This one was painted bright blue. But it was the symbol painted on the door that got Ruben's attention: A gold five pointed star and the words COUNTY SHERIFF. Maybe the police were here to stop all of this. Maybe the madness was over. But the glimmer of hope sputtered and died as the man who called himself "General" walked out to greet the imposingly large gray-haired man in the brown uniform that climbed down out of the huge truck. The two men shook hands as another pair of men got out of the white van. Both were dark-haired and pale-skinned, dressed in jeans and leather jackets. One of them was carrying a briefcase. The four men conferred briefly and the General took the briefcase. He and the Sheriff went into Building Three while the other two walked toward the women's building.

"Come on," the guard holding his gun on Ruben and the other men spoke up. "Let's move. We ain't got all fuckin' day."

Ruben turned his head to watch what was happening as they walked toward the gate. Several women walked out of the barracks, with Kinney and his rifle behind them. The group met the two men from the van, and the women lined up, just as the men had a few moments ago. Ruben spotted some of the women from the group he'd come with; he didn't recognize the others. One of the men from the van walked up and down in front of the line. He pointed at one of the older women, then another. Kinney said something and the women walked away from the rest of the group, heads down. The rest of the women were marched toward the van. Ruben could hear some of them weeping.

"Keep moving," the guard said. Ruben had to turn away to keep walking. The van passed them as they walked to the field, kicking up a cloud of dust that made some of the men cough. Ruben saw Diego's sister looking out the window as they passed. Her eyes were blank and hopeless. "Where are they going?" Edgar whispered. Ruben just shook his head. He knew where the women were being taken, but couldn't bring himself to say it to his brother.

Today, it wasn't field work they were doing. It was construction. Instead of being marched to the fields, they were taken to a broad flat area. There were lots there—and roads—marked off by stakes, string, and small plastic flags on thin metal rods. There were poured concrete foundations on two of the lots, with piles of freshly cut lumber beside them. A few of the men had done construction before, and they had become the de *facto* foremen of the project. They'd told Ruben they were building houses. No one knew for whom, but they all knew it wasn't for them.

IMPRESSIVE VEHICLE," THE GENERAL SAID.

Sheriff Cosgrove grinned. Surprised you didn't recognize it. That's an MRAP." He pronounced it "Em-rap." He pronounced the next words with evident relish. "Mine Resistant, Ambush Protected vee-hicle. Now that that whole Iraq mess is over, the Army's givin' 'em away to police departments."

The General was amused. "Are you expecting that the local blacks are going to be acquiring land mines?"

"It's a dangerous world, General," Cosgrove said. "We need to be prepared."

"You don't have to tell me," Walker replied. They had entered the office at the back of the building. Walker placed the briefcase he'd been given on his desk.

"Not going to count it?" Cosgrove said.

"Should I?"

"The Croatians haven't shorted me yet."

"No doubt they're afraid to," Walker said. "You might run over them with your big Army truck."

Cosgrove didn't answer that. Both men loathed each other, and both men knew it. But their relationship had been mutually profitable enough that they would let insults slide, if they were veiled and subtle enough. Plus, Walker knew that the Sheriff enjoyed the fringe benefit of getting to sample the "product" before it was sold to the Croatians. "So, when can we expect another shipment?" Cosgrove said.

"Soon," Walker said. "I'm told very soon."

"Good. That last group was a good 'un."

Walker kept his face expressionless. "Because of the young girl."

"Yeah," Cosgrove said. "See if you can get me some more like that."

"I don't control what's sent north. I only utilize it."

"To do the Lord's work," Cosgrove sneered.

"Yes. You think I'm a hypocrite? The Lord gave us dominion over the beasts of the earth, Sheriff." *Of which you are one.* "We use them as we see fit."

"Whatever," Cosgrove said. "Just let me know when the next one gets here. I'll notify the Croatians." He smiled "After I've had a little time to sample the merchandise."

"I will. But there's something else we need to discuss with you."

Cosgrove turned back from the door. "What's that?"

"I hear you've hired a black for your department."

Cosgrove sighed. "Don't start this with me, Walker."

"Why would you trust one of them? Knowing what you know."

"The guy's a war hero. They gave him a goddamn parade when he came home."

Walker knew that the blasphemy was intended to make him angry. He kept his voice controlled. "This was not a good idea."

"Look, *General*," the Sheriff put extra contempt into the word, "you may not have to run for office, but I sure as hell do. I need the nigger vote. And when I have to go to the churches and smile and pretend I give a shit about them, it helps to have one of their heroes up on the podium."

"Hopeless," Walker thought. "Too entwined with the cares of the world. He can't see the greater picture. God would provide a shield for him if he just believed."

"Just call me when the next load's due," Cosgrove said, "and let me worry about my own business." He turned and left without another word.

CHAPTER TWENTY-FOUR

"**I** DON'T THINK WE HAVE THAT much to talk about," Keller said. "I came to find my friend here. I've found him. Now we'll be going."

Mandujano shrugged. "As you wish. I have no desire to detain anyone against their will. But there will be a condition."

"What's that?"

"That you leave Mexico. That you not come back. And that you stay far away from any of my businesses from now on."

"Great," Keller said. "No problem." He caught sight of Oscar's face and his heart sank. "Why do I get the feeling that there's a problem?"

Oscar smiled sadly. "I haven't found my boys yet, Jack."

"Ah," Keller said. "Well, Maybe Mr. Mandujano here can tell us something."

"Sadly, no," Mandujano said. He gestured at the table again. "Please. Sit. I will explain the situation."

Keller looked from face to face. Despite his unease, he walked over and took a seat. The rest followed. It was cooler under the shade of the umbrella, but not much.

Mandujano raised his voice. "Andreas!" he called out. "Have Esmeralda bring us some cold beers." Keller noticed the fat man standing by the doors. He looked even unhappier as he disappeared back into the house. Mandujano sighed. "My associate does not feel that it is a good idea to take you into my confidence. But Mr. Sanchez tells me you are an honorable man."

"I do okay," Keller said. "But maybe your associate is right."

"Maybe," Mandujano said. "But this is one of those situations where all our alternatives seem bad."

"I'm not sure what you mean by 'our' alternatives," Keller said.

A girl came out of the house. She was carrying a tray with several bottles of Sol beer balanced on it. Keller recognized her as the girl from the bar, the one who'd tried to put the tracking device on his vehicle. She was dressed in tight white shorts that contrasted with the rich caramel color of her skin and a black bikini top. She brought the beers to the table and set them down. She didn't speak, and she wouldn't look at Keller. As she turned away, Keller saw that her back was mottled and bruised, the contusions striped as if someone had beaten her with a belt. He put the beer down. "Hey," he said. "Esmeralda."

She stopped in mid turn and looked back at him. Her eyes were blazing with hate. "*Que?*" she said. She made it sound like a curse.

"Nothing," Keller said. The girl turned and walked away without looking back. Keller turned to Mandujano. His voice was tight with anger as he said, "Was that supposed to be for my benefit?"

"Failure has consequences, Mr. Keller," Mandujano said mildly.

Keller stood up. "Okay," he said. "I get it. You're a vicious prick who beats innocent women to intimidate people. Message delivered." He turned to Angela and Oscar. "Come on, let's go."

Angela started to stand, but Oscar spoke up. "Please, Jack, hear him out."

Keller just stared at him for a moment. "What the hell is going on, Oscar? How are you okay with this?"

"I'm not," Oscar said. "But sometimes we must do hard things to protect what we love."

That hit home. He remembered Lucas's words, *You did what you did to protect what you love.* He slowly sat back down. "Okay," he said to Mandujano, "I'm listening."

Mandujano took a sip of his beer. "I truly do not know what happened to those people. That shipment, like one before it, simply disappeared."

"Shipment?" Keller said. "Those were *people.*"

Mandujano shrugged. "What would you call it? Load? Group? Shall we sit here and argue word choice? The point is, I would like to find out what happened as much as Mr. Sanchez here." Keller started to speak again, but Mandujano raised his hand. "I know. I did not have family on board that truck. But I had a valued employee driving, one of whom I was fond. Most importantly to me, someone has attacked my business. Someone has made me look foolish. If that happens, I must respond, or others might be tempted to do the same."

"So you want me to find out what happened," Keller said.

"I want you to find those people," Mandujano said. "You are good at finding people, I hear."

"Why don't you get your own people to do it?"

"I have. But they have turned up nothing so far, beyond what I have told you. And now you are here. A successful hunter of men, or so I hear. Perhaps you can succeed where others have failed."

Keller shook his head. "For all we know, they're all dead." He looked at Oscar. "Sorry, man, but it's true."

Oscar nodded. "I have considered this. But..." He gestured at Mandujano, urging him to go on.

"There were two bodies found," Mandujano said. "My driver and one other. If the rest were killed, then why not leave their bodies in the same place?" He shook his head. "No, those people were taken."

Keller looked down at the table and took a sip of his beer. "And you want me to find where they were taken. And by whom."

"Yes," Mandujano said. Keller didn't answer. He only stared at the label on his beer. "I ask you this," Mandujano said. "Why would they be taken and not killed? What use would someone have for a truckload of workers?"

Keller looked up. "You're talking about slavery."

Mandujano nodded. "Some of the group taken were women. Young women. I trust I do not have to paint you a picture."

Keller knew he was being manipulated. But what Mandujano was saying made sense. And if Oscar's sons were being held in captivity, Forced to work, or worse...

"Okay," Keller said. "Say, just for the sake of argument, I agree to do this. What happens when I find these people?"

"You just need to tell me where and when," Mandujano said. "My people will deal with it from there."

"Bullshit," Keller said. "If I find someone is holding people as slaves, in the U.S., I'm calling the law."

"As you wish," Mandujano said, "as long as you stop whoever is doing it." He smiled and took another drink. "Permanently. I think you are beginning to comprehend where our interests are the same."

Keller looked at Oscar and Angela. "And are you going to beat them if I fail?" he asked Mandujano. "Like you did that girl?"

"No," Oscar said, "I am coming with you."

"Whoa," Keller said. "Time-out. That's not going to happen."

Mandujano smiled. "Mr. Sanchez seems a very determined gentleman. He told me the only way to stop him looking for his sons would be to kill him. I do not mean to be threatening; I am merely stating a fact, when I tell you that option is still on the table."

"Oscar," Keller said, "you're not a bounty hunter. You're a schoolteacher."

"I am also a father, Jack," Oscar said. "And a man. I will not sit safely while another man risks himself for my sons."

Keller looked at him in shock. When he'd met Oscar, the older man had been quiet, almost meek. He was still quiet, but Keller nearly didn't recognize the calm, determined man who sat across from him. He could tell what Mandujano said was true. You'd have to kill Oscar to get him off this hunt. And he'd be safer with Keller. But Angela... Keller pointed at her. "You let her go back to the States," he said.

"Agreed," said Oscar.

"Of course," Mandujano said.

"No," Angela spoke up.

"Angela," Oscar said gently. "You can't come with us."

"I'm not spending all this time to find you," she said, "just to lose you again." For a moment, Keller wondered whom she was talking to.

"Angela," Keller said. "There's only one way for us to do this. That's to go north with one of these," he looked at Mandujano and nearly spat the next word, "shipments." Oscar nodded.

"And hope someone attacks you," Angela said. "Great plan."

"It's the only one I can think of," Keller said. "And it's not one you can be part of." He looked at Oscar. "Right?"

Oscar looked at him thoughtfully for a long moment. Then he looked at Angela. She turned her eyes away. "Yes," Oscar said.

"Okay, then." Keller looked at Oscar. "I don't suppose there's any way to talk you out of it, buddy."

Oscar shook his head. "Sorry."

"Okay," Keller said. "It's decided. But one thing," he said to Mandujano.

"What is that?"

"We don't go with a load. I'm not going to put a lot of innocent people in the line of fire. We mock it up just like a real shipment, but we run empty."

Mandujano thought it over, then nodded. "Agreed."

"This is insane," Angela snapped.

"All the more reason for you not to go," Oscar said.

She shook her head. "Fine." She stood up. "Get yourselves killed."

Oscar and Keller stood up as well. "May I have a moment to say good-bye to my wife?" Oscar said.

"Of course," Mandujano answered. "We will pick you up at the hotel."

"You knew where we were staying," Keller said.

"Of course," Mandujano answered.

"So why put a tracer on our car?"

"I knew where you were," Mandujano said, "but I didn't know where you were going. When you made it impossible for me to find that out..." He shrugged. "I had to go with another plan."

"So you took Angela because I found your tracking device?"

Mandujano smiled coldly. "I said a minute ago that failure has consequences. When you are opposing me, so does success."

"Mr. Mandujano?" Keller heard Angela say. Keller turned to see her standing a few feet away. "Will you do me a favor?" she said, adding, "Sir?"

"What would that be?" Mandujano said.

"Take your sunglasses off."

He looked puzzled. "*Que?*"

"Please," she said, "take them off. I'd like to look you in the eye when I say what I have to say."

He hesitated a moment, then removed the glasses. His eyes were pale brown, almost tan, set a little too far apart. Angela leaned down and put one hand on each arm of his chair. Her face was inches from Mandujano's when she spoke.

"If anything happens to them," she said in a low, steady voice, "either of them, I'm holding you responsible." He didn't flinch or blink, just looked back at her calmly. "I don't know how. But believe me, I will devote the rest of my life to killing you, after destroying everything you love." He didn't answer, just stared back at her without blinking. She straightened up. "Now call your dog to see us back to our car. This place is beginning to turn my stomach."

Mandujano put his glasses back on. "ANDREAS!" he called out. The fat man appeared at the glass door, as if summoned like a genie. "Take them back to the car. Let them go in peace. In fact," he said, "escort her to the border. See that no harm comes to her." The man shook his head in evident disgust, but motioned to Angela. She walked to him, head held high, not looking back. When she disappeared into the house, Mandujano chuckled. "Much woman, that one."

"You have no idea," Keller thought.

CHAPTER TWENTY-FIVE

"SO," ANGELA THOUGHT TO HERSELF, "you found what you were looking for. How do you like it?" The three of them were following the fat man—Andreas, she'd heard Mandujano call him—down the flagstone path toward the gate. Her legs were hurting, the fatigue and stress of the last few days caused her old injuries to ache. She glanced over at the cage in the shade of its canopy. The lion watched her, his golden eyes unreadable. She was frightened down to her very core, for herself, for Oscar, and for Keller. She wondered if any of them was going to get out of this alive. And if they did, she didn't know what she was going to do afterward.

"I'll drive," Keller said. "I know the way." Oscar nodded and got into the front passenger seat. She experienced a brief flash of irritation at that. She'd gotten used to riding shotgun. With Keller. Now her husband was back, and..."*Why is everything so complicated?*" she asked herself as she climbed in the back. They set off in silence. She noticed a black SUV pulling out to follow them.

"You realize how crazy this is," she said to them.

"A little bit, yeah," Keller said.

"It is the only way," Oscar said.

"No," she said, "it isn't. You can go back and talk to the—" She stopped.

"To who?" Oscar demanded. "The police? Immigration? They would lock me up and send me back to Colombia. Without my sons and without you. We have talked about this."

"No, Oscar," she said, "*you've* talked about this. I haven't had any say in it. None at all. And I've about had it with that."

He was silent for a moment. "This is what I have to do," he said.

"*God*," she snapped. "You are so goddamn pigheaded." She turned to Keller. "And you're no better. You're on the hunt again. I know that makes you happy. But you're going to get both of you killed. You know that." Keller didn't answer.

"Please," Oscar said, "let's not fight. Not now."

"Jesus." She shook her head and gazed out the window.

KELLER DIDN'T SPEAK BECAUSE HE didn't know what to say. Angela was right. This plan was likely to get both he and Oscar killed. But he couldn't deny the feeling he was getting, the rising excitement. He was going back on the hunt. Back to war. And he loved it. God help him, he loved it.

They pulled into the courtyard of the hotel, the black SUV following. Angela got out without speaking. Keller looked at Oscar. "She's right. We can still bail out on this."

Oscar shook his head. "You don't have to come, Jack. You've done enough as it is."

"I'm not letting a friend go up against these people alone. Whoever they are. Besides, someone kidnapping people, keeping them as slaves…" He shook his head. "Hard to believe it, in this day and age."

"It is evil," Oscar said. "And we will try and stop it."

Keller nodded. "Okay."

"Excuse me," Oscar said. He got out of the car. Keller did the same as the black SUV pulled into the parking lot. Angela was coming back down the stairs, her bag in her hand. Oscar motioned her over to the side, a few feet away. Keller didn't look, but he could hear them whispering. He stole a glance out of the corner of his eye and saw them embrace. He kept his face expressionless. They broke the hug, and Keller caught one softly murmured phrase from Oscar. "*Mi corazon.*"

My heart.

"*Mi corazon,*" she whispered back. She was looking at Keller over Oscar's shoulder as she said it. After a moment, she broke the hug and walked over to Keller. "Take care of him, okay?" she said softly.

"I will," he said. She embraced him tightly. "And take care of yourself, Jack," she whispered in his ear.

"I will," he whispered back.

"We'll talk when you get back." She pulled away and got into the Jeep.

Keller looked at Oscar. He was looking at the black SUV. Keller saw Mandujano in the passenger seat.

"Well," he said, "let's get going."

ANDREAS ZAVALO KEPT HIS FACE impassive, even as he raged inwardly. He wasn't used to having his counsel disregarded, especially in such an open and humiliating manner. If it had been up to him, the woman, her Colombian husband, and the crazy *gringo* who'd accompanied her would be dead and buried in an unmarked desert grave. But Mandujano seemed intent on using them to find out what was happening to his shipments of illegals. That was something Andreas Zavalo could not let happen, because what was happening to them was entirely due to the enterprise of Andreas Zavalo.

He wondered if his boss had figured out what he'd been doing, but quickly rejected that idea. People who skimmed from the cartels did not live to see old age. If Mandujano really knew that he'd been skimming not just profits, but people, Zavalo would be dead, or dying slowly and in agony at that very moment. He was under suspicion, for sure. That was why the *jefe* wouldn't use his own people. He didn't know who to trust. But using outsiders, even ones so easily expendable...that was madness.

He could hear the woman's footsteps behind him. He'd been too far away to hear the actual words, but he could see the way she'd confronted the *jefe*. If he was a man given to regret, he would regret what he was about to do to someone with such courage. But he was not that kind of man. That kind of man did not survive long in the seas he and Auguste Mandujano swam in.

They reached the gate. Zavalo opened it with a flourish. The three of them, the two men and the woman, stepped through without speaking. One of Mandujano's men was pulling around the front with their vehicle. He closed the gate and turned away, pulling out his cell phone and dialing a number he knew by heart. The person on the other end picked up as Zavalo paused in front of the lion cage. "Yes?" was all he said.

"The next shipment," Zavalo said, "won't have any workers. It's a trap. Mandujano is sending a couple of freelancers to try and find out where his shipments are going."

"Understood," the voice said. "We'll deal with it. And the payment for the last batch should be in your account by this afternoon."

"*Gracias*," Zavalo said, using Spanish because he knew it irritated the man on the other end. The only answer was a click as the man broke the connection. Zavalo smiled. He might be doing business with these racist *pendejos* and their phony "General," but he didn't have to like them. He looked forward to the day when he didn't have to do either. He was almost ready, the pieces almost in place for him to move against Mandujano. The sale of the "shipments" to the General had provided the seed money, as well as causing Mandujano to lose respect. No one would come to the aid of someone so weak he couldn't protect his own business.

He stopped in front of the lion cage. He shook his head at what having such an animal on his property said about Auguste Mandujano. He had heard that another trafficker had a leopard, and he would not be outdone. He'd spent hundreds of thousands of dollars to prove he could have a more extravagant pet than a competitor. Zavalo regarded that as another sign of his weakness.

The beast looked up from gnawing on a length of bone to regard him with those impassive golden eyes. Zavalo stared back, unwavering, as he hit the speed dial for one of the Mandujano "soldiers" loyal to him. When the man answered, he said in Spanish. "The woman who just left here. When the two men with her leave…" He was going to say "kill her," but a last moment thought occurred to him. "Take her," he said. "Keep her at the safe house." His man acknowledged the order and hung up. Zavalo slid the phone back into his pocket, still maintaining eye contact with the lion. "Who knows," he said out loud, "the stupid bastards might get lucky and survive." In that case, they might very well come back. Maybe even after him. The woman would give him a handle on them. But once they died, she'd be of no further use.

The lion broke eye contact first. He always did. He went back to chewing and licking on the bone held between his paws. Zavalo noticed a tuft of blond hair on the ground. He couldn't tell if there was still scalp attached. That and the bone the lion was worrying were all that was left of Mandujano's last playmate. "You weren't as docile as we thought, *chica*," he said, "but you shouldn't have tried to run."

CHAPTER
TWENTY-SIX

THE MAN WHO HAD MET Keller at the gate drove them from the hotel. Mandujano sat in the passenger seat of the black SUV, with Keller and Oscar in the back. A small red pickup followed with a couple of other gunmen in the truck bed, guns at the ready. Keller wondered if this was the normal security or if Mandujano was worried. It was impossible to tell from the man's face. Keller wondered if he ever showed any emotion at all.

They made the ride in silence, the only sound the blast of the car's air conditioner. Keller noticed Oscar glancing at him from time to time, but he didn't speak.

After fifteen minutes or so, they entered an area of large gray and dark blue industrial buildings, many surrounded by chain-link fence topped with razor wire. The air began to take on a tang of smoke and chemicals, even filtered as it was through the air-conditioning. They pulled to a stop in front of a gate guarded by a single man slouching in a shabby wooden booth. The man straightened up when he saw who the passenger was. He pressed a button and the gate rolled aside.

Mandujano acknowledged the man with a slight wave as they rolled through.

A warehouse sloppily painted in barn-red paint loomed over the cracked concrete of a parking lot, empty except for a battered white moving van backed up to the concrete loading dock. A man with a gun slung on his back stood in the opening of one of the bays. He was dressed in the usual BDU pants, black T-shirt, and sunglasses. Another man joined him as the SUV pulled to a stop beside the truck. The second man was dressed in jeans and a loose-fitting *guayabera* shirt. He had a low forehead, a weak chin, and a wide mouth, giving his face the squashed look of a toad's. He wore thick horn-rimmed glasses and a small gold cross around his neck.

"Almost have enough for a run, *jefe*," the man said as they got out of the car. Mandujano took the lead, with Keller and Oscar following behind, and the driver bringing up the rear. The man glanced back into the warehouse behind him. "It's been a little slow." He rubbed his hands together nervously.

"Change in plans, Manuel," Mandujano said. "We're running the next truck empty." He glanced at Keller and Oscar. "Mostly."

"Empty?" Manuel's brow furrowed in confusion. "I don't understand."

"You've heard what's been happening to the shipments," Mandujano said. "These men are going to try and get to the bottom of it."

Manuel wiped the back of his hand across his thick rubbery lips. "But…these people have paid to be on the next run."

"They'll wait," Mandujano said. He gave Manuel a thin smile. "What else can they do?"

Manuel's head bobbed in agreement. "Of course. Of course." He pointed at the truck. "It's gassed up and ready to go."

Mandujano nodded and turned to Keller. "There's a GPS in the truck," he said. "It is pre-loaded with the way you should go. The place where we lost contact with my trucks is about six miles from the border. It's an empty place. No towns, no traffic. That is where I think they were taken."

"Wait a minute," Keller said. "In case you didn't notice, we're unarmed. I expect the people we're hoping to meet aren't going to be."

Mandujano hesitated. Then he turned to Manuel. "Take them inside. Give them what they want."

Manuel goggled at him in disbelief for a moment, then bobbed his head again. "Of course. Gentlemen. Come this way."

Keller put one hand on the edge of the dock and hopped up. He turned and extended a hand to pull Oscar up with him. The two of them looked down at Mandujano.

"I expect this will be the last time we see each other," Mandujano said.

"I think we all want that," Keller said.

"*Vaya con Dios*, Mr. Keller. Mr. Sanchez. I hope you find your sons."

"*Gracias*," Oscar said.

"This way," Manuel said.

Inside, the warehouse was dimly lit. Keller had to stop and let his eyes adjust. As they did, he saw that the front of the warehouse had been partitioned off from the back half by a plywood wall that went up about ten feet, halfway to the high ceiling. There was one door in the wall, marked with a store-bought plastic sign: PELIGRO. NO ENTRE. There was a group of people in the empty space between the wall and the loading dock. Some stood as they came in, others stayed seated on the floor, backs against the wall. The group seemed to be mostly composed of young men, although there were a couple of women who stood together. There was also what looked like a family, with a woman holding a baby in her arms next to a stocky young man in a Def Leppard T-shirt. All of them looked suspiciously at Keller and Oscar as Manuel led them to the door. Manuel didn't seem to take any notice of them.

The door led to a corridor, with walls made of the same cheap plywood and doors along its length. As they walked down the corridor, Keller glanced into some of the open ones. A couple of the rooms appeared to be offices, but one contained a pair of bunk beds. A larger room near the end of the corridor was piled high with bundles of some white powder wrapped in clear plastic. It looked like more than people were being smuggled out of this place.

Manuel stopped at the end of the corridor and fumbled in his pocket for a moment, looking at them with an apologetic smile. He came out with a key and opened the door. Keller whistled as he stepped inside.

"*Madre de Dios,*" Oscar said softly.

The place was an arsenal. A conference table with a few leather chairs was placed in the center. A rifle was set on top of a blanket spread on the table, broken down into its components. The walls were lined with long guns resting on pegs set into the wall. Shelves set chest-high contained a selection of handguns. A heavy machine gun sat atop a high tripod at the far end of the room.

"Looks like you guys are expecting trouble," Keller said.

Manuel shrugged, still with that unctuous smile on his face. "It pays to be prepared, no?"

"Yep." Keller walked to the wall and considered. He spotted a familiar looking weapon and took it down. It was an M4 carbine, a smaller and lighter version of the M16 he'd trained on in the Army. The fat tube of an M203 grenade launcher hung beneath the barrel. He slung the weapon on his back and picked a Glock Model 22 pistol from the shelf. A shelf closer to the floor yielded up a leather shoulder holster. Keller put it on and slid the gun into it. He looked at Oscar, who was gazing around the room with a look of confusion on his face. "I'd suggest the shotgun," Keller said, pointing at a 12-gauge Mossberg on the wall. "You've used those before." Oscar just nodded and took the gun down. Keller pulled down a .38 caliber revolver. "Take this one, too," he said and handed it over.

Oscar took it, so that he was holding a weapon in each hand. He looked at them as if he couldn't believe what he was holding. Keller felt a deep sense of dread as it came to him how unprepared the former schoolteacher was. He wondered if he was leading his friend to his death. "*Then there'll be nothing keeping you from her,*" a voice whispered in his head. He shook it violently. No. He wasn't going to think like that. He was going to bring them both through this and get them home. "*Like you did for your men in Kuwait?*" the voice said.

"Jack?" Oscar said. "Are you okay?"

"Yeah," Keller said. "I'm fine." He looked at Manuel. "Ammo?"

"Of course. Of course," Manuel said. It seemed to be his favorite phrase. "In the other room. Follow me."

They loaded up on as much ammo as they could carry. Keller saw a familiar-looking olive drab box in the corner. "We'll take those grenades as well."

Manuel looked unhappy, but he nodded anyway. "Of course."

CHAPTER
TWENTY-SEVEN

ANGELA WAS ON HER WAY, moving slowly over the potholed road on the outskirts of town. The father north she got, and the farther away from the town center, the poorer the houses got and the more rusty and battered the vehicles, which is why she noticed the black car right away. It was a Mercedes that looked as out of place here as a diamond tiara on a beggar. It was gaining rapidly. She thought of turning off to try to see if the car was following her but she knew she'd immediately be lost in the side streets. She sped up. The black Mercedes kept pace, then accelerated, and pulled out to pass. She saw another car, an identical black Mercedes — right behind.

"Shit," she said. She stomped the accelerator to the floor. The engine of the old Jeep whined with the strain as the vehicle shot ahead. She hit a pothole hard enough to make her teeth snap together painfully. The first Mercedes outpaced her easily and got in front. The second one pulled up, right on her tail. The one ahead braked sharply, causing her to have to do the same. The wheels of the Jeep locked up and the tires squealed as she slid to a stop, her front bumper inches away from the back bumper of the blocking car. The second car pulled up directly behind her, so close she couldn't back up without hitting it.

She looked around frantically. No one was on the street; the people who'd previously been outside in the dirt front yards and alleyways had disappeared at the obvious signs of trouble.

A man got out of the car in front. She recognized the man from the bar last night, the one who'd been talking to the girl Esmeralda. He was dressed in black again. There was a gun in his right hand, held down by his hip.

"Oh, no you don't," Angela said grimly. She slammed the gearshift into reverse and stomped the accelerator again. The tires barked sharply as the Jeep lunged backward, smashing into the grille of the vehicle behind her. She heard the sounds of rending metal and breaking glass. Her head snapped back against the seat. The man in black was raising his gun. She whipped the wheel to the left and prepared to floor the gas pedal as he fired—into the front left tire. She swore as he fired again, into the radiator. Only then did he raise the gun to point through the windshield at her as steam began pouring out from beneath the hood. He gestured to her with his free hand to get out of the car. Angela bent down and put her forehead on the wheel, trying to get her breathing and heart rate under control. When she looked up again, the man in black was at the driver's side door, tapping on the window with the butt of the gun. "Okay, damn it," she muttered as she opened the door.

"*Senora* Sanchez," the man said. "You will come with me. You won't be harmed."

Not yet. She got out of the car. "Where are we going?"

"Someplace safe. Come."

She went. There was nothing else she could do.

THEY SAT BY THE BROKEN road at the edge of the vast scrubland, a few miles from the border. It wasn't a desert exactly, but it was so dry and arid that nothing grew taller than thick, gnarled bushes no higher than a man's knees. The sky seemed endless, only a few high wispy clouds making light brushstrokes in the darkening blue as the sun sank in the west behind a distant line of low hills.

They'd decided to wait for the cover of darkness, keeping to the pattern of the other smugglers who'd disappeared before them. Keller glanced over at Oscar. The older man had gone silent as they'd approached the border. Both of them were apprehensive, but Keller sensed that there was something else bothering his friend. "You okay?"

Oscar nodded, and then took another drink from the plastic water bottle he held in his hand. The other held the shotgun upright, the butt resting on the floor of the truck cab. He turned the bottle up, swigging the last few drops out, then dropped it to the floor. "Jack," he said, not looking at Keller. "I need to ask you a question."

"Sure, buddy," Keller said.

Oscar turned to look at him. "Did you sleep with my wife?"

Keller felt a tightening in his gut, but he looked back at Oscar steadily. "No," was all he said.

Oscar looked back, gazing out at the scrubland through the windshield. "Sorry," he muttered. "It was a foolish question."

"Oscar —," Keller began, but Oscar silenced him with a raised hand.

"No, I believe you." Oscar sighed. "But she still cares for you. And you for her."

"That was a long time ago," Keller said. "And, as you remember, it didn't work out." Oscar didn't answer. "You think if she still had a thing for me," Keller said, "she'd have come looking for you?"

Oscar looked at him, his brown eyes solemn. "She came looking for you first."

"Because she knew I'd help find you."

Oscar nodded and looked away. "I am lucky to have a friend like you. Thank you."

"Hey," Keller said, "you put your ass on the line for me when you barely knew me. If it hadn't been for you, I'd be rotting in a cell right now."

Oscar chuckled. "I felt bad for pulling a gun on you then." The chuckle died. "It was the first time I ever held a gun on anyone."

"Not the last," Keller said.

Oscar nodded. "This will be the last time for me. I am not meant for this. I know that. Not like you." He stopped. "I didn't mean that the way it sounded."

"I know," Keller said. "But you're right. And you can still go back."

Oscar shook his head. "No. These are my sons. I will find out what happened. If they're alive, I'll get them back. If not…" He rubbed his hand over his face. "They will have justice. One way or another." He turned to Keller. "You can go back, too. This isn't your fight."

"Maybe," Keller said, "but it's the only one I've got."

Oscar laughed out at that. "You know that's crazy, right, Jack?"

"Oh, yeah." Keller looked out the window. "It's almost dark."

"Yes," Oscar said. "Let's go."

Keller started the truck and they headed into the gathering darkness.

CHAPTER
TWENTY-EIGHT

THE GENERAL ALWAYS SAID THEY were doing God's work, keeping America pure. He could go on for hours about the subject, telling his little army about how God had appointed the white man to rule the earth and America to be His instrument for the purpose. Rance Colton didn't know about God. He only knew this job gave him a chance to fuck with Mexicans, and that beat the hell out of stocking merchandise in some Walmart in his hometown of Huntsville, Alabama. All the factory jobs had gone south, down the very road he and his little fire team were watching, and that made messing with the little brown monkeys that had taken those jobs that much sweeter when they dared to try and come north to take what little was left. He was a little disappointed that there wouldn't be a truckload of them this time. One of the men that was supposed to be coming, though, was some sort of Colombian tough guy, maybe some cartel goon. Well, that would have to do. Colton pulled the night vision goggles that had been perched high on his head down over his eyes and adjusted the straps. He looked down the hill where he and the other two men were lying prone. They already had their NVGs pulled down. The road they were overlooking went from a vague line in the darkness to a thoroughfare that appeared bathed in a bright green light. A brief cloud of dust blew across his vision. The wind was picking up.

Colton was just sorry he wouldn't get to see the looks on the faces of the monkey and his race-traitor partner when they sprung the surprise he'd brought. He looked over at the new guy, Fincher, who was holding a short metal tube with a pistol grip. The rocket protruded from the business end of the tube, its fat warhead looking like two large metal cones soldered together at their bases. Colton had seen the Soviet made RPG-7 demonstrated during his brief stint in the Army, but he'd never fired one. The explosive in the warhead would turn the truck to a heap of burning and twisted metal and anyone inside into charred meat. The bastards would never know what hit them.

Colton looked down the road, towards the south, the direction from which the trucks always came. In the distance, he saw a flicker of headlights. He smiled and got to one knee. The wind ruffled his hair. He looked up at the sky. The clouds were getting thicker overhead. He saw a flash of lightning branch out like a great electric tree across the expanse of sky. A storm was moving in, and the wind was picking up. They were going to have to be quick.

"Fincher," he said. "Gimme the RPG."

"ARE WE GETTING CLOSER?" KELLER asked. "Check the GPS." Oscar leaned forward and peered at the screen of the GPS device stuck to the dashboard. The arrow representing their truck moved slowly down the narrow ribbon representing the road they were on.

"Five and a half miles north of the border," Oscar said. He looked out the passenger window. "An empty place," he quoted.

Keller squinted out the front window. The wind was kicking up dust devils that swirled in the headlights. "I can't see a damn thing." He applied the brakes, which groaned as the truck began to slow.

FINCHER LOOKED UP. "YOU EVER fire one of these?"

"You point it, you pull the trigger," Colton said irritably. "At this range, you can't miss."

"Okay," Fincher said, "but there's something you should know."

The truck was almost abreast of them now. It seemed to be slowing.

"Just give me the damn thing," Colton snapped. "And shut the fuck up."

"Suit yourself," Fincher said. He handed over the RPG, looked at the other member of the fire team, and shrugged. The third man, a new guy who Colton only knew as Shippen, shrugged back and went prone, aiming his rifle at the road beneath.

Colton flipped up the sight and positioned the weapon on his shoulder. *That wind is really getting stronger. Coming from my left, so I adjust left to compensate...* Colton moved the warhead to the side.

"Wait," Fincher said. "You don't..."

Colton ignored him. The rocket ignited, leaving the shoulder-mounted launcher with a loud hiss. Colton's goggles were filled with a brilliant green-white light as the RPG streaked off into the darkness.

THE SOVIET RPG-7 HAS A quirk that is counterintuitive to the inexperienced user. When the rocket-propelled grenade leaves the barrel, a set of large stabilizing fins deploys in a split second. In a crosswind, the broad fins catch the wind like sails, pushing the back of the rocket around. This causes the rocket to actually turn *into* the wind.

Jack Keller saw the rocket streak past, a few feet in front of the truck, trailing a tail of white fire. In an instant, he was transported back to another desert, thousands of miles and twenty-two years away.

Missile, he thought. *MISSILE.* He heard the *crump* of the warhead detonating, saw the Bradley fighting vehicle he'd been riding in moments before going up in a ball of flame, heard his men screaming in pain and terror as the Hellfire missile fired out of the darkness took their lives.

Burning, they're burning oh my god it's happening again...

"Jack!" Oscar was screaming. The voice brought him back to the present. He saw Oscar's terrified face through a red haze. *Got to get him out, he'll burn, they'll all burn…* He dimly heard the metallic thumps as small-arms rounds smacked into the left side of the truck. *Ambush.*

He turned to Oscar. "OUT!" he bellowed. "Get out and get to the ground."

Oscar scrabbled at the door handle in a panic. He found it and slammed the passenger door open. The driver's side window shattered and another round clanged off something in the interior. Oscar bailed out, carrying his shotgun with him. Keller followed. He reached up to pull the M4 and the bag of ammo from where he'd stashed them behind the passenger seat.

"What's happening?" Oscar said.

"Someone just fired a goddamn missile at us," Keller said grimly. His heart was still pounding, but he was back in the present. The rage he'd felt for years, however, wasn't going away. It was building again, taking him to the dark place that felt far too much like home. He heard a round strike the gas tank. The truck wouldn't be decent cover for much longer. *Who the hell are these guys? They're not pros.* Something savage answered him from deep within, an inner voice from the most primitive part of his mind, the lizard brain that lies beneath the layers of thinking and reasoning tissue that evolution and civilization have grafted onto the killer beneath. *"Whoever they are,"* the voice said, *"they die today."* Keller felt his breathing slow, his heart rate drop.

The hunter was awake.

"What are we going to do?" Oscar said. He was breathing hard, but Keller's outward icy calm seemed to settle him down.

Keller worked the charging lever of the M4. "I'm going to kill them," he said.

"WHAT THE FUCK?" COLTON SAID.

"I tried to tell you," Fincher said. "In a high wind like this, the round turns upwind." He squeezed off a short burst from his AK-47 assault rifle toward the truck. A few feet away, Shippen followed suit.

"Gimme another round," Colton demanded.

"Get it yourself," Shippen answered. He sounded disgusted as he fired another burst. "In the bag."

Colton realized how exposed he was and dropped to the ground, taking cover behind the lip of the hill. He trained his own rifle on the truck below and fired. "Okay. We've still got them outnumbered. And outgunned." He fumbled for the green canvas bag that lay on the ground between him and Shippen. After a moment, he found the second rocket. It was the last one they had. He rolled to his back and groped for the launcher. "Keep firing at the gas tanks," he ordered. When he had the round seated in the launcher, he rolled to his belly again and looked down.

He saw someone step out from behind the truck and fire, the muzzle flash sparking brightly in his NVGs. "Get that bastard," he whispered. He heard the sharp reports of his teammates' weapons and saw dirt and dust kick up at the feet of the person below. That person fired back and ducked away behind the truck. "Okay, you son of a bitch," Colton said. He raised up to one knee and took aim. He wasn't going to miss again.

KELLER COULD SMELL THE ACRID stench of gasoline as more rounds hit the tank slung beneath the truck. If one of those rounds kicked up a spark, the truck was going to turn from cover into a death trap. He heard someone bark a command from the overlooking hill.

"Oscar," he said, "back away from the truck. See if you can keep it between us and them."

"I'm not even sure where they are," Oscar said.

"Just follow me." He started backing away. The trick would be to keep from getting so far back that he'd move into the field of view of the men above. He suspected they were using some kind of night vision equipment. "Okay, this way," Keller said. He started to move in the direction of the back of the truck. As he did, he heard a familiar hiss coming from up the hill.

"GET DOWN!" he yelled. He went to the ground, grabbing Oscar and pulling him down. with him.

COLTON WHOOPED AS HE SAW the round hit the truck and explode in a shower of white sparks. The gas tank went up next, a rolling ball of flame that flared in the NVGs, so bright and sharp that Colton pulled them off. He rubbed his eyes and looked down the hill. The flames had turned from white to orange, streaked with thick black smoke. The glow illuminated the valley beneath him, shadows wavering across the ground.

He put the launcher down and picked up his assault rifle. He couldn't see what had happened to the men in the truck. From out of the darkness, he heard a soft report, duller than the crack of a rifle. It was a sound he could have sworn he'd heard before. He had only a moment to process it before something landed a few feet away, just in front of Shippen. A split-second later, he recognized what it was.

"GRENADE!" he shouted.

CHAPTER TWENTY-NINE

"**C**OME ON," KELLER SAID AS he sprang to his feet. The two of them were moving up the hill even as the grenade exploded just below the crest. He heard someone screaming in pain. He stopped, fired off a three-round burst, and ran. The rattle of answering fire came from the top of the hill, but the grenade must have disoriented the shooter, because the rounds whined harmlessly overhead. Keller fired again, then charged the last few feet to the top of the hill. As he came over the crest, he was panting for breath, eyes filled with sweat.

He saw a man, on his back, rolling on the ground and howling in agony, hands over his face. Another man looked up from where he knelt over the wounded one. All Keller could see was a flash of white face in the darkness. As the man started to rise, Keller fired. In the dimness, he couldn't see where the round hit, but the figure fell backward, landing bonelessly on his back, without a sound. He didn't move. The man on the ground kept screaming.

"Drop the gun!" Oscar shouted, his voice cracking, the blast of the shotgun following almost immediately.

Keller spun around. A man was falling backward, hitting the ground with a thud, followed by the skittering of rocks and the sound of the body sliding backward down the reverse slope of the hill. Oscar stood panting at the top of the hill, the shotgun in his hands, and fell to his knees.

"Oscar," Keller called out as he ran over. He dropped to his knees beside Oscar and put an arm around his shoulder.

"I'm fine," Oscar wheezed. "I'm not hurt." As his breathing steadied, he racked another round into the chamber. He had a stricken look on his face. "I didn't give him time to drop the gun," he whispered.

"He wasn't going to," Keller said. "Next time, don't bother asking." He gave Oscar a slap on the shoulder, then stood up. "Good job."

"Good job," Oscar whispered. He shook his head and staggered to his feet.

The one remaining man was still writhing on the ground, but his screams had trailed off to dull moans. Keller walked over and looked down at him. After a moment, he nudged the wounded man with his foot. "Hey," he said. The man only whimpered. "HEY!" Keller said louder. He kicked the man in the side, not too hard.

"Jack," Oscar said.

Keller looked up. "This cocksucker and his buddies here just tried to kill us, Oscar." He leaned over and picked up the launcher for the RPG. "With this. If he'd had his way, we'd be," he tossed the launcher aside and pointed to the flaming wreckage of the truck, "burning to death down there." He kicked the man in the side, harder. There was no response. "And he may be the key to what happened to your boys. So forgive me if I don't much care about hurting his feelings."

"I think he's dead," Oscar said.

Keller lowered his gaze, then bent down, and felt for a pulse. "Shit," he said. He moved the man's hands away from his face. They fell limply to his sides.

"*Madre de Dios*," Oscar said as he saw the ruin of the man's face. He crossed himself.

Keller stood up and looked around. "They had to have come here in something. Maybe that'll give us some clue. At least we can drive it out."

"Jack," Oscar said. "These men are dead."

Keller looked at him steadily. "I know," he said. "We killed them."

"Shouldn't we bury them?"

"We don't have time. They may have friends nearby who'll come looking if they don't report in. We need to get whatever information we can and haul ass." He gestured with the barrel of his rifle to where the man Oscar had shot had fallen. "Go look through that guy's pockets," he said. "Look for ID. Anything with an address on it. Restaurant or hotel receipts. Anything."

Oscar looked down the hill, into the darkness. He didn't move.

"Come on, buddy," Keller said. "I know this is hard. But these aren't just random assholes. They didn't just wake up this morning and say 'Hey, let's go blow up some dude's truck we never heard of.' They have to be connected with the people who took your boys. And I don't want to sound like a broken record, but they did just try to kill us. The only reason I'm sorry they're dead is we can't get them to talk. Now come on, we need to get moving."

Oscar shook his head again and walked down the hill, into the darkness. Keller knelt by the dead man and went through his pockets, turning him over to try and find a wallet. Nothing. He repeated the process with the other man. He noted the web of tattoos on the dead man's arms and chest. There were a number of Nazi symbols: a swastika, the paired lightning bolts of the SS, a cross in a circle. The arms of the cross were of equal length. Keller recognized it as the Odin Cross. It was another symbol used by white supremacist groups. He rocked back on his heels and thought for a moment.

He'd had to bring back a few bail jumpers who'd been affiliated with white supremacist and neo-Nazi groups. One particularly chatty jumper who he'd had to bring back from Georgia had railed for hours about how the "invasion" of what he called "mud people" was going to destroy the United States if someone didn't stop it. The man had finally annoyed Keller so much that he'd spent the last two hours riding in the trunk of Keller's old Crown Victoria with a strip of duct tape over his mouth.

Oscar came trudging out of the darkness, his head down. "Find anything?" Keller asked. Oscar just shook his head. Keller stood up. "Let's look for a vehicle," he said. "At least we can find a ride out of here."

Oscar nodded. "Okay," he said in a low voice.

"Oscar," Keller said. "I know this is rough on you. But you'll get used to it."

Oscar looked up. "I don't want to get used to it," he snapped. "I don't want to become like—" He stopped.

"Like me," Keller said. "I get it."

"I'm sorry," Oscar said. "I shouldn't have..."

"No," Keller said, "you're right. You don't want to become like me. Hell, *I* didn't want to become like me. But shit happens. Shit happened to me, and it happened to people I cared about, and here I am. Believe me, Oscar, I know just how fucked-up I am. But how I am is what I need to be to get this job done. To find your sons. And to get you home to your wife."

Oscar nodded sadly. Keller realized that at least part of the sadness was for him. Oscar felt badly for him. He felt a brief flash of anger at that, then it died. He didn't have the time for anger. The hunt was on, and there was only one way it led.

Forward. Just keep moving forward. Do the next thing. Don't think too much about what you've become. If those boys are in the hands of some white supremacist wackos, then they don't have much of a life expectancy.

"Come on," Keller said, "let's find that vehicle."

CHAPTER THIRTY

THE TINY ROOM WAS NOT what Angela would have called comfortable, even if she hadn't been locked into it. There was only a single cot with no blankets or sheets, a rickety wooden table, and a chair so old and flimsy she hesitated to sit down on it. At least everything was clean.

They hadn't bothered to blindfold her. That worried her. If they weren't concerned about her finding the place again, that might mean they intended for her not to be alive to try. But then she recalled the confusing journey through increasingly narrow streets. Maybe they were confident she'd never find her way back, even with her eyes open. There was one narrow window in the room, set high in the wall. The window was dirty to the point of being opaque and there was a metal grate screwed into the wall over it. She could hear city noises filtering dimly through the window: horns, traffic, the occasional shout. At one point, she thought she heard children playing, but she couldn't be sure. She wished she had a book to read, a newspaper, a radio, anything to pass the time. With the window obscured, she couldn't even be sure

159

if it was day or night. The old injuries in her legs ached the way they always did at night, but that could have been the result of stress.

A sound came from overhead, someone walking in the room above her. She heard voices, then there was silence. A few moments later, she heard a rhythmic squeaking of bed springs, followed by a woman's voice crying out, over and over. It lasted for about a minute, then stopped. Footsteps again, then silence.

She got up for what felt like the hundredth time and prowled the room, considering what she might use as a weapon. She could possibly break the chair into a club, but the thing seemed about as substantial as balsa wood. The table was too unwieldy, the cot too hard to take apart with no tools. "Come on," she told herself, "think. You've got to get out of here."

She heard the jingle of keys outside and the scrape of a key in a lock. She went over and sat on the cot, trying to listen as closely as possible. A lock clicked, then another, then she heard a bolt snap back. The door swung open and Esmeralda, the girl who she'd last seen at Mandujano's, came in carrying a tray. She glanced sullenly at Angela, then away as she crossed the room, and set the tray down on the table.

"Thank you," Angela said softly, then, "*Gracias.*"

"*De nada,*" the girl said automatically, then looked away again.

"Esmeralda, isn't it?" Angela asked in Spanish.

"I'm not supposed to talk to you," the girl replied in the same language.

Angela nodded. "Okay. I don't want you to get hit again. I know what that's like." Esmeralda looked at her in surprise, then her face went blank again and she walked to the door. "But could you maybe get me a blanket?" Angela said. "Or a pillow? And I'm going to need to use the bathroom."

The girl hesitated. "I'll see what I can do," she murmured. As she exited, Angela caught a glimpse of the hallway outside. There was a man there, carrying a machine gun. As the door closed, he said something to Esmeralda in a low, insinuating voice. The closing door and the rattle of the locks being fastened cut off her reply.

Angela walked over to the table. There was a bologna sandwich on a plate and a plastic tumbler of milk. So they weren't going to starve her, and they weren't going to shoot her. Yet. She sat down and started eating, looking at the door. She picked up the plate as she held the sandwich in one hand. It was plastic, like the tumbler. She might be able to break it, but there wouldn't be any edges sharp enough to use as a weapon. *If I'm going to get out of here, I'm going to have to talk my way out. And I'm not sure I can do that.*

On the floor above, she heard the squeak of the bedsprings again, the woman's voice crying out.

Great. I'm in the basement of a whorehouse. Well, it wasn't like I was going to get any sleep tonight anyway.

THEY FOUND THE VEHICLE AT the bottom of the ridge. It was a large, black Dodge crew cab truck. Keller climbed up into the driver's seat. The keys were still in the ignition. "Oscar," he called out, "look in the glove box. See if you can figure out who this is registered to." Oscar climbed into the passenger seat. Keller heard him rummaging among the papers. He turned the key and the engine roared to life. He looked around. A GPS system was secured to the dashboard by a suction cup, and Keller pulled it off. After a few false starts, he figured out how to scan through the preset destinations in the device's memory.

Oscar spoke up from the other seat. "I think I have found the registration, but...this makes no sense."

"Let me see it," Keller said. He turned on the overhead light and took the crumpled paper from Oscar's hand. It was a South Carolina registration, in the name of The Church of Elohim, LLC.

"What kind of church needs that kind of weapons and employs that kind of men?" Oscar asked.

"A really scary one," Keller said. "We may have more trouble here than we thought."

"That seems to happen to you a lot," Oscar observed.

"Can't deny it," Keller said. He checked the address of the Church of Elohim against the stored destinations. One of them, designated as "Farm" appeared to be located in South Carolina, near a town called

Hearken.

"Maybe this is too big for us," Oscar said. "Maybe we *should* alert the authorities."

"Not sure how we'd explain being armed like we are, driving a truck across the border, a truck that could probably be traced with a little work to a notorious drug dealer, with, no offense, an undocumented immigrant on board."

Oscar sighed. "You're right. Of course."

"Only one way out of this," Keller said, "And that's forward. We need to check these people out."

Oscar nodded. "I could see what I can look up on my phone," he said, "but it was in the truck."

"Well, shit," Keller said. "So was mine. Hang on a sec." He rummaged through the center console. The only thing he found was what appeared to be a motel key card in a small paper envelope. FREY MOTOR LODGE, the legend on the envelope read, FREY, TEXAS. The room number was written on the envelope in blue pen. Keller pocketed the key card.

They'd have to use the dead men's vehicle to get out of there. He didn't like the idea; one traffic stop could end in questions being asked that would get them locked up. And he couldn't shake the sense that they were running out of time.

"So what do we do now?" Oscar said.

Keller reached into his pocket and pulled out the key card. "Somewhere around here is a town called Frey," he said. "They were staying there. Let's see what they left behind."

CHAPTER THIRTY-ONE

ESMERALDA WAS BACK THE NEXT morning. At least Angela assumed it was morning, because this time there were eggs on the plate, with a little salsa spread across the top, and a single piece of toast. Angela thanked Esmeralda anyway. "Remember what I said about needing to use the bathroom?" she added. "It's gotten kind of urgent."

Esmeralda nodded. "Okay," she said. "Wait." She seemed a little friendlier today. She slipped out the door.

Angela noted that she didn't lock it behind her. She heard the muffled sounds of conversation outside, low at first, then Esmeralda's voice rose in anger. Angela took a bite of the toast and waited.

In a moment, Esmeralda was back. Her eyes were narrowed and her jaw set with anger. "He says you can use the bathroom, but you have to leave the door open. So he can see you."

Angela took a deep breath. "Okay. I guess I don't have any choice." She stood up. "Is there a sink, too? So I can wash?"

Esmeralda nodded. "I'm sorry," she whispered.

Angela smiled. "It's not your fault. Thanks for asking for me."

Esmeralda opened the door. The guard in the hall was young, with a wispy attempt at a mustache that looked like a smear of dirt on his upper lip. He leered at Angela as she walked out of the room, with Esmeralda behind. "This way," he said in accented English, gesturing down the hall with the shotgun he held in his hands. She saw an open door down a short hallway. She held her head up as she walked down the hall, the guard and Esmeralda behind. As they reached the end of the hallway, Angela noticed a door to her left that opened onto a set of rickety wooden steps. She mentally filed that away and turned back to the door ahead.

It was a half bath, with a toilet and sink, but no shower or tub. Without looking at the guard, she unbuttoned her jeans and took them down. She heard the guard's quick intake of breath as he saw the scars on her legs—from the old burns and the ones caused by the surgeries to put her broken leg bones back together. She sat down and did what she needed to do, still not looking at the guard. When she was done, she stood up, and pulled up her jeans. She looked at the guard for the first time. His smile was gone. "May I wash?" she asked in Spanish. Esmeralda stepped into the doorway with a washcloth and a bar of soap. "Thanks," Angela said. She turned to the sink and washed her face. She could see the guard's face in the mirror over the sink. She stole a look at him as she slowly removed her blouse. He turned away when he saw the burn scars on her back and arms. She could see Esmeralda put her hand over her mouth. She washed her body quickly, and then put the blouse back on. She turned back to the guard. "See everything you came to see?"

He didn't look at her, just mumbled something in Spanish and gestured back down the hall to her room. They walked back the same way they'd come, in the same order. The guard stayed outside as she entered the room, sat down, and began to eat.

Esmeralda stood by the door, her pretty face unreadable. Finally, she spoke. "Is there anything else you need?"

"Other than a way out of here?" Angela said.

"That will happen soon," the girl said.

"I wish I could believe that. Can you at least tell me why I'm here? Why did *Senor* Mandujano lie about letting me go? Where are my husband and my friend?"

The girl just shook her head and walked to the door. "I'll be back," she said. "I'll try to bring you something to read."

"Thank you," Angela said. She turned back to her meal. When she heard the door close and the locks click shut, she bent over and put her arms on the table. With her head cushioned within her arms, Angela began to cry, releasing all of her fear, anger, and humiliation through her muffled sobs. She wasn't going to let them see how afraid she was. But she didn't know how much longer she could keep this up. Or how much longer they'd let her live. She let herself cry for a few minutes, then sat up and wiped her eyes on her sleeve. "Okay," she said aloud to the empty room. "You're no princess, this whorehouse isn't a tower, and there's no knight in shining armor coming. If you're going to get out of this, girl, you're going to have to do it yourself." She thought of adding a "you can do it," but she'd always hated that pep-talky bullshit. She walked over and lay back on the bed, eyes open, staring at the ceiling...thinking.

CHAPTER
THIRTY-TWO

BACK IN THE DAYS BEFORE NAFTA, Frey had probably been a mirror image of Ciudad de Piedras. But where globalization had created a boomtown south of the border, time had passed Frey by and left it a dried husk of itself. The town's main street was mostly empty storefronts. Only a lone, sad looking diner and a dusty convenience store showed any signs of life. A couple of men in folding chairs sat outside the convenience store, their gazes tracking the pickup truck as it drove past.

They found the Frey Motor Lodge on the far side of town, beside the road heading north. It looked as sad and dispirited as the rest of the town, with only a few units extending away from a small office. The whole place was painted a pale yellow that looked washed out in the bright hard sunlight of a Texas late-summer morning.

Keller pulled the truck into a parking space outside the unit whose number was written on the envelope. As he turned the engine off, a man stepped out of the office at one end of the building. He was an older man, with a full head of gray hair. He was dressed in jeans, a white shirt with a string tie, and cracked leather boots. He eyed them suspiciously as he leaned against a post and crossed his arms against his chest.

"What are you going to do?" Oscar said.

"Have you got a business card?" Keller said. "From the bail bonding company?"

"Yes."

"So we're tracking a jumper," Keller said. "Just follow my lead."

"How will we..." Oscar said, but Keller was already climbing down from the driver's seat.

"Howdy," he said as he approached the gray-haired man.

"That ain't your truck," the man said.

"Actually," Keller said, "it is. At least it's going to be."

The man's eyes narrowed. "You repo men or somethin'?"

"No," Keller said. "We're bail bondsmen." He stepped forward and presented a business card. The man took it. "The guy we're looking for put up his vehicle — this one — as security. He didn't show for his court date. And he took the truck."

"We're here to bring him back," Oscar said. "And the truck."

Keller nodded. "We saw it at the diner, and, well, I guess we did kind of repossess it. Sort of. The guy we're after took off, though. We lost him. Found the key to his room in the truck and figured he'd come back here for his stuff."

The man didn't look convinced. "Which one you after? They was three people in that room."

"The...um...one with all the tattoos," Keller said lamely.

"You don't know his name?" the man said.

"His name is Jefferson Hager," Oscar said. "But he was probably using an alias here, no?"

The man nodded. "Yeah. Called himself Colton."

Oscar nodded. "Colton. Yes. That is one of his aliases."

"So can we look around in his room?" Keller said. "Maybe get some idea of where he went?"

"I think you're fulla shit," the old man said.

"No, really," Keller said. "We just want to—"

"Fifty bucks," the old man said.

"Pardon?" Oscar said.

"I don't know who the hell y'all are, or what you're really up to. No good, most likely. But I know for damn sure they was. Up to no good, I mean. But gimme fifty bucks an' you can go on in there an' do whatever bidness you need to do. I'll look the other way for fifteen minutes. After that, I want you two out of here. An' take their shit with ya. Whatever trouble this is, I want it gone from my place."

"Yeah. Okay." Keller reached into his back pocket, pulled out his wallet, counted out the money, and handed it to the old man.

"Another twenty," the man said, "an' I never saw y'all here. In case someone comes askin'."

Keller sighed and pulled out another bill. "Whatever."

The inside of the room smelled of spilled beer and body odor. The occupants had stacked beer cans in a ragged pyramid on the dresser. Clothes were thrown carelessly over the two double beds. There was an unfolded cot next to one of the beds.

Keller turned to Oscar. "Jefferson Hager?" he asked. "Wasn't that the name of Angela's ex-husband?"

Oscar shrugged. "First name I could think of at short notice."

Keller grunted. A laptop computer was plugged in and closed on the desk next to the TV. "We'll take that," he said. "It may tell us something."

The only luggage was a pair of army-surplus duffel bags on the floor. Keller bent down and rifled through one of the duffels. He came up with a wallet and opened it. "Belongs to a Rance Colton," Keller said. "Address is Hearken, South Carolina." He tossed the wallet back in the duffel. "Same address as on the GPS."

"You think that's where they took people?" Oscar said. "My sons?"

"If not," Keller said, "that's where people are who'll be able to answer some questions. So I guess that's where we're going." He started throwing things in the bags. Oscar did the same.

Suddenly, Oscar straightened up, holding something in his hand. It was a large roll of bills. "Jack," he said.

Keller looked over. "Great," he said. "Because we're starting to run low."

Oscar nodded, but he still looked unhappy. "This feels like stealing."

"Probably because it is," Keller said. "But they won't miss it. And it's time they contributed to a good cause."

That brought a smile to Oscar's face. "Well, if you put it that way."

CHAPTER
THIRTY-THREE

THEY DROVE STRAIGHT THROUGH, STOPPING only to ditch the truck on a street in San Antonio within walking distance of a used-car lot, where they picked up another vehicle using the cash they'd taken.

Oscar had nudged Keller, as they had walked down the rows of used cars, and pointed to a faded, but serviceable looking, Crown Victoria. The car looked like the older sibling of the car that Keller had driven during the years he'd worked for Angela. The dealer was a little suspicious of the large wad of cash they used to pay for the car, but when they offered to pay five hundred more than the price written on the windshield in exchange for expediting the paperwork, his misgivings seemed to vanish. After swinging back by the truck to transfer the duffels and weapons to the trunk of the Crown Vic, they hit the road again.

They quickly found the interstates and headed east, booming through Texas and Louisiana, skirting the Gulf Coast in Mississippi, turning north through Alabama and Georgia, stopping only briefly to eat, relieve themselves, and switch drivers at faceless truck stops along the way. They spoke little. Their longest conversation occurred at a nearly empty Arby's outside of Biloxi. Oscar took advantage of the free Wi-Fi to open up the laptop computer they'd taken from the motel room in Frey. He put it on the table next to the sandwiches and drinks, and rubbed his eyes tiredly as they waited for it to boot up.

"I'll drive the next leg," Keller said. Oscar nodded and looked out the window and the night outside. There was nothing visible beyond the orange glow of the lights in the parking lot. The computer chimed. Oscar looked at the screen. "Asking for a password."

"Shit," Keller said. "Any ideas?"

Oscar nodded and reached into his back pocket. He pulled out a creased and stained index card. "This was in one of the duffel bags." He showed it to Keller.

Keller shook his head. "They password-protect the computer, then write the password down someplace nearby?"

"You'd be surprised," Oscar said. "A lot of people actually tape the password to the top of the screen. These men probably thought they were being clever."

"Jesus." Keller took a bite of his sandwich as Oscar put in the password. The computer chimed again. Oscar frowned as the screen came alive.

"What?" Keller said. Oscar turned the screen around. A black Odin Cross, like the tattoo one of the dead men had worn, filled the screen on a white background. Large capital letters in a pseudo-Germanic script beneath it proclaimed CHURCH OF ELOHIM-GOD'S TRUE ISRAEL.

Keller nodded, remembering some of the doctrine his chatty bail jumper had spewed. "Oh, yeah. I've heard this shit before. They think the Jews rejected Jesus, but white Europeans didn't, so now they think that they're the chosen people. They're the real Israelis." He saw the look on Oscar's face and shrugged. "So to them, white Christians are the real Jews."

"I thought people like that hated Jews."

"I didn't say it made sense." Keller gestured at the computer. "Open up the browser. Let's see where these guys have been."

Oscar nodded and clicked an icon along the bottom of the screen. A website popped out that looked as if a third grader learning basic Internet skills had created it. The screen was dense with text on pastel-colored backgrounds and symbols, some of them blinking. The Odin Cross sat in the center of a banner atop the page, surrounded by the words RACE SURVIVAL DEMANDS RACISM.

"Charming," Keller said.

Oscar's brow furrowed as he squinted to read the text. "They certainly don't like black people." His frown deepened. "Or Latinos." He read on for a few moments.

"Oscar," Keller said as he saw a grim expression cross his friend's face.

Oscar looked up. "This...this *church*," he nearly spat the word, "says Latinos...people like me, like my family, have no souls. We are meant only to serve this 'True Israel.'" His face twisted in anger. "They call us *mud people*." He shoved the computer away from him so hard Keller had to catch it to keep it from sliding off the edge of the table.

"Easy, man," Keller said. "I get it. These people are assholes. But we could spend hours down this rabbit hole. We need to move, *now*, which means we need to find out more about this place where they are. Is there any mention of some farm, or 'the Farm' or something like that?"

Oscar stood up. "You look. I have to use the bathroom." He walked off, shoulders hunched. He was as angry as Keller had ever seen him.

Keller pulled the laptop over in front of him and started clicking and scrolling. It took him a few minutes to master the touch pad, but in a few minutes, he was adeptly paging through the browser history. White supremacist and Christian Identity Movement sites were frequently interspersed in the visited sites list with hard-core pornography, Craigslist ads, and sports scores. Keller focused on the movement sites. The Church of Elohim had pages and pages of "doctrinal statements," along with ads for books and tapes espousing the church's philosophy and various conspiracy theories. One book purported to be a frame-by-frame dissection of the famous Zapruder film, which would prove that Jacqueline Bouvier Kennedy had been the one who'd killed JFK, in her role as a dedicated Mossad assassin and agent of Communist Zionism. But there was nothing about any facility matching the "Farm" he'd seen on the GPS.

Oscar returned and sat down. "Sorry," he muttered. "I let my anger get the better of me."

"Don't be," Keller said. "I'm pissed off, too. But we need to focus on finding these people."

Oscar looked at him. "My sons are in the hands of madmen, Jack. Men who think they have no souls. If they are even still alive." He looked back out the window. "It's easy to kill something that has no soul. Even a child."

"They're still alive, Oscar," Keller said. "We have to believe that."

Oscar nodded. "I know. We keep moving forward. But now I know what we're up against. And I am afraid. But more than afraid, I am angry."

"Good," Keller said. "Go with that."

Oscar rubbed the back of his neck. "You know, for a while, somewhere in the back of my head, I think I still had this foolish hope that we could talk to these people. Bargain with them. Get my sons back." He shook his head, "but they won't be reasoned with."

"No," Keller said, "but maybe they can be intimidated." He leaned forward. "These people are cowards. They take women and children and people who are helpless. They shoot from ambush, out of the dark. They're afraid. Hell, read all this crap they write. It's all about how the world's collapsing, there are enemies behind every tree, and everything is going to hell. They're *scared*, Oscar."

"Frightened people can be dangerous."

"Not as dangerous as angry ones. And you're pretty angry right now."

"Yes," Oscar said, "I am."

"Finish your sandwich," Keller said.

As Oscar ate, Keller kept tapping away on the computer. He did a Google search on the Church of Elohim. "Looks like these guys originally came out of Southern Ohio," he said. "Offshoot of one of the Aryan Nations groups. The original leader, a guy named Elihu Stone, got busted for shooting a black cop in the head, then for conspiracy to bomb the local NAACP office, and the whole thing fell apart. The second in command, some guy named Martin Walker, came down to South Carolina with a few of the holdouts and started it up again."

"The Sword Arm of the Lord," Oscar said through a mouthful of fries.

"What?"

He swallowed. "That's what he calls himself on the website."

Keller went back. "Yep. Here he is. 'General Martin Walker, Sword Arm of the Lord.'" He looked at the picture. "Ugly fucker."

"Sounds dangerous," Oscar said.

"Sounds stupid," Keller said. "You done?" Oscar nodded. "Okay," Keller said, "let's get back on the road. We'll be in this Hearken place by daybreak. We need to scope this 'church' out for ourselves. And maybe have a little talk with the 'General.'"

CHAPTER
THIRTY-FOUR

THE GENERAL HUNG UP THE phone. No answer again. Not even voice mails. He was becoming increasingly uneasy about the loss of contact with the capture team. He wondered if he should have gone with them, like he had before. But he couldn't watch his soldiers all the time. Sometime, they would have to learn to do things without their General holding their hands.

Once the bloodshed began in Mexico, he thought, he'd put an end to the use of the illegals as workers. It had shown some profit, especially the sale of the women to the Croatian syndicate Cosgrove had steered him to, but not as much as he'd hoped. And he was getting more and more uncomfortable with the way his soldiers indulged their lusts with the women.

Now, two men were poking their noses into what had been happening to the illegals being brought north. Two amateurs. Not law enforcement. His contacts in the government had assured him of that. Two amateurs — one of them a brown monkey — should have been easy to deal with, especially with the firepower the team had taken with them.

He made his decision. Picking up the phone, he dialed the Sheriff. "Two men," the General said when he answered. "An American and a Mexican. They may be coming this way." He listened to the response, cutting it off in the middle. "Pick them up. Hold them. Let me know." He hung up.

Cosgrove would obey. He was in too deep. He'd taken some of the profit from the sale of the women, but not before amusing himself with some of the younger ones. He'd been foolish to think his sins wouldn't go unrecorded or that the General wouldn't use them as leverage. *Once again, men's own weakness and depravity is my greatest weapon in doing the work of the Lord* .

Now, to the other matter. Zavalo had let him know the men were looking for a pair of boys who were taken in one of the raids. The Mexican's sons, Zavalo had said. Or maybe he'd said the man was Colombian. Whatever. The boys in question could only be the impertinent young monkey, who'd talked him into letting Diego be buried, and his brother. He considered simply killing them, but decided against it. If by some insane chance, the two men made it this far, they'd most likely do almost anything to keep the General from hanging the two brats from the Judicial Tree. Even lay down their weapons. And when they did that, he'd see how many monkeys could hang from one limb of that tree. He imagined quite a few.

"Funny," the General said aloud. "The tree is where monkeys belong." He chuckled at his own witticism. A sudden thought stifled the laughter. He needed to make sure nothing happened to them, at least until they were no longer needed. He'd need to keep the boys close to him. Until the end.

ESMERALDA WAS BACK IN A few hours, bearing another plate. This time, the sandwich was peanut butter. No jelly. The girl didn't leave this time. She sat on the cot and watched Angela eat.

"So, that man, the one you were with. In the bar. The blond." Esmeralda gestured at Angela's body. "Did he do those things to you?"

"No," Angela said. "My ex-husband did."

The other woman looked doubtful "The other man? At Mandujano's house?"

"No. That man is my husband now. He'd never do anything like that. He's a good man. A good husband. The man who hurt me was my first husband."

Esmeralda hugged herself involuntarily. "Why?"

Because he was a fucking psychopath. "Because I told him I was sick of being beaten. I told him I was leaving him. He couldn't stand that. I was his. He told me that a lot. If he couldn't have me, no one would. So he broke my legs with a baseball bat, so I couldn't get away when he set the house on fire. Then he killed himself — in front of me."

"*Dios Mio,*" the girl whispered.

"Esmeralda," Angela said, leaning forward and fixing the girl's dark eyes with her own pale ones, "that guy. The one who hit you. He's not going to stop. It's going to get worse. It's probably going to get a lot worse."

Esmeralda shook her head. "He says he's sorry."

"Yeah," Angela said. "And he loves you and it won't happen again, that he's just under a lot of pressure. Right?"

The girl looked back at her, mute, her eyes glistening.

"I heard that bullshit too, honey," Angela said. "Right up till the day the man I still loved shattered both my legs, made me beg for my life, and then tried to burn me to death."

Esmeralda stood up. Tears were running down her face. "You're just trying to mess with my head, so I'll help you get out of here."

"I admit it. I want out. And I want you to come with me. Out of here. Away from these people. Before this..." she pulled up her right sleeve to show the web of scars that ran up it, "happens to you."

Esmeralda shook her head desperately. "You don't even know me."

"No," said Angela, "but I wouldn't want anyone to go through what you're going to go through." Esmeralda turned as if to flee. "Don't walk out looking like that," Angela said. "If they see you crying, they'll know something's up. They'll ask you what. And if they don't like the answer, they'll beat it out of you."

She turned back to Angela, furious. "You don't know anything," she spat. She fled the room.

Angela listened for the sound of the locks being refastened. If the girl was upset enough, maybe she'd forget. Her heart sank as she heard the metallic clinks and clicks.

"Shit," she said aloud. She didn't expect to ever see the girl again. Or to ever get out of that room alive.

SOMETHING WAS WRONG. RUBEN COULD sense it. The guards, whose bullying of their prisoners was usually almost as jovial as it was cruel, were grim and unsmiling. The routine remained the same, but there was an edge to their voices. As the prisoners worked, they stood together, conversing in low voices. Once when Ruben drifted near, he overheard something about a "capture team." He recalled Kinney's conversation with Colton, the other guard, and realized that he hadn't seen Colton since.

The guards cut the day's work shorter than usual. That would normally have made the men happy, but they'd caught the tension in the guards' demeanor as well, and they looked at each other apprehensively as they were marched back to the barracks. As they walked through the gate, Ruben heard a voice call out to him.

"Boy." He stopped at the sound of the General's voice. The General was standing a few feet away, next to a large vehicle Ruben recognized as a civilian model Hummer. "Come here," he said. Ruben hesitated as the other men moved on, not looking at him.

"Well?" Kinney snapped, "Move!"

Ruben walked over, trying not to drag his feet. He stood before the General. The older man didn't speak at first, but Ruben could feel the General appraising him. Ruben kept his eyes down.

Finally, the General spoke. "Can you read and write English as well as speak it?"

Ruben nodded. "Answer out loud!" the General snapped.

"Yes," Ruben said, "Yes, sir. I can read and write English."

The General grunted. "Can you do sums?"

"Sums?"

"Add. Subtract. Mathematics."

That's arithmetic, not mathematics. What kind of backward place does this man think I'm from? Ruben had been first in his calculus class in school. "Yes," he said, "I'm good at math."

"We'll see," the General said. "And if you're lying, you'll be punished. Severely."

"I'm not lying," Ruben said.

The General acted as if he hadn't heard. "The man who assists me in recordkeeping has been unavoidably detained. This leaves me shorthanded of able men to keep you people in line. So. Follow me." He turned and began walking toward Building Three. Ruben's stomach knotted in fear, but he followed. They walked inside, through the room where they'd been taken for "trial" when they'd first arrived, and into a smaller room with a desk and filing cabinets. The office was immaculate, the desk empty except for a clipboard. "Here," the General said, picking up the clipboard. "Go to Building Four. Inventory the supplies." He handed it over.

Ruben looked down at the clipboard. Along the left hand side of the page was a list of foodstuffs — flour, beef, ham, beans, and others — followed by a column showing the quantity of each as of a week before. It looked simple enough. Ruben looked up. "I have to look after my little brother," he said. "The other men, they pick on him. Take his food when I am not there." Their suspicion and distrust of Ruben as a collaborator had affected Edgar as well. The other men in the barracks ignored them when Ruben was there, but when they were apart, the smaller and more timid Edgar had a rough time of it. "And it will g worse if I'm doing this."

The General shook his head in disgust. "Animals. It will be taken care of. As long as you do your job, and do it well, the two of you'll be protected."

"Yes, sir," Ruben said. "Thank you, sir." He turned away with the clipboard. *Now who will protect us from you?*

CHAPTER THIRTY-FIVE

BY MIDMORNING, THEY'D ARRIVED AT the city limits of Hearken. Though they were stiff and bleary-eyed from the road, neither one of them felt like resting. They felt their goal getting nearer. Somewhere around here was the answer, and maybe Oscar's sons.

Keller had written down the street address of the Church of Elohim. The town was small, even tinier than Frey, with only the one main street. The address they eventually located was a storefront on a side street, without signs or any evidence of occupancy. The front plate glass was covered with paper on the inside so they couldn't see in. They got out of the car and stood looking at the building. Keller walked over and tried the door. The place was locked.

"Maybe they closed down," he said.

Oscar shook his head. "The website is being maintained. Last posting was three days ago."

"So this address is a front." He was walking back to the car as a brown and white Sheriff's patrol car pulled in behind them. He tensed as the officer inside put on his flashers and activated the blue light bar on top. "Let me do the talking," Keller said.

"Not a problem," Oscar said.

The officer who slowly unfolded himself out of the front seat was a tall and lanky, light-skinned African-American. He had the rawboned look and big hands of a farm boy, and the slow amble to match, but his eyes were shrewd and appraising as he looked them over. "Mornin', fellas," he drawled. The nameplate over the pocket of his short-sleeved khaki shirt read CASTLE.

"Morning," Keller said.

"You gentlemen new in town?"

"Here on business," Keller said. "Mind if I take my card out of my back pocket?" The deputy nodded. His eyes never stopped moving between Keller and Oscar, who sat in the car.

Keller handed over the card. Castle took it and studied it. "Bail Bonds," he said. "Y'all are a ways from home."

"So's the guy we're looking for," Keller said. "My boss here," he nodded at Oscar, "has some serious cash on the line."

"Your…" he looked at Oscar sitting in the car, who smiled. Castle looked back at the card. He walked around to the passenger side and motioned for Oscar to roll down the window. Oscar complied. "Oscar Sanchez?" the deputy said. "The business is yours?"

"Mine and my wife's." Oscar's smile grew wider. "So I guess I am only the boss when she's not around."

That brought a ghost of a smile to the deputy's lips, but it quickly vanished. He slid the card into the pocket of his uniform shirt, straightened up, and looked at Keller. "License and registration, please." Keller slid into the car and pulled the bill of sale out of the glove box. "We just bought the car," he said, handing it to Castle along with his driver's license.

Castle's brow furrowed. "In Texas?"

"I'm telling you," Keller said, "this guy's led us all over the damn place."

"What's his name?" Castle said.

"Hager," Oscar answered. "Jefferson Hager."

"We'd heard he might have joined up with this Church of Elohim,"

Keller said, watching the deputy's face closely. "This was the address we had for it."

Castle shook his head. "They moved out of town," he said. "And the land where they moved is posted. No trespassing."

"Okay," Keller said. "I understand." He tried another tack. "Maybe you've seen Hager around. He sometimes uses the name Rance Colton."

There was still no reaction. "Never heard of him. Wait here." Castle took the license and registration back to his car.

"Jack," Oscar said, "if he looks in the trunk…"

"We're just working stiffs trying to do our job," Keller said, "and exercising our Second Amendment right to bear arms."

"Would that include the rocket launcher?" Oscar said.

"It's South Carolina," Keller said. "You never know. They probably hunt deer with the damn things down here."

The deputy came back with his slow amble, but his eyes no longer held that watchful wariness. "License checks out," he said, handing the license and bill of sale back to Keller.

"Any idea where we might find our bail jumper?" Keller asked.

Castle shook his head. "Like I said. Never heard of him. But I will tell you this." He looked directly at Keller. "Stay away from that church's property. Like I said, it's posted, and they don't like trespassers. I or one of the other deputies gets called out there, they *will* press charges. Understood?"

Keller nodded. "Understood."

"You fellas have a nice day, now," Castle said.

As he turned away, Keller caught a glimpse of a tattoo on the deputy's bicep, peeking out from under his short-sleeved uniform shirt. It showed a shield with a black silhouette of a horse's head in the upper left corner. "Hey," he said. The deputy stopped and turned back. The wariness was back in his eyes. "First Cav?"

Castle nodded. "Yeah."

"Me, too," Keller said. "Desert Storm."

"That so?" Castle said. "Bosnia for me, then the second go-round in the Gulf."

"Fallujah?"

Castle nodded.

"Bad as it looked?"

"Worse."

"Sorry," Keller said.

Castle shrugged. "Embrace the suck," he quoted.

"Heard that," Keller replied.

"Have a good day," Castle said, a little more pleasantly this time.

"You, too." Keller got back in the car as Castle climbed back into his. He waited for the deputy to start his car before he turned the key.

"That was close," Oscar said. "Have we made a friend?"

"Maybe," Keller said, "or maybe he's calling those Elohim assholes right now."

"Unlikely," Oscar said. "Given he's a black man."

"Stranger shit has happened."

"So what do we do?" Oscar said.

"We move forward," Keller said. "We need to check out the farm."

"That officer said..."

"That they don't like visitors. That they're really insistent on keeping people away. Wouldn't you do that if you were holding people as slaves?"

Oscar nodded. "Do you think that is where they are?"

"I think it's the next place we look," Keller said. He put the car in gear and pulled away. "But I want to find a library first."

"A library? Why?"

"If we're going to find a way in," Keller said. "We need a map. And where's the best place to find a map?"

"The library?"

"Maybe. But also, online. But we'll need a printer."

Oscar nodded. They were pulling out onto the main street. "There." Oscar pointed to a small, older building, set back from the street and surrounded by trees. A sign out front read HEARKEN PUBLIC LIBRARY.

"Great," Keller said. He pulled into a parking space in front.

CHAPTER THIRTY-SIX

RAY CASTLE STEERED HIS PATROL cruiser through the streets of Hearken, eyes moving over the familiar homes and storefronts of the town where he'd grown up. All quiet today. He smiled to himself. Quiet was good. He'd had enough excitement over in the Sandbox to last a lifetime. He'd come back with a Silver Star, a Purple Heart, and a deep desire never to leave his hometown again. The first two had given him enough local fame to ease his way into a job in the Sheriff's department despite the prejudice that still existed. It never hurt a politician's chances to be seen giving a break to a serviceman. Sheriff Cosgrove had even invited Castle to a few of his fundraisers and campaign stops, especially those at AME Churches and Black Community Centers. He knew he was being used as a prop, but he tried hard to let it go. For all the bullshit, this place was home. His whole family was here.

The radio crackled with static. "All units, base." He recognized the voice of Sheriff Cosgrove. His brow furrowed. That was odd. He keyed his mic. "One-seven," he responded. He heard the four other units on patrol in various sections of the county call in.

"All units," Sheriff Cosgrove said over the channel. "Be on the lookout for any unfamiliar or strange subjects in or around Hearken. Particularly subjects showing interest in the Church of Elohim or its properties."

"What the…" Castle whispered to himself. He keyed the mic again. "Sir, this is one-seven. I just talked to a couple of subjects outside the church's old headquarters. The place they had before they moved out to the farm."

There was a brief silence. "One-seven, meet me back at the substation."

"Ten-four," Castle said. He wondered if he'd screwed up by letting the two men go. Still, there'd really been nothing to hold them for. He began to sweat, even with the air-conditioning turned up high.

Cosgrove was standing by his personal vehicle, a white Cadillac Escalade, out in front of the small sheriff's substation on Main Street. He still had the broad shoulders and massive build of the star middle linebacker he'd been at the University of South Carolina, even though his brush cut shock of hair had gone gray and his face was lined from years in the sun on his family farm. The Cosgroves had done well for themselves for generations in Hearken, which is how Castle figured the Sheriff could afford vehicles like he drove on what the county paid him.

"What's up, sir?" Castle said as he got out.

"Castle," the Sheriff said, "tell me about this stop you just made."

"Yes, sir," Castle said, nearly snapping to attention by sheer reflex at the commanding tone. He gave the Sheriff the full story, trying to keep it as straightforward as possible, as if he was giving testimony in court.

"A white guy and a Hispanic?" Cosgrove said when he was done. Castle nodded. "Good," Cosgrove said. "Find them. Pick them up."

"Sir?"

A scowl appeared on Cosgrove's face. "Do I stutter, son? I said pick their asses up. Bring them here." He gestured at the substation. "And let me know. But use your cell phone. Stay off the air."

"Yes, sir," Castle said. This was making less and less sense. The tiny substation had been the old Hearken police department until the town had decided their money would be better spent if they let the county Sheriff pick up the slack. Officers joked that the place reminded them of the Sheriff's office in the old *Andy Griffith* show: A couple of desks, an ancient computer, an even more ancient radio that was a relic of the 1970s, and a pair of old cells in the back. There wasn't even a magistrate on duty. Which reminded him. "Sir?"

Cosgrove had been turning away toward his car. Now he turned back, the scowl deepening. "What now?" he snapped.

"What's the charge?"

The Sheriff stared at him incredulously, as if the question were the most absurd thing he'd ever heard. "Charge?"

"Yes, sir," Castle said. "Why am I bringing them in?"

"Questioning," the Sheriff said.

"Questioning," Castle repeated.

"Yes. Questioning. They may be material witnesses in an ongoing Federal investigation. Any more dumb-ass inquiries, son?"

"No, sir," Castle said. *Other than what bug has got up your ass.*

"Good," Cosgrove said and turned away again. "Now do your damn job."

"Yes, sir," Castle said and got back in the patrol car. He took a moment to get his anger under control as he watched the Sheriff drive off. Then he started the engine.

"JACK," OSCAR SAID. HE WAS making no move to get out of the car.

"Yeah?" Keller said.

"When we find this place," Oscar said, "what are we going to do?"

"We're going to go in and get your boys," Keller said.

Oscar shook his head. "I do not think that will work."

Keller's grip tightened on the wheel. "Why not?"

Oscar looked at him sadly. "You really haven't thought this through, have you?"

Keller felt a brief stab of frustration. "What are you..."

Oscar nodded. "Think, Jack." He gestured toward the trunk of the car. "We've seen what kinds of weapons these men have. And we know there will be more of them at this farm." He shook his head. "I have known you for years now. I have worked with you. I know your first thought is to kick down doors and start grabbing people."

It's all I have. The thought came to Keller unbidden. Oscar saw his look and nodded again. "I know that is what you live for. What keeps you feeling alive. But I don't think it will work this time. And it might get my sons killed."

"So what do you suggest we do?"

"We look. We see what we can see. And then we do what we should have done a while ago. Alert the authorities."

"Who?" Keller said. "Local cops?"

"No," Oscar said. "I think the locals may be protecting these people. Certainly they do not seem to want to know what is going on out there. But the FBI, even the Immigration…" he shrugged. "We let enough people know that someone is practicing slavery, here in America, in the twenty-first century, someone will do something." He sighed. "If nothing else, they will come once they know illegals are here."

Keller tried to keep the frustration out of his voice. He didn't entirely succeed. "Maybe it's you who hasn't thought this through, Oscar. Best-case scenario is, they believe you, and being the Feds, they hem and haw and take forever to put something together. Who knows what happens in the meantime? Worst case is, they don't believe you, don't do anything, and they figure out you're not here legally, and they lock you up, then they deport you. Actually, in any scenario, they lock you up and send you back to Colombia. And your sons. If those crazy racist fucks don't kill them first."

Oscar nodded. "I know that. I have decided I'm going back anyway. With my sons."

"You'll…what?"

"I can't keep living like this, Jack. Outside of the law. It's making me crazy." He looked at Keller. "I came here to be safe. So my sons could be safe." He threw up his hands. "Look at this. Am I safe? Is my family safe? Since I came to America, I have been kidnapped and shot by drug dealers, I've had crazy men try to kill me, and now this. *Mierda*, I was safer in Colombia, teaching school, than I am in this place. Than I am with—" He stopped.

"Than you are with me," Keller said.

"Jack, I didn't mean—"

"No, no, you're right," Keller said. He thought back to another man's words: *You bring death, and hell follows with you.*

"You are not responsible for what has happened to my boys," Oscar said quietly. "Without you, I wouldn't be this close to finding out what happened to them. I thank you for that. But we're going to do this my way."

Keller still felt the burn of his frustration. But Oscar was right. He knew that a head-on attack was probably suicide, for him and for Oscar. Still, something in him clamored for, as Oscar said, kicking down doors and grabbing people, even if it would get both of them killed. He took a deep breath.

"Okay," he said. "We'll do it your way."

"Good," Oscar said. "Now let's go see what we can see."

CHAPTER
THIRTY-SEVEN

SHE HADN'T GOTTEN BREAKFAST THAT morning. The only way she could even tell it was morning was by the sounds outside. That worried her. If they'd stopped feeding her, then whatever reason they had for keeping her alive might have gone away. She wished she knew what was going on. She wished she knew what time it was. And she really had to pee again.

When she heard the locks working again, Angela got up off the bed and stood behind the chair, grabbing it with both hands. If someone came through that door with a gun, she was going to pick it up and try to club him with it. The chair might be flimsy, it might not be much of a weapon, but she wasn't going without a fight.

It was Esmeralda, and she wasn't carrying a gun. She was dressed in black jeans and a white blouse with ruffles on the front. She wore dark glasses. Angela couldn't see the usual guard behind her. She stood inside the opened door, not speaking.

"Hi," Angela said. "I was wondering if you'd be back." It was then she noticed the marks on Esmeralda's wrists, ugly blue bruises that looked fresh.

Esmeralda saw her looking and her jaw tightened. She took off the dark glasses to show a blackened eye. "So, I guess you were right."

"It doesn't make me happy," Angela said. "And no, I'm not going to say I told you so."

The girl shook her head, her face a mask of fury. She wiped her glistening eyes with the back of her hand. "You still want to get out of here?"

"Yeah," Angela said. "What about the guard?"

The girl gave her a savage smile. "Come see."

The guard was stretched out full length in the hallway, snoring, with an empty tray next to him. Next to the tray was an equally empty bottle of beer lying on its side.

"I put pills in his food...and in his beer. He'll sleep for a while. I had to wait till Miguel and the others were gone."

"Where did they go?"

Esmeralda shrugged. "Something to do with their big plan. Against the boss."

"Miguel is making some sort of move against Mandujano?"

Esmeralda nodded. "He works for the fat man. Zavalo."

"So Mandujano has nothing to do with bringing me here."

"I don't know why you were brought here. I hear about some things. Not others. Do you want to leave or not?"

"Oh, yeah," Angela said. "But first things first." She gestured at the guard. "You get his guns. I'll be back."

When Angela exited the restroom, Esmeralda was standing in the hallway looking impatient. She was holding the guard's submachine gun in one hand, a 9MM Beretta in the other. "You know how to use either of those?" Angela asked.

"The pistol. A little."

"Okay," Angela said. She held out her hand for the machine gun. It was an H & K MP5.

"You know how to use this?" Esmeralda said.

"A little," she said. She retracted and released the bolt with the charging handle. "Okay. Let's go."

"Where?"

"You know where the American consulate is?"

"I think so."

"Then there," Angela said.

"But I'm not American," Esmeralda protested.

"There may be some people there ready to overlook that," Angela said. "If you're willing to talk to them."

"Talk...you mean inform?" The girl shook her head. "No. I won't do that."

"Esmeralda," Angela said, "you may not have a choice. You won't be able to come back here. You know that."

Esmeralda's eyes grew wide. "I...I..."

"When you opened that door for me," Angela said, "you crossed a line. Miguel finds out you did that, he'll hurt you. Badly. Maybe kill you. He'll almost certainly kill me. And he probably won't do it quickly."

The girl was beginning to panic. "She didn't really think this through," Angela thought. It came to her that, despite her outer hardness, she was a terribly young girl. "Come on, honey," she said. "We can talk about this in the car. You do have a car, don't you?"

Esmeralda nodded. "Outside. In the alley."

"Okay." Angela heard the sound of footsteps on stairs, the clamor of upraised male voices.

"*Mierda*," Esmeralda said. "They're back early."

CHAPTER
THIRTY-EIGHT

KELLER DROVE, WITH OSCAR IN the passenger seat studying the stolen GPS, which he held on his lap. In his other hand was the map they had printed out on a computer in the Hearken Library. Both of them had their pistols, Keller's stuck down into the gap between his seat and Oscar's, and Oscar's between his seat and the door. The long guns were in the backseat, under a rough blanket they'd taken from the trunk. Occasionally, Oscar would look up from the GPS as they approached one of the infrequent crossroads. At each one, he'd quietly call out a direction: "Left. Straight ahead. Right." The Glock Keller had taken from the warehouse in Mexico was shoved down alongside Oscar's between his seat and the passenger door.

Outside of town, the terrain turned to pine forest that crowded in on the sides of the narrow road. From time to time, the land on either side of the road fell away and they drove along a raised roadway with blackwater swamp on either side, the water stained to the color of strong tea by decaying vegetation. The trees seemed closer, arching over the road as if they contemplated making their final move and blocking them from in front and behind. Then, as suddenly as they'd entered, they'd burst out into sunlight, the swamp giving way in its turn to open fields thick with crops—soybeans, cotton, tobacco, and corn. They saw farmhouses set back from the road, surrounded by trees, some bright and shiny and new, some looking as if they were frozen in the midst of their collapse.

"We're getting closer," Oscar said. "This is the beginning of the church's lands."

"I can tell," Keller said. Where the other fields had been open, here a chain-link fence ran between the road and the open land. The fence was high, at least twice the height of a man, and topped with a double strand of barbed wire. Every few feet, a sign was wired to the chain link, stating POSTED. NO TRESPASSING in white letters on a black background. Other signs, bright yellow in color, warned DANGER. HIGH VOLTAGE.

"An electric fence?" Oscar said.

"That cop was right," Keller said. "They really *don't* like visitors."

The fields behind the fence had been mowed, but not planted. Then the pines took over again, blocking their view of what lay beyond. Keller slowed as he saw something up ahead. "There's the gate," he said.

It was a double gate, made of dark, heavy wood, standing as tall as the fence. More signs announced PRIVATE PROPERTY. NO TRESPASSING. But it was the Odin Cross painted on each wing of the gate that interested Keller.

"Yep," he said, "this is the place."

It was then that they noticed the man behind the fence. He was dressed in khaki pants, a light-brown shirt, and heavy military-style boots. He wore a ragged boonie hat pulled low, and dark sunglasses that hid his eyes. He carried an AK-47 rifle loose in his hands.. As they slowed, he pulled a radio from where it was clipped to his belt and raised it to his face. They could see his lips move as he spoke.

"Don't think we'll be getting in that way," Keller said. He sped up and pulled away. He checked the rearview to see if anyone was following, dropping his hand to the pistol beside him.

"Next crossroads," Oscar said, "take a right. We'll see if there is another way in."

They never got the chance. As they neared the crossroads, a brown and white sheriff's car, like the one they'd seen in town, came up behind them, fast. Almost as soon as Keller saw it, the blue lights came on.

"Damn it," he said. He thought of punching the accelerator, trying to outrun the sheriff's cruiser. He could have made a go of it in his old Crown Vic, itself a former police car. But the car they'd bought in Texas was a tame, civilian model of his car, which Keller had last seen burned out on a mountainside in Western North Carolina. The cops would run them down, force them off the road, and things would go downhill from there. He pulled the car over to the narrow dirt shoulder.

"What are you doing?" Oscar said.

"Just follow my lead," Keller said. He saw the officer getting out. It was Castle, the deputy they'd met in town. He didn't look happy. Keller rolled the window down. He kept his hands on the wheel in the ten and two position.

"I thought I told you two to leave this place alone," Castle said as he reached the car window.

"We're on a public road," Keller said. "We're not breaking any laws."

Castle hesitated. "Out of the car," he said finally.

Keller saw the hesitation. "You know I'm right."

Castle's face reddened. "I *said*, out of the car." He reached down to the Taser riding on his belt.

Keller felt the adrenaline rising in him, that exquisite, knife-edge excitement that always came over him at moments like this. His senses seemed especially acute. He could hear Oscar stirring restlessly in the passenger seat. They both had guns within reach, cocked and locked, ready to fire. He could see it playing out in his mind—pull the weapon, come out of his seat, take the shot, put this small-town cop down, and...then what? *Then you bring death*, a voice said inside his head, *and hell follows with you.*

"Okay, okay," Keller said. He opened the door and slowly got out. Oscar started to do the same.

"You!" Castle barked. "Stay where you are."

Oscar looked at Keller, who nodded. Oscar slid back into the car. Keller straightened up.

"Turn around," Castle said. "Hands on the roof of the car."

Keller did as he was told. "You know something's wrong here, Deputy Castle," he said as Castle patted him down.

"You need to be quiet, sir," Castle said. He finished his frisk. "Okay. Hands behind your back." He took a pair of handcuffs from his belt.

"Wait," Keller said, "you're arresting me? For what?"

"I said be *quiet*," Castle snapped. "And I'm not going to tell you again. Put your hands behind your back." Keller took a deep breath, but complied. Castle fixed the handcuffs around his wrists, tight but not too tight. He walked around to the other side of the car and motioned Oscar out.

Keller stood by the driver's side door, watching. He heard the passenger door open...and then the sound of something clatter to the ground.

A look of shock crossed Castle's face as he looked down. He leaped backward, drawing his weapon.

No, Keller thought. *No. Not Oscar. Please.*

"OUT OF THE CAR!" Castle bellowed. "GET ON THE GROUND! NOW!" Keller heard Oscar's soft answer. He couldn't make out the words, but he saw Castle's weapon lowered to point at something on the ground, so he assumed Oscar was complying. Castle holstered his weapons and knelt down out of Keller's sight. In a moment, Keller saw Oscar jerked upright, hands behind his back. He looked at Keller with an apologetic smile.

"Castle," Keller said.

"Shut up," the officer replied.

"There's another gun between the seats. It's mine. Two long guns in the backseat."

Castle stared at him, then bent to look inside the car to confirm. He straightened back up, holding Keller's Glock. "You're both under arrest for carrying a concealed weapon, going armed to the terror of the people, and trespassing. You have the right to remain silent..."

"We could have taken you out, Castle," Keller said. "You know it's true. You never would have seen it coming. But we didn't."

"What the hell do you want for that?" Castle said, his voice tight with tension. "A medal?"

"No," Keller said, "but maybe you can hear me out."

"You can say whatever you want, back at the station," Castle said. "Right now, you have the right to remain silent…"

CHAPTER THIRTY-NINE

MIGUEL WAS THE FIRST ONE down the stars. He was calling out Esmeralda's name, irritation evident in his voice. He trailed off in midshout as he saw the machine gun in Angela's hand. He was wearing a pistol in a fancy tooled-leather shoulder holster. Another man was following him down the stairs, a kid with unruly hair who looked no more than sixteen. Miguel's sudden stop caused the kid to pile into him from behind. Miguel stumbled forward and Angela raised the gun higher to point at his face.

"Stop," she said in Spanish.

"What the hell," the kid said. His hand went to the gun stuck in his waistband.

"Don't," Angela said. "I don't want to have to kill you."

Miguel's eyes narrowed. He looked back and forth from Angela to Esmeralda. "What's going on, baby?" he said to the younger woman.

"She doesn't want to end up beat all to hell and left for dead like I did," Angela said. "So we're getting out of here."

"Shut the fuck up, bitch," Miguel said. He looked back at Esmeralda.

"Baby," he said in a soft voice, "is this what it's about?" He gestured at Angela. "What kind of nonsense has she been putting in your head?"

Angela stole a look at the girl. She was holding the pistol out in front of her with both hands, but her hands and arms were shaking visibly. Her voice trembled a little too, but from anger. "You beat me," she said. "You beat me like a fucking *dog*. Then you said you wouldn't do it again. But you *did*."

"Okay," Miguel said, holding out his hands, palm open. "I know. I'm sorry. I know you're angry with me. I was wrong. But this…this is crazy. This is going to get the both of us in trouble, more trouble than you can imagine. The both of us are going to get hurt." The girl didn't answer, but a single tear rolled down her face. "If Zavalo knows I let her get away, he'll blame me. And you know what that means. I could even live with that, baby. But he'd find you. You know he would. And you know what he'd do."

Angela felt sick. The girl was weakening, she knew it. She knew that calm reasonable tone, that persuasiveness. She'd heard it all before. And she'd fallen for it.

"Take the guns out," Angela said. "Two fingers. Thumb and forefinger. Drop them on the ground."

Miguel ignored her. He never took his eyes of Esmeralda. "You know I love you, don't you? It would kill me if anything happened to you." He put one hand on his chest. "You're my heart."

Angela almost pulled the trigger on him right there. He sounded so much like her husband Jeff, just the sound his voice sent a hot bolt of rage through her. She saw the kid smirking. Still, she couldn't bring herself to pull the trigger.

The kid looked at her and his smile widened. "Fuck this," he said. "She won't shoot us." He reached for the pistol stuck in his waistband. Angela's gun bucked in her hands. She saw the first round strike the kid in the chest, knocking him back into the stairwell. The gun rode up with the uncontrolled recoil and the second round struck him in the face. The third splintered the wood of the stairwell. Angela had no recollection of pulling the trigger.

Miguel roared with rage and yanked his own gun from the shoulder holster. Angela heard the blast of Esmeralda's pistol, saw Miguel stagger backward clutching his belly. He looked at Esmeralda, his eyes wide with shock. "You BITCH," he shouted. "You fucking SHOT me!" He raised the gun, and Esmeralda sobbed and fired again. Her second shot was spoiled by the tears in her eyes. It went into the doorjamb. Miguel and Angela fired at the same time. She was ready for the recoil this time and all three rounds struck Miguel in the chest and neck. He fell backward and lay still. Angela looked at Esmeralda.

The girl was sitting on the floor, clutching her belly with one hand. The other still held the gun. Blood stained her white blouse and covered her fingers. She looked up at Angela reproachfully, as if to say *this was your fault.*

"Oh no," Angela said. She knelt by Esmeralda's side. "Esmeralda, can you hear me?"

Esmeralda nodded, but didn't speak.

"We have to get you out of here, honey. Someplace safe. Someplace with a doctor. Can you get up?"

"I don't know," the girl whispered. "It hurts. It hurts bad."

"I know," Angela said, "I know. Come on." She got herself under Esmeralda's arm on one side and tried to stand her up.

The girl cried out in pain with the first attempt. The second one, she whimpered, but struggled to her feet. "I feel dizzy," she said.

"Stay with me, girl," Angela said. "Stay awake. You're not dying today. Not if I have anything to say about it." She guided Esmeralda toward the stairwell.

When they reached Miguel's body, Esmeralda looked down and started to cry. "You shot him," she sobbed. "You killed my man." She reached out to him as if she wanted to sink down beside him to mourn.

Angela was panting with the effort. "We don't get you to a doctor, Esme, he'll have killed *you.* Now *move.*"

"Noooo," Esmeralda wailed. "Let me be with him. Let me die with him."

"Goddamn it," Angela said. "I said *no.* Now come *on.*" She half dragged, half carried Esmeralda to the stairs. The climb seemed endless, Esmeralda a dead weight on Angela's shoulder. The gun in her other hand seemed to weigh a ton as well.

The door at the top of the stairs opened onto a kitchen. Dirty dishes were piled in the sink, and the stovetop looked as if it hadn't been cleaned in years. There was a back door, leading to the outside. Angela tried it. It had been nailed shut.

"I want to sit down," Esmeralda whined.

Angela was tempted to just let her do it, leave her burden on the floor, and get out of there. She fought the feeling down. "When we get to the car, you can sit down," she said. "Where's the car, Esme? Come on, stay awake, and tell me where the car is."

"Other door," Esmeralda mumbled.

"Where?" Angela demanded. There was no answer. Esmeralda's head lolled. Angela gave her an angry shake and she cried out in pain. "Wake up," Angela said. "Where's the fucking *door*?"

A young girl entered the kitchen, dressed only in a short white robe. She was Latina, but her hair was dyed a brilliant blond not found in nature. She squeaked in surprise at the apparition she saw before her.

"We are probably a rare sight," Angela thought, "two women covered in blood, one toting a machine gun."

"Who are you?" the woman asked in Spanish. "Where's Miguel?"

"Miguel's dead," Angela replied. "His little buddy, too."

The blonde's hand went to her mouth. "Dead?"

"Yeah," Angela said. The girl just stared. Angela raised the gun. "How do we get out? Show me."

"This way," the blonde said. She led them down a back hallway, Esmeralda staggering and mumbling protests all the way. There was a door at the end, which opened onto a landing above an alleyway. There were two cars parked in the alley—the black Mercedes they'd seen in town and a lemon-yellow Mini Cooper. Angela figured the Mini for Esmeralda's car, but there'd be more room for the girl in the Mercedes. "You," she said to the blonde, who was staring at them, trembling. "Check that black car and see if the keys are in it." The girl complied immediately, running down the stairway to the alley, her short robe flapping. Angela could see she wore nothing underneath. The blonde reached the car, looked inside, then looked up and nodded vigorously.

"Good," Angela said. "Now come up here and help me get her in."

A few minutes later, Angela was in the front seat, Esmeralda strapped in and semiconscious in the passenger side. Angela looked at the blonde. "I don't suppose you know where the American consulate is, do you?"

The girl looked blank. "The what?"

"Never mind," Angela said. "But if you or any of the other ladies have been wanting to leave, now might be a good time."

The blonde looked back at the house, then out at the end of the alleyway, where traffic was rolling by on a busy street. She looked back at Angela. "Did you really kill Miguel?" she whispered.

"Yeah," Angela said. "I kind of had to."

The woman leaned into the car window, grabbed Angela's head, and kissed her full on the mouth. Angela tried to pull away, but was blocked by the seat's headrest. The woman broke the kiss and looked into Angela's eyes. "Thank you," she whispered. "Thank you so much."

"Don't mention it," Angela said. "You can come with us if you want."

The woman looked at the mouth of the alley. "Go," she said, "before anyone else comes. I need to get the other girls. *Vaya con Dios.*"

"*Vaya con Dios,*" Angela replied as she started the car.

CHAPTER FORTY

THE AMERICAN CONSULATE IN CIUDAD de Piedras looked more like a prison than a diplomatic post. It was a plain, three-story building made of smooth gray concrete, located far back from the street behind an equally featureless high concrete wall topped with concertina wire. A line of metal bollards set into the concrete kept vehicles away from the wall, funneling all traffic into a two-lane driveway. White-painted guard posts flanked the metal gate.

It had taken Angela a half hour to find the place. She'd fled the neighborhood of the brothel at high speed, barely stopping at intersections, constantly checking the rearview mirror to see if she was being followed. As soon as she was satisfied that no one was behind her, she pulled over to where a man was standing on the corner, as if looking for a ride. As Angela motioned him over, the man approach with a smile on his face. The smile died as he saw the unconscious girl in the front seat.

"*Donde esta el consulada Americano?*" Angela called out, but the man was already backing away. "Shit," Angela said.

She put the car back in gear and rolled on. It was then that she noticed the mobile phone nestled in a cradle attached to the dashboard. She couldn't figure out at first if it was a hands-free system, much less how to turn it on, so she yanked the phone from its cradle and dialed 040 for information. As soon as the operator came on the line, Angela asked the address of the American consulate. After that, it was a matter of finding the car's GPS system and making her way there.

As she turned into the long drive and neared the gate, she saw the Marine guard unsling his weapon. He began speaking rapidly, head bent in the direction of a microphone on his lapel. Puzzled, she slowed down and looked in the mirror. There was a black SUV in the street behind her, parked across the entrance to the driveway. *Shit.* She accelerated and pulled up to the guardhouse. The Marine looked impossibly young to Angela, but he held the rifle as if he knew how to use it. The sight of Esmeralda slumped in the front seat caused him to blink in confusion. "I'm an American citizen," she said. "My name is Angela Sanchez. I've been held prisoner by one of the local drug traffickers. This girl was wounded helping me escape."

The Marine looked back up the drive, then back to Angela. "We got a report that someone was going to show up here in a stolen vehicle. Robbed one of the local businesses and killed the manager." He swung the weapon to bear on Angela.

"You have *got* to be kidding me," she said.

He didn't look like he was kidding. "Stay in the car, ma'am."

"Damn it," Angela said, "we don't have time for this. This girl is bleeding to death, if she hasn't already. We need *help.*" The Marine didn't answer or budge. "Look," she said desperately, "look at who's behind me. Does that look like the local cops?"

"No," the Marine said, "but that does." He nodded toward the top of the drive.

Angela looked. A blue and white pickup with a light bar on top had pulled up. The word POLICIA was stenciled on the side with a gold star beneath it. She turned back to the Marine. He was speaking into his mic. "Please," she begged. "The cops here work for Mandujano. Or Zavalo. If you let them take us, they'll kill us." A thought occurred to her. "Tell someone upstairs we have information about Auguste Mandujano's involvement in human trafficking and illegal immigration. Please."

"Wait one," the Marine said. He spoke again. Angela looked back. A pair of stocky men in police uniforms had gotten out of the pickup and were approaching. One appeared older, with gray streaks in his hair. Otherwise they were almost identical with their brush cuts and mirrored shades. They might have been father and son. The Marine got done speaking and exited the guardhouse, holding his weapon at the ready. "Help you fellows?" he said in English.

The older cop on the right seemed to be the one in charge. He answered in Spanish. "This woman is under arrest for robbery and murder."

The Marine smiled apologetically and shrugged. "Sorry," he said in English. "*No comprendo.*"

The younger one spoke up in English. "These two are wanted criminals. We're taking them in."

The Marine nodded. "That's what I hear. Thing is, one of 'em's an American citizen, and the other one's hurt. I got to kick this one upstairs. Kinda above my pay grade. Sorry. If you guys would just wait a couple minutes, maybe we can—"

"We're not waiting," the young one said. He reached for the pistol on his belt.

The Marine raised his rifle and pointed it. "Ah-ah," he said, "Let's not do anything silly, now."

"There are two of us," the young cop said, but his hand had stopped midway to his holster. "You are alone."

Angela heard a metallic rattle and a grinding sound. She looked forward and saw the gate slowly moving aside. Sitting several yards behind it was a desert sand-colored Humvee. A turret atop the vehicle held a multibarreled minigun, pointed at the men in the driveway. The man behind the gun looked grim.

The Marine was still smiling. "Gentlemen, I am a member of the United States Marine Corps. I am *never* alone. Now why don't y'all trot on back to your vehicle and sit in the AC while we get this straightened out? It's a hot day."

The two men, frozen in place, stared at the Humvee. The younger one slowly lowered his hand. Then he mumbled something and turned away. The older man followed. They walked back to the police truck, heads held high, and backs stiff.

"Assholes," the Marine muttered. He leaned over and looked inside the Mercedes. "Sit tight, ma'am, we got a medic coming."

"Thank you," Angela said.

Another young man in a Marine uniform was striding out past the Humvee, a medical bag slung under one arm. He reached the car and yanked open the passenger door. He had red hair and fair skin scorched by the sun. He knelt and slid two fingers to Esmeralda's neck looking for a pulse. He grimaced. "She's alive, but barely. She needs a hospital." His voice had a country twang that reminded her of home.

"If you take her there," Angela said, "the people after us will kill her."

"Well, that settles it, then," the red-haired medic said. He stood up and motioned at the Humvee, which began to slowly back up.

"Get the car inside," he said to Angela.

"We ain't got authorization to let 'em in yet, Sergeant," the guard warned.

"And I give a fuck about this why, exactly?" the medic responded. "You got a problem, talk to Mr. Huston. He'll back me up." He looked back at Angela. "Get a move on, lady."

Angela moved forward, letting out her breath as she cleared the gate. A pair of Marines ran up with a stretcher. As she got out of the car, they began carefully loading Esmeralda onto it.

"Excuse me," a voice said.

Angela turned. The man standing next to her was tall and slender, dark-complected, with large dark eyes and a neatly trimmed beard and mustache. Despite the heat, he was dressed in a dark suit, which fit him as if tailored, and a red tie.

"My name is Huston," he said, holding out his hand. "I work here at the consulate. If you would come with me, please."

CHAPTER
FORTY-ONE

THEY WERE HEADED BACK INTO town, both Keller and Oscar cuffed in the back of Castle's patrol car. Oscar said nothing, just sat and stared out the window. Keller leaned forward and spoke through the metal grating, which separated the front of the car from the prisoners in the back.

"Castle," he said.

"Shut up."

Keller ignored him. "Do you know what's going on out at that farm? What that church is up to?"

"Don't know," Castle said. "Don't care. Now sit back and shut up.

"They're kidnapping people. Illegals. We don't know what they're doing with them. Not for sure. But we both know it's nothing good. Especially for the women. You know what I'm talking about."

Castle said nothing.

"You ever read any of their literature? Seen their website?"

"They mind their business," Castle said. "I mind mine."

"They're white supremacists, Deputy," Keller said. "They think people like you and my friend here aren't even human. They think God appointed them to be supreme."

Castle snorted. "I let myself get all bent out of shape every time some crazy-ass white man puts somethin' stupid up on the Internet, I'd go outta my goddamn mind."

Oscar spoke up. "Do you have children, Deputy?"

"No," Castle said, "if it's any of your business. Which it ain't."

"I believe that those people have kidnapped my sons," he said. "They're holding them."

Castle looked in the rearview mirror, back at them. His brow furrowed in concern. "Why do you believe that, sir?"

Oscar and Keller looked at each other. "It's kind of a long story," Keller said.

"Uh-huh. Maybe you should tell it to your lawyers, then." He was pulling to a stop in front of a small building set back from the street, with a narrow strip of grass and shrubs in front of it. A fading wooden sign attached to the front said SHERIFF.

Castle got the two of them out of the car and shepherded them to the front door. He had to pause to take the front door key out of his pocket and unlock the glass front door.

"Kind of small for a sheriff's department," Keller remarked.

"It's a substation," Castle said. "Don't use it much."

"So why bring us here?" Oscar asked. "Not the main station?"

"Orders," Castle said. "This way." He led them into a tiny office with a pair of empty desks—the tops bare as if no one worked there. The lights were off, the only illumination provided by bars of light filtering through the partially opened venetian blinds.

"Orders," Keller repeated. He looked at Oscar, then back at Castle. "Don't those orders seem a little odd to you?"

"I just work here, sir. Stand over there." He pointed to a spot a few feet away, on the other side of the desks. Keller and Oscar shuffled over to stand side by side in the place indicated, as Castle found another key on his ring and opened a metal door covered in flaking red paint that stood across the room. The door opened with a shriek of hinges long unused. "In here."

"What is in there?" Oscar said.

"Holding cells. Come on, move it."

"Holding cells?" Keller asked. "For what?"

"Holding," Castle said. "Now get in."

"If I go in there," Keller said, "What are you going to do?"

"Wait for the Sheriff," Castle said.

"Instead of taking us in and booking us. And this still makes sense to you?"

Castle dropped his hand to the Taser on his belt. "You going in there, or you wanna ride the lightning in?"

Keller considered his options. He didn't have many. He'd counted on his instinct about Castle, thought he could talk him into helping them. He'd apparently been wrong, and that miscalculation was going to get him and Oscar locked up. After that, he sensed, things were going to get very, very bad. But he was unarmed, handcuffed, and faced by a man with a variety of ways to take him down and force him into the cell that awaited him beyond that door.

"Okay," he said. "We'll go. But promise me one thing."

Castle rolled his eyes. "You are not in any position to bargain here, Mr. Keller."

"I'm not bargaining. I'm just asking. It'll cost you nothing."

"Tell me while you're walking," Castle said.

Keller moved toward the door. "If you've got access to a computer, go online. Look up Church of Elohim. E-L-O-H-I-M." He walked through the doorway. There was a short hallway in front of him, with a barred window set high in the wall at the end of it providing the only light, and old-fashioned barred cells on either side of the hallway.

"I'll do that," Castle said, "in my abundance of spare time. Keller to the right. Mr. Sanchez to the left."

In moments they were in the cells, facing each other across the hallway. There was nothing in each cell but a pair of bunks and a metal toilet. "Remember what I said, Castle," Keller said.

The only reply was the clang of the metal door closing. The deputy didn't speak as he walked down the hallway and out of the door.

"**S**O," ANGELA SAID, "IS HUSTON your first name or your last name? Or is it like Madonna? Or Cher?"

She sat across from him at a table in a featureless room with only the table and chairs for furnishings. Angela assumed, however, that there would be others listening.

Huston smiled. "Let's go with that last one."

"Are you FBI?" Angela said. "DEA? CIA?"

Still the same smile. "Officially, I'm a cultural attaché."

"CIA, then. How's the girl I came in here with?"

"I understand she was badly shot up. I don't know anything beyond that."

"She's got a lot of information you might want," Angela said. "About drug trafficking, human trafficking, arms across the border, you name it. You should take really good care of her."

Huston nodded. The smile didn't waver. "Believe me, we've considered that." The smile faded a bit. "But," he said with a shrug, "she is apparently a Mexican national. The subject of an investigation by the local state police, but not the Federals. The *Federales*, according to what we can find out, know nothing about any killing in any whorehouse in Ciudad de Piedras. And that in itself is pretty interesting." The mask dropped away and Huston's face suddenly looked as cold and merciless as an Aztec idol's. "So, Mrs. Angela Sanchez, most recently of Wilmington, North Carolina, maybe you should be as honest as you possibly can about what the hell is going on here, before we decide to throw you both back in the lagoon and let the sharks figure out who wins and who loses."

"I'm going to tell you," Angela said. "You don't need to bully me."

Huston studied her for a moment, his dark brown eyes locked on hers. Then he nodded. "Okay," he said, "I'm going to break protocol here, and tell you I'm sorry. I know you want to help, and I know why. So." He smiled, and it was the first genuine smile Angela had seen from him. "Please, Mrs. Sanchez, tell us what you think we need to know, paying special attention to the smuggling of people and weapons into the United States."

She took a deep breath, then she told him everything. Huston sat across from her, nodding from time to time. She noticed after a while that he wasn't taking any notes, and mentioned it.

"Don't worry," Huston smiled. "We've got that covered."

"You've got the room wired."

"Of course."

Angela kept talking. When she finally wound down, Huston nodded.

"Thank you," he said. "This may be of use. If true."

"I hope so," she said. "Because it's true. All of it."

He went on as if he hadn't heard her. "We've been picking up lots of chatter, seeing lots of movement of people and assets. Those trucks found empty out in the desert, with no sign of what happened. Sources tell us that everyone's jumpy, as if something big is about to happen. Up until now, we haven't known what that is. And now, thanks to you, we have some more pieces of the puzzle. Andreas Zavalo's about to make a move on Auguste Mandujano." He smiled at her. "Assuming everything you've told us is true."

"What are you going to do?" she said, adding, "Assuming this is all true."

He shrugged. "Well, there's an argument to be made for letting them do it. One less *narcotraficante*, or a few dozen if this thing turns bloody, wouldn't be such a bad thing."

"But a lot of innocent people might get killed."

He sighed. "There is that." He stood up. "I'll have someone show you to a room where you can freshen up. Maybe get some rest."

"Has anyone found out what happened to my husband?" Angela asked. "And my friend Jack Keller?"

Huston shook his head and sat back down. He studied the backs of his hands for a moment, as if considering what to say.

She felt her throat constricting in fear. "What's happened?"

Huston seemed to come to a decision. He looked up at her. "Border Patrol found a burned-out truck just north of the border. There was a lot of spent brass around. Evidence of some kind of firefight. A lot of blood." He hesitated. "Three bodies."

"Who?" the word came out as a whisper.

"They haven't identified them yet."

She took a deep breath, tried to calm her thudding heart. "Was one of them Latino?"

He looked sympathetic. "I don't know. I'll see if I can find out."

"Please do," she said. "And thank you. Now, I think I need to lie down."

He stood up again. "Of course," he said. "Follow me."

CHAPTER
FORTY-TWO

KELLER PACED THE CELL LIKE an animal, going back and forth from the bars to the bed to the toilet, over and over, looking for something, anything he could use to try and get them out. Oscar sat on the bed, watching him from across the hall.

"You're going to wear yourself out doing that," Oscar said finally.

Keller paused at the cell door, leaning his head against the bars. The iron felt cold on his forehead. "I'm sorry, Oscar," he said. "I screwed up. I thought I could get that cop to trust us."

"Because he was a fellow soldier," Oscar said. "He'd been where you'd been."

"Yeah. Maybe. I don't know."

Oscar shrugged. "This is not over. Maybe he will have a change of heart."

"I can't depend on that," Keller said. He looked back at the bed. "Only thing I can think of is I try to clog the toilet. Maybe with the blanket from the bed. I flood the cell. The cop has to come in and stop the water. I rush him."

"And then?" Oscar said.

"Then we get the hell out of here."

"I mean, what happens to that young officer? You'll have to injure him. Maybe kill him. Do you think he deserves that?"

"I don't care what anyone deserves," Keller said. "I need to get us out."

Oscar shook his head. "I think you do care," Oscar said. "If he's an innocent man, doing his job, then you must not harm him. And I think we both believe that's what he is."

Keller sat down on the bed, clenching and unclenching his fists. He recalled Lucas's words. *You never killed anyone that didn't try to kill you first.* "I need to get us out of here," he repeated.

"You will," Oscar said. "You will think of something. Or opportunity will present itself. When it does, you'll know what to do. I have faith in you. Perhaps you should as well." He lay back on the bed, arms crossed behind his head. "I'm going to rest now," he said. "And think. Try to do the same." Then he was silent.

Keller thought for a moment. Then he got up and went to the bars again. He looked down the hall to where the metal door blocked his access to the rest of the world. *Come on, Castle. Come on. Do the right thing.*

RAY CASTLE SAT AT THE desk and rubbed his eyes. Keller was right. What he'd been ordered to do didn't make any sense. But then, it wasn't the first time he'd been ordered to do things he didn't completely understand. And now he was back to thinking about Fallujah, and that was something he tried to avoid thinking about as much as he could.

Orders. Right. He pulled out his cell phone and dialed the Sheriff.

Cosgrove answered on the first ring. "You get 'em, Ray?"

"Yes, sir," Castle said. "They're locked up in the substation. I caught them outside the perimeter of the Church of Elohim farm."

"Were they trying to break in?" Cosgrove said.

"No, sir. They didn't have a chance. They were checking it out, though. And I took some weapons off them. Two pistols, a shotgun, and, get this, an assault rifle with a grenade launcher on it."

"No shit," Cosgrove said.

"No, sir," Castle replied. "The rifle looked military. I'm getting ready to run them all through NCIC, see if any of them come up stolen."

"No," Cosgrove said hastily. "Don't do that."

"Sir?"

"Don't do anything until I get there. And keep this completely quiet. Completely. Understand?"

"No, sir," Castle said. "I really don't."

"Just do it, son," Cosgrove said. "I'll explain everything when I get there." He hung up.

Castle stared at the cell phone, then put it down on the desktop. He looked around the deserted substation, thinking. Then he booted up the computer.

"I HAVE THEM," COSGROVE TOLD WALKER.

"Both?"

"Both. They're locked up in the substation."

"Who picked them up?"

"Castle," the Sheriff said. "The new kid."

"The black?" Cosgrove could almost see the General's sneer.

"Don't worry," he said. "He'll do what he's told."

"None of those people can be trusted," the General said. "He's a potential weak link. You'll have to get rid of him."

"Get rid of—"

"Make it look like Keller tried to escape and shot him. Then you kill Keller. My sources have been filling me in on him. He's a lunatic with a history of violence. He should have been locked up years ago. You'll be the man of the hour, having stopped a dangerous and unstable killer threatening your town."

"No," Cosgrove said. "No way. I'm not shooting one of my own men."

"He's not a man," Walker said, "and he already knows too much.

Especially if the prisoners are talking to him. Telling him about what's happening. Do you think he'll just go along with that?"

Cosgrove was beginning to sweat. "No," he said finally. "Okay. I'll take care of it."

"See that you do," Walker said. "Save the wetback for me. I'll be there in a bit to pick him up."

"What are you going to do?"

"He came here to find his sons. I'm going to give them the family reunion they want." He paused. "Then I'm going to hang all three of them."

CHAPTER FORTY-THREE

RAMON ORTEGA WAS SITTING ON a bench on the street, eating his lunch, when the call he'd been dreading for years came. The cell phone in his shirt pocket buzzed. He put down the sandwich he'd been eating and pulled the phone out. When he saw the number, the food turned to a lump in his gut. The phone buzzed again. He answered. His hand was shaking as he put the phone to his ear.

"*Bueno*," he said. His voice came out as a dry croak. He took a sip of the bottled water on the bench beside him and answered again, more strongly. "*Beuno?*"

"Ramon," a voice said. "It's time to pay the debt you owe." The voice spoke in Spanish, the words distorted by some sort of filter so that he couldn't tell who was speaking.

"I'm ready," he said.

"There are two women who have been taken into the consulate. They are probably in the guest quarters. One is wounded. They must not leave there alive. They must certainly not be allowed to reach the United States."

"I...I don't know if I can get into the guest quarters. I'm only a file clerk—"

"You will find a way. Or your debt will have to be paid in some other fashion. Perhaps your sisters can pay it for you. Or your wife. Do you understand?"

"Yes," he whispered. "I understand."

"Do you still have the object we gave you?"

"Yes," he said. He thought of the gun in his bottom desk drawer, buried under a pile of old magazines and meaningless junk paper. He had never fired it, and had hoped he never would.

"Good," the voice said. "Do not fail us. We will know if you do. But if you succeed, your debt will be wiped clean. If you can get to the street, we will protect you. And your family. We will know you can do important work. And Ramon?"

"Yes?"

"This must be done immediately. As soon as you get back. So finish your lunch."

It was only then that he saw the black SUV across the street. The windows were so darkly tinted he couldn't see inside but he could feel the eyes on him and knew they were watching.

"I won't fail you," he said, looking at the vehicle as he spoke. He closed the connection and put down the phone. His hands were shaking worse now.

He'd worked at the consulate for five years, filing and occasionally translating documents. He made a good living, but there was no honest living he could make that could keep up with even the interest on the money he owed Andreas Zavalo. One day a man had come to him with a gun and a proposition. They would defer the debt until such time as Ramon could do a job for them. They hadn't specified what the job might be, but the gun they had given him had made it clear that it wasn't going to be anything small. It had rested in the bottom drawer for three years now, and Ramon had dared to wonder if maybe they'd forgotten him. He saw now how foolish that idea was. These people did not forget. Nor did they forgive. He was trapped. He'd never killed anyone before, but now it was kill or be killed. Or worse. He stood up and shoved his lunch bag and empty water bottle into a nearby trash can. A thought occurred to him. He reached into the trash can and pulled the bag back out. The bag was brightly colored, emblazoned with the name of a local chicken restaurant. He looked down the street to where the consulate rose, gray and forbidding, above the surrounding buildings. Trudging like a man with a heavy load on his shoulders, he began his walk back, holding the empty bag in one hand. Lunch was over, and so was life as he knew it.

THE GUEST QUARTERS WERE ON the third floor, down a long carpeted hallway that reminded Angela of a college dormitory. Huston led her toward one of the rooms on the end. As she passed one room with an open door, she looked inside and saw Esmeralda. The girl was lying on the bed, her eyes closed, breathing shallowly. There was an IV bag on a stand beside the bed, filled with what looked like blood. The red-haired medic she'd seen earlier was seated in the chair next to the bed. He held Esmeralda's wrist in one hand, and he was looking at the watch on his other wrist. There was a cart next to him, piled high with bandages, syringes, and vials of unidentified medications.

"How is she?" Angela said, stepping into the room.

"She needs a real hospital," the medic replied. "She's a tough little gal, but she's lost a lot of blood, and she's gonna lose more. I can't just keep pumping it into her." He looked at Huston. "This ain't my usual gig, sir," he said. "I need that medevac. ASAP."

"Working on it, Bentley," Huston said.

"So work harder. Sir."

Angela looked at Huston, who only grinned. "Understood, Sergeant."

Bentley just grunted, then bent over to check his patient's dressing.

"Come on," Huston said. He led Angela back into the hallway and opened the door to a room across the hall. Angela stepped inside. It was small, but clean, with a bed, dresser, chairs, and a small desk. There was one window, with bars on it.

"Rest here," Huston said. He indicated a door across the room.

"Private bathroom, with a shower if you want it."

She wanted one desperately, but she stopped Huston as he started to step out. "That Marine seems to think you're a lot more than a cultural attaché," she said. "He seems to know you pretty well, in fact."

Huston gave her that inscrutable smile again. "Sergeant Bentley has an active imagination."

"And a big mouth," she said.

"He's good at his job," Huston said, "Several jobs, actually. So I indulge him."

"So tell me. What's really going on here?"

"Mrs. Sanchez," Huston said, "I would like to be able to tell you. But I truly can't."

"Can you still at least find out if my husband's alive?" she said. "And my friend?"

"I have people working on that right now," he said. "I hope to be back to you within the hour. Now, just rest easy. You're on American soil. You're completely safe."

"Thanks, Mr. Huston," she said. "But I guess that's not your real name."

That smile again. "It'll do as well as any other. See you in a bit."

CHAPTER
FORTY-FOUR

RAY CASTLE SHOOK HIS HEAD in disgust as he closed the web browser. He'd taken the time he'd normally have spent checking NCIC for the stolen weapons to do as Keller had suggested and check out this Church of Elohim. What he'd seen had amused him at first, then angered him, then made him almost physically ill. He recalled a quote his Uncle Leonard used to use, something from one of Unc's favorite movies, "White folks get stranger all the time."

The sound of a vehicle pulling up outside startled him out of his reverie. He got up and went to the door. The Sheriff's white Escalade was parked at the curb. Castle frowned as he saw another, unfamiliar vehicle pull in and park behind. The frown deepened as he saw a man in what looked like military fatigues without insignia and a soft flat-topped patrol cap. He'd just been looking at the man's picture online. It was Walker, the man who called himself "The Sword Arm of the Lord." There were two men with him — both dressed in khaki pants and black T-shirts. One was long haired, with a bushy beard. The other was a blond man who wore his hair slicked back and gelled. Both men's arms were dark with tattoos. They were carrying assault rifles. Castle felt tightness in the muscles of his back, along with a tingling along his spine. It was a feeling he hadn't felt since he'd left the Army. He'd experienced it more times than he could count in Iraq. He called it the "creepy crawlies," and it had never failed him as an indicator that serious shit was about to go down. The other guys in his squad had kidded him about it, but they'd learned to respect it on patrol.

Castle eased his sidearm out of the holster and racked the slide. In the quiet town of Hearken, where the most violent thing he usually encountered was a noisy drunk, he didn't often carry the weapon cocked and locked. But he was having a really bad feeling about this. He gently slid the weapon back into the holster, leaving the holster unsnapped, and stepped back from the door. He saw the Sheriff stop and confer with Walker for a moment. There was a brief discussion, apparently some disagreement, but eventually, Walker nodded. The Sheriff entered alone. Castle was standing at attention by the desk.

"Afternoon, sir," he said.

"Afternoon, son," the Sheriff said. The look on his face made Castle even more nervous. He looked ten years older than the last time they'd met. He was dressed in his brown uniform pants and Smokey Bear hat. Despite the heat, he wore his brown uniform jacket. Cosgrove stopped, looked around, spotted the metal door. "They back there?" he said.

"Yes, sir."

"Separate cells?"

"Yes, sir."

"Good. Give me the keys."

Castle hesitated. "Are you okay, sir?"

Cosgrove's face hardened with irritation. "I'm fine. Give me the keys."

He didn't want to do it. Everything was telling him that it was a bad idea. But it was a reasonable and lawful order. Castle took the keys from his belt and handed them over. Cosgrove went to the front door and opened it. The two gunmen came in, followed by Walker. The gunmen were grinning. Walker's face looked as if it were made of stone. Cosgrove handed the keys to Walker, who went to the cellblock door and opened it.

"What's going on, sir?" Castle asked.

"Mr. Sanchez is going with some friends of ours. We'll be taking Keller."

"Where, sir?"

"To the county courthouse for arraignment."

Castle could hear yelling from inside the cellblock. He started toward the door. "That won't be necessary," Cosgrove said, but the nervousness in his face belied his calm words.

"All due respect, sir," Castle said, "I can see transporting the prisoners separately. But why use these guys? Why not call another deputy?"

"Everyone else is tied up. I've...deputized these men as an emergency measure."

The gunmen came out, leading the Latino prisoner, Sanchez, to the door. As they passed, the little guy looked at him. Castle would remember the calmness and dignity in that face for the rest of his days. "You know this is not right," Sanchez said to him.

The blond gunman with his hair slicked back smacked him in the back of the head. "Shut the fuck up," he growled. The other one laughed. Their smiles were the ugliest things he'd seen since Iraq.

Walker came out. "Enough," he said to the blond. He ignored Castle.

"Sir..." Castle said helplessly. He knew he should be doing something, but it was three on one, and two of them had high caliber long guns. He watched as the three of them took Sanchez out the door. When they were out of Castle's view, the Sheriff turned around.

"Now," he said, "let's go get Keller. But I'm going to need you to give me your sidearm before you go in."

It was actually protocol. The officer who had actual physical contact with the prisoner didn't carry his pistol, to discourage attempts to grab it from him. But after what he'd just seen, there was no way in hell Castle was going to turn his weapon over. He felt strangely lightheaded, but calm, the way he'd always felt when the apprehension of waiting for combat had given way to the adrenaline clarity of the real thing.

"No, sir," he said as he drew his pistol and pointed it at the Sheriff.

THE RED-HAIRED MEDIC, BENTLEY, STOOD up and stretched. Angela heard a strange whirring and clicking sound as he did. She'd though she'd noticed it in the driveway, but hadn't been able to figure what it was, and events had distracted her from considering it further.

"I need more blood," Bentley said. "Can you watch her while I get it?"

Angela nodded. "Please," she said, "help her. She saved my life."

"Yes, ma'am," Bentley said. "I'll do everything I can."

"You said this wasn't your regular job," she said. "What do you usually do?"

He stopped and smiled at her. It was the first time she'd seen him smile, and it made him look slightly off-kilter. "I blow stuff up, ma'am." He walked out, that strange sound following him. With a start, Angela realized that Bentley was walking on two artificial legs. She wondered where he'd lost them, and wondered how he'd managed to stay on active duty. *Not your average Marine.* She thought of Huston, then to the confrontation at the gate. *Talk to Mr. Huston,* he'd said. *He'll back me up. Maybe not a Marine at all,* she thought. She really wished she knew what was going on here. She reached out and took Esmeralda's small hand in hers.

"Hang on, Esme," she said, "we're safe."

RAMON WALKED DOWN THE HALL, hoping no one would see him and notice his shaking. He came to the door of the guest quarters, at the foot of a short flight of stairs. A Marine in fatigues stood by the door. Ramon recognized him. He was an easygoing Californian named Barbour who liked baseball. He and Ramon had had a few conversations about it.

"Hey, Ramon," Barbour said. "What's up?"

Ramon held up the bag. "I got lunch. They told me to bring some back for those two that just came in."

Barbour looked dubious. "No one told me about this."

Ramon shrugged. "Nobody tells us anything, huh?"

Barbour laughed. "Roger that. Go on up. But hurry."

Ramon quickly mounted the stairs, his heart pounding with more than the exertion. The gun inside the bag seemed to weigh a ton. At the top of the stairs, he ran into another Marine, this one a short, pugnacious-looking redhead.

"Who the fuck are you?" he demanded.

"My name's Ramon. I work here. They asked me to bring the ladies something to eat."

"It's okay, Sergeant," Barbour called from below. "I know Ramon. He's good people."

The redhead grunted. "Okay, but don't be all fuckin' day."

"No, sir," Ramon said. "This won't take long."

CHAPTER FORTY-FIVE

COSGROVE'S FACE DARKENED WITH ANGER. "Have you lost your mind, son?" he barked. "Give me that weapon. That's an order."

"I don't think so, sir," Castle said. "Something is way fucked-up here, and I ain't doing a goddamn thing until I figure out what it is."

"Deputy," Cosgrove said, "you are buying yourself more trouble than—"

Castle interrupted him. "I'll need your weapon, sir. Reach down, pull it out with two fingers, and put it on the ground. You know the drill."

Cosgrove looked about ready to explode. "Come and take it, you son of a bitch. Or are you going to shoot me? Right here, when I haven't got a weapon in my hand?"

"No, sir," Castle said. He let go of his two-handed grip and lowered the gun to his side. "I won't shoot you when you don't have a weapon in your hand." He slid his gun into the holster.

Cosgrove seemed to relax. Then his hand moved quickly toward his belt. Castle didn't have time to think. He drew and fired in a smooth motion he'd practiced a thousand times on the range. The first two rounds caught Cosgrove in the chest and knocked him backward. He stumbled back, against the closed metal door, cursing, but didn't go down. Castle saw the Sheriff's pistol clear the holster as if in slow motion.

Body armor. That's why he wore the jacket. The barrel was coming up, up...Castle's hands seemed to move independently of his thoughts as he adjusted his aim and put the third round into the center of the Sheriff's forehead.

ANGELA TENSED AS HE HEARD the knock on the door. "Sergeant Bentley?" she called out.

"No, ma'am," a voice said. "My name is Ramon." The door swung open. "I...I brought you lunch."

She immediately knew something was wrong. The young Latino man standing in the doorway was sweating profusely. It ran down his face and stained the armpits of his shirt. He wouldn't look at her.

"Thank you," she said as calmly as she could, backing toward the bed. "But I'm not very hungry. And as you can see my friend here is—"

"I'm sorry," Ramon said as he reached inside the bag. His hand came out holding a gun. As soon as it did, Angela reached back onto the cart next to the bed, her hand going unerringly to the scissors she'd noticed earlier.

"No!" she screamed as she leaped forward. The sound made him flinch and his shot went wild, smacking into the plaster of the wall behind her. She brought the scissors down with all her might in a vicious downward strike that buried them to the hilt in the shoulder of his gun hand. He shrieked in agony and dropped the gun. As he fell to his knees, crying in pain, she yanked the scissors out with another howl of rage. "LEAVE ME THE FUCK ALONE!" she screamed and prepared to bring the scissors down again, this time into his brain.

The young man cried out in fear again and began to propel himself backward across the floor. Angela followed, the scissors still raised high. She was consumed with killing rage, all the anxiety and anger and naked fear of the last few days preparing to channel itself into that last murderous strike.

"ANGELA!" she heard a voice bellow from down the hall. She stopped, but didn't turn. She stood over the crying man, breathing hard. She wanted to kill him so badly. But the voice had stopped her. That, and the thought that had come unbidden to her mind as she'd raised the scissors high.

This is how Jack must have felt.

It was exhilarating and it made her sick to her stomach at the same time.

"Angela," the voice said, more softly. She lowered the scissors. She turned toward the voice, but not before locating the gun on the floor and kicking it out of reach.

Huston and Sergeant Bentley were there, a few feet away. They had identical black handguns trained on the man on the floor. Huston was down on one knee, Bentley standing in a slight crouch beside him.

"Ma'am," Bentley said, "could you back up, just a smidge? I won't miss at this range, but Mr. Huston's been lazy at gettin' his range time in lately, an' I'd rather him not hit you."

"Sergeant," Huston said, "when this is over, we'll both go to the range. Loser buys the other a steak."

"I thought you was vegetarian, Doc."

"I'll make an exception for the purpose of watching you buy me steak."

"Please," the man on the floor sobbed, "Don't let her kill me."

"You're on," Bentley said, and straightened up. "But business before pleasure, I reckon." He walked over to Ramon, looked down, and shook his head. "I knew you was up to no good. You want me to take a look at that shoulder?"

"Please," Ramon said again. "I didn't want to hurt anybody."

"Funny way you got of showin' it," Bentley said as he bent over. He tore Ramon's dress shirt aside. Blood flowed from the wound Angela had made in his shoulder. "Missed the arteries," he observed. He looked up at Angela and grinned that crooked grin again.

Angela wondered if he was completely sane.

"You want, I can show you how to be a little more effective with those next time." His face turned serious. "You're not lookin' so hot, ma'am," he said. "You may wanna sit down."

"Thanks," Angela said faintly, "I think I will." She stumbled back into the room and sat down. The world seemed to fade away for a bit. When she recovered her senses, Huston was kneeling next to her, taking her pulse. The room was full of people, some in suits, some in uniform. They all seemed to be talking at once.

"I thought Bentley was the doctor," she said muzzily. "Why'd he call you 'doc'?"

"Sergeant Bentley is a man of many talents," he muttered, looking at his watch to time her pulse, "And we cross-train. Never know what you might have to do."

"As a cultural attaché," she said.

"Shhh," he said, but he was smiling. She noticed the watch face. It was a grinning cartoon cat, his front legs forming the hands. "That cat...I remember him. Felix—"

"Okay," he interrupted. "You're good." He stood up and clapped his hands. "All right," he said in an authoritative voice. "Everyone out." They all stopped talking and stared at him. He made "go away" motions with his hands. "Go on, now. Shoo. We'll be medevacing these ladies out of here within the hour."

"Hold on a damn minute here," a wiry bald man in Marine fatigues with a major's clusters on the lapel spoke up. "I wasn't made aware of any—"

"Sorry, Major," Huston interrupted. "We had to jump a few rungs on the normal chain of command." He fished in his jacket pocket, took out a small white card. "Please call this number. Ask for a Mr. Weaver. He'll give you any authorizations you need."

The major looked at the card and his eyes narrowed as he looked up at Huston. "This card says The White House."

Huston's face was bland. "That's where Mr. Weaver works."

"All right," the major said. "Wait here." He left the room.

"Why Felix?" Angela asked Huston.

He turned to her. "What?"

"Why Felix the Cat? On your watch. Seems like kind of an unusual bit of jewelry for a cultural attaché."

Huston smiled. "My spirit animal."

"Felix the Cat is your spirit animal?"

"Since childhood."

The major returned. He looked shaken. "So," he said to Huston in a low voice. "Iron Horse. It's not just a rumor."

"Major," Huston said softly, "not everyone in the room has the clearance to hear that name." He cocked his head as if listening to something. The room fell silent.

In the sudden quiet, Angela could hear the unmistakable thudding pulse of rotor blades.

"Ah," he said, "that would be our helicopter."

CHAPTER
FORTY-SIX

KELLER HAD BEEN STANDING AT the bars of the cell when he heard the corridor door opening. He turned toward the sound, getting ready for another try at negotiating with Castle. The men who came in, however, weren't deputies. The first two who came in looked like thugs, arms heavily tattooed, assault rifles cradled in their arms. He recognized the third from his picture on the website. It was Walker, the self-proclaimed 'General' of the Church of Elohim. *Oh, shit.* Out of the corner of his eye, he saw Oscar stand up. The three didn't speak until they reached the end of the hallway and the cells. Walker gave Keller only a glance before turning to Oscar.

"Oscar Sanchez," he said. "You are under arrest."

Oscar raised an eyebrow. "That much would seem obvious."

"Shut the fuck up, monkey," one of the gunmen snarled. He raised the weapon to point into the cell.

"Hey," Keller said. "Walker."

Walker acted as if he hadn't heard. "You will be taken from this place to appear before a people's tribunal, where you will answer for your crimes against the United States, specifically that you have violated its sovereign and sacred borders and defied its lawful authorities."

"I would like to speak to a lawyer," Oscar said.

"Denied," Walker said.

"Walker," Keller said, more loudly. "Look at me, you son of a bitch."

Walker still ignored him. He took a ring of keys from his belt and opened the cell door. He stepped back. "Out," he said.

Oscar stepped back from the door as well. "I don't think I'll be going with you."

"Even to see your sons?" Walker said.

"WALKER!" Keller yelled.

Oscar stepped forward. The eager look on his face broke Keller's heart. "You have them?"

"Oscar!" Keller said. "Don't listen to him. He's fucking with you."

"They want to see their father," Walker said. "Come with us if you wish to see them."

Oscar squared his shoulders and walked out of the cell. The two gunmen stepped aside to let him out. The grins on their faces enraged Keller. He threw himself against the bars, reaching out for Walker. "Let him go," he snarled through gritted teeth. "Let him go, you cocksucker."

Oscar looked at Keller. He seemed very calm. "Come help me if you can, Jack."

"I'll do it, buddy," Keller choked out. Oscar walked out in front of the gunmen, head held high. Walker lagged behind. Only then did he look at Keller.

"You two have caused me a lot of trouble," he said. "You, in particular, have betrayed your own race. That's unforgivable. I hope that, when you get to hell, they give you a seat where you can watch your friend and his brats slowly choking to death when I hang them."

"I'm going to kill you, Walker," Keller said.

"I'll see how long I can make them last," Walker said. "Let them down, let them catch their breath, then hoist them back up to die a little more. Think about that." He strode out without looking back.

As the metal door clanged shut, Keller screamed with rage and shook the bars futilely. They didn't budge. He looked desperately around for anything he could use to get out or use as a weapon. As he did, he became aware of voices raised on the other side of the door. Then the unmistakable sound of a gunshot. Another in quick succession. Then a third. He froze, waiting, for what seemed like a very long time. Finally, the metal door swung open. Castle walked in, shuffling like a sleepwalker. He held his sidearm down and away from him in his hand. Keller tensed. Castle reached the cell and looked inside at Keller.

"What the *fuck* is going on here?" he whispered.

"Those people," Keller said. "The ones that just took my friend? They're going to kill him. And his children. They're going to torture them to death. You've got to help me stop it."

Castle looked at him as if he was speaking in tongues. "My boss just tried to kill me."

Keller nodded. "And I'm betting I was supposed to be next. He was probably going to try and make it look like I was trying to get away. You'd have been a hero. A dead hero."

Castle shook his head as if trying to clear it. "This is crazy. This is nuts."

"You'll get no argument from me. But it's happening, and we've got to stop it. Let me out of here."

"No," Castle said, "You're under arrest. You stay where you are. I'll call the State Police. Maybe the Feds."

"We don't have *time*," Keller said. "Right now, while you dither around, they are taking that man to the place where they're holding his sons, and probably a lot of other people as well. And as soon as they get there, from the sound of it, they're going to give them some sort of fake trial, and then they're going sentence them to death, and then they're going to kill them. Slowly. And the only to people who can stop it in time are you and me. Now LET ME THE FUCK OUT OF HERE!" the last words rose to a scream that seemed to jolt Castle out of his reverie.

He stared at Keller, considering. "Okay," he said finally. "Okay." He went back out and got the keys, then let Keller out of the cell.

"Thanks," Keller said.

Castle nodded. He still seemed subdued. "What do we do now?"

"You still have my weapons? And the ammo?"

Castle nodded. "In the locker."

As they stepped out into the main room, Keller saw Cosgrove's body. He took note of the neat wound in the center of the forehead. "Good shooting," he said.

"Thanks," Castle murmured.

They retrieved the shotgun and M4 carbine from the evidence locker—actually a closet with a heavy padlock added to the door. "You've used one of these before, I figure," Keller said, holding the M4 out to Castle, who looked at it for a moment, then took it.

"Once or twice, yeah," he said. He examined the weapon and grimaced. "When was the last time this thing was cleaned?"

"No idea," Keller said. "But it shoots just fine."

"Do I even want to know where this came from? Or the grenades?"

"You probably do," Keller said, "and the Feds'll be real interested, too. But first things first. We need a vehicle. You got one?"

"Yeah," Castle said. "I know just the one."

CHAPTER FORTY-SEVEN

"**B**EFORE WE LEAVE," HUSTON SAID, "there's one more thing we'd like you to do."

"Mr. Huston..." Angela said wearily.

He held up a hand. "It won't take long. I promise. Please, this way." He led her down the hallway. As he walked, she heard him whistling softly. It was a familiar tune, but so jaunty as to seem completely incongruous in this place. It was a cartoon theme she remembered from her childhood.

Whenever he gets in a fix,
He reaches into his bag of tricks...

He noticed her staring and stopped. He chuckled. "Sorry," he said, "old habit." He stopped near the end of the hallway.

There was another room there, furnished with only a desk, two chairs, and a phone. The man sitting behind the desk stood up as she entered. He was tall and slender, with salt and pepper hair in a short military cut. He had the most arresting eyes she'd ever seen. They were bright blue, and there was a look of calm confidence in them. *This is the man in charge,* she realized. The air of command was unmistakable.

"Mrs. Sanchez," the man said, extending a hand. His voice was deep and as reassuring as his eyes, giving her the impression that everything would be all right if only she would listen to him. It put her on her guard immediately. She hesitated a moment before taking his hand. He smiled and shook it. "I regret all the cloak and dagger, ma'am. You've stumbled into a rather complicated situation."

"Complicated," she said, pulling her hand back. "I'm not sure I like the sound of that."

He cocked his head quizzically, still smiling. "Pardon?"

She looked back at Huston, who was closing the door. "Complicated," she said, "usually means something's about to be pushed under the rug. You know, to make things simpler for someone."

"Ah," the man said. He gestured to a chair. She sat down slowly, her eyes still suspicious. "I can assure you," he said, "that we're here to deal with the matter of Mr. Mandujano. And his associates. That's not getting pushed under anything. It's just that our methods are a little unorthodox."

"Who is this 'we'?" she said, "and I didn't get your name."

"I know you didn't," he said, "and you won't. Who we are is, I'm afraid, also complicated."

She sighed and stood up. "Look, whoever you are, I'm not in the damn mood for this. I just want to go home."

He nodded. "And you will, ma'am. We're not keeping you here against your will. A friend of mine will be asking to debrief you when you get back. She's with the FBI. You can trust her." He held up a hand to stop her reply. "I know that recommendation doesn't carry a lot of weight, since you don't trust me. You'll have to make your own assessment when you meet Agent Saxon. I'm confident it will be the right one. But in the meantime, I would like to ask you a favor."

She remained standing. "What?" She knew she sounded ungracious, considering how polite he was being, but she was too tired to give a damn.

He took a cell phone out of the desk. "I'd like you to call Mr. Mandujano," he said, "and tell him what happened."

Angela stared at him. "You're serious."

Huston spoke up, sounding amused. "He's rarely anything else, ma'am."

She turned and glared at him, then back at the man behind the desk. "You want me to warn him about Zavalo."

The man nodded.

"You're taking sides?"

"In a way. What you told Mr. Huston was correct. If the war goes on as planned, it could get bloody. Innocent people will be killed."

"Collateral damage, I believe you military types call it."

His eyes narrowed. It was the first anger she had seen in him, and the force behind those eyes took her aback.

"I never use those words," he said in a low, dangerous voice. "Those are coward's words."

She held up her hands. "Okay, okay."

He relaxed a little and smiled at her again. "Sorry," he said. "But we've assessed the situation. If there's going to be a war, a short, one-sided one will be better."

"But that will leave Mandujano in place."

He nodded. "For the moment."

"Still smuggling people," she said, "and drugs."

"And arms," Huston said, "and the occasional terrorist across the southern U.S. border. Which is how he came to our attention."

"And this is somehow okay with you people?" she demanded, her voice rising.

The man behind the desk was unperturbed. "Not at all. As I said, we'll deal with Mr. Mandujano in our own way. Perhaps if he feels himself in our debt that can be turned to our advantage."

"What," she said, "he's just going to say, 'oh, thank you for saving me, in return I'll give up my life of crime'?"

The man shrugged. "Stranger things have happened."

She shook her head. "If I make that call," she said, "I'm signing Zavalo's death warrant."

"Yes."

"It'll be as if I pulled the trigger myself."

"Yes. In fact, he is at Mandujano's house, right now. Alone. He's that confident in the tightness of his security."

She thought about it for a moment. Zavalo and his people had kidnapped her, held her prisoner, were probably going to kill her when they had no further use for her. Still, it was a hard thing to think about doing. "And what if I don't make the call?"

"You get on the helicopter and go home," the man said. "I told you, your participation in this is entirely voluntary."

"Why don't you make the call?"

"He doesn't know me. He's met you. Knows your voice."

She thought some more. She thought of the girl in the other room, hovering near death because of Zavalo's machinations. If the man behind the desk was right, there'd be more people caught in the crossfire if the war he planned went down. *If he can be trusted.* But looking into those arresting blue eyes, she somehow did just that.

"Okay," she said. "Make the call. But answer me one question first."

"If I can," he said.

"Who or what is Iron Horse?"

He shot a look at Huston, who shrugged. "Mr. Weaver told the major. The major mentioned it to me, but in her presence. I don't think anyone else heard him."

The man sighed and looked back at Angela. "Iron Horse is something that doesn't exist," he said. "Not officially."

"Wait, wait, don't tell me," she said. "It's complicated."

He smiled tightly. "Extremely." He picked up the phone. "Any more questions?"

"No," she said. "Let's do this. And then get me out of here."

CHAPTER
FORTY-EIGHT

AUGUSTE MANDUJANO STOOD IN THE cool dimness of his living room, phone to his ear, listening to a familiar voice on the other end of the line. He spoke little, responding only with an occasional "yes" or "go on" when the narrative seemed to flag. As he listened, he looked out the glass doors where Zavalo lay on his stomach by the pool. A stunning blonde wearing only a bikini bottom was rubbing lotion on his back. When the American woman on the other end of the line wound down, he said merely, "*Gracias,*" and cut the line. He stood looking out toward the pool. He had taken a gamble on letting the woman and her friends go. But he'd found what he hoped to find, if from an unexpected source. Now he knew the person who'd been working against him. He had no doubt now who it was that was behind the disappearance of his shipments. He'd had his suspicions about some of Zavalo's recent absences and the new men he was gathering around him. He'd been giving his oldest friend more and more autonomy in the running of his end of the businesses, even allowing him to branch out into some new ventures of his own, with the idea that when Mandujano retired in a few years, Zavalo would step in as head of the whole operation. Perhaps Zavalo saw that as weakness. Perhaps he just didn't want to wait.

Mandujano had always prided himself on his quickness to reach a decision and his resolve to see those decisions through immediately. This time was no exception. He strode over to the bar that dominated one corner of the room and reached beneath, coming out with a cut-down pump shotgun. He jacked a round into the chamber and walked out onto the pool terrace.

The girl saw him coming first. She blinked in confusion, her wits still addled by the pills Zavalo kept her wasted on. When the realization of what was happening finally found its way through the fog, she stood and stumbled backward. She fell over the lounge chair behind her and went sprawling. Zavalo's head jerked up at the commotion. He looked at the girl, saw the terror in her eyes, and looked back to see death approaching. As he rose, Mandujano pulled the trigger of the shotgun. The pellets of double-ought buckshot shredded Zavalo's chest. He fell backward, narrowly missing the now-screaming girl. Mandujano pumped a second round into the chamber and walked over to stand astride the body of the man he'd known since childhood. Zavalo was still breathing, but the air bubbled out wetly through the holes in his lungs. Mandujano aimed the gun and fired again. Blood, bone, and brains splattered out around the destroyed skull. Some of the debris landed in the pool, staining the water with streaks of red. He looked up at the girl.

She'd stopped screaming. Her eyes were wide and unseeing, he knew her mind had fled deep inside, far away from the horror that had just played out in front of her. Mandujano didn't hesitate. She might be no part of Zavalo's plot, but at the very least, she was a witness. He raised the gun and fired again.

From behind him, he heard the sound of running footsteps. He turned, pumping another round into the gun, and raised it. Two of his guards had come pounding up, most likely drawn by the sound of gunfire. He watched them carefully, alert to any sign they were part of the betrayal. They stopped and stared, their eyes narrowed, but they made no move to raise their weapons to him. He relaxed, let the shotgun drop to his side. "Find someone to clean this up," he said. He looked at the blood in the water. "And tell the man to drain the pool."

ANGELA WALKED ONTO THE ROOFTOP helicopter pad, with Huston following close behind. A U.S. Army Blackhawk helicopter was sitting there with the doors open. Two men were loading Esmeralda onto the chopper on a stretcher. She turned to Huston. "Thank you for helping get us out of here."

He smiled. "It was the least we could do. By the way, we got an answer back regarding the truck that was found in the desert."

She could feel her heart thudding inside her chest. "And?"

"None of the bodies answered the description you gave us of your husband and Mr. Keller."

She closed her eyes, suddenly weak with relief. "Thank God," she murmured. She opened her eyes again. "Do you have any idea where they went?"

"We have some idea, yes. And we're following up."

"Following up on what?"

"The men who were killed have connections to a white supremacist organization known as the Church of Elohim. Given what we've found, we believe that, as you suspected, they may be kidnapping people. Selling them into slavery."

The helicopter's engine coughed to life and began spooling up. Angela had to raise her voice to be heard over it. "Mr. Huston, if Jack Keller found the same connection you did, he'll be going after this church."

"He shouldn't do that," he shouted over the roar of the rotor blades. "These people are well armed. They're dangerous. You've got to try and persuade him to stop."

She laughed. "You've clearly never met Jack Keller. He won't stop, Mr. Huston. You'll either need to get there first or..." She'd reached the helicopter door. A young soldier in a flight suit extended a hand to help her up.

"Or what?" Huston called to her.

She turned back to him. "Or you'll need to send in people to pick up the pieces and recover bodies."

He nodded. "Understood. I think I might like this Keller. *Vaya con Dios*, Mrs. Sanchez."

"*Vaya con Dios,* Doctor…what is your real name anyway?"

He winked at her, raised his right arm, and tapped the cartoon watch with his left index finger. "And my first name's Armando," he said.

"Thank you, Dr. Felix," she said.

"*De nada.*" He stepped back. When he was clear, the whine of the helicopter engines increased to a roar and they lifted off the pad. Angela looked back to see him waving as they lifted up and away, leaving the consulate and the city behind.

CHAPTER
FORTY-NINE

WALKER WAS THE FIRST ONE out of the car when they arrived back at the compound. "Bring him," he barked at his two guards. He strode off toward one of the wooden barracks as they took Oscar from the vehicle. He didn't resist as they steered him to the building where the General had just gone. He saw the large numeral 3 painted on the outside of the building. He looked around at the other buildings. There didn't seem to be anyone else around.

"Come on," one of the guards said, taking him by the shoulder. "This way to your trial."

"I haven't done anything wrong," he said quietly. That earned him another slap to the back of the head from the other guard.

"Shut up and move your ass."

He kept his head held high as he walked between them to the building. They entered a large room, empty except for the table at the other end. Walker was standing in front of the table. There was someone standing beside him.

Oscar stopped. He couldn't believe what he was seeing.

"Boy," Walker said, "go and greet your father." Then Ruben was running toward him, arms outstretched. Oscar held out his own arms and the boy ran into them, crying. Oscar wrapped his arms around his son.

"Papa, Papa," Ruben sobbed into his chest.

"Ruben," Oscar whispered, the tears running down his own face. "My son." *The pictures your aunt and uncle sent didn't do justice to how much you've grown.* He took the boy by the shoulders and held him at arm's length. "Let me look at you," he said. "*Dios mio*, you're a man." *But so thin. And more careworn than a boy should be.* "Your brother," he said. "Where is Edgar?"

Walker answered for him. "Working, but don't worry. He'll be back soon."

"Papa," Ruben whispered. He switched to Spanish. "This is a terrible place. These men are monsters. Please get us out of here."

Oscar hugged his son again, felt the boy's thin body racked with sobs as he held him tight against his breast. "I will," he said. "I will." *Please God, show me how.*

Walker spoke to the guards. "Go get the others," he said. "Bring them here. I want them to see what happens."

"OKAY," KELLER SAID AS THEY stood in the doorway of the garage, "you have my attention."

The giant armored truck nearly filled the garage, leaving barely enough room on either side for a man to get past it. Keller had seen vehicles like it on television, images broadcast from far away, from a part of the world he hoped never to see again. "What the hell's something like that doing *here*?"

Castle looked at the MRAP sourly. "Some government program," he said. "With the wars winding down, I guess the Army has a lot of these they don't need. And there's plenty of sheriffs and police chiefs all over the country who'd just looooove to have a bigger badder truck than the guy down the road."

"Your boss really thinks he needs something like this to serve warrants and break up fights at the high school football game?"

Castle looked at him without smiling. "I don't know what the fuck my boss was thinking. I thought he was just trying to be the biggest bad-ass in the neighborhood. Now," he looked at the MRAP, "I don't know."

"Whassup, Ray?" a voice said. They turned. A man dressed in grease-stained jeans, a shirt with the sleeves cut off, and a grimy trucker hat was standing behind them, wiping his hands on a rag.

"Hey, Junior," Castle said. "I need to take the truck."

Junior looked puzzled. "What for?"

Castle shrugged, smiling. "Sheriff wants to show it off to some high muckety muck from out of town."

"I ain't heard nothin' about that," Junior said.

"It'll only be for a while," Castle said. "We'll bring it back."

Junior jerked his chin at Keller. "Who's this guy?"

"The high muckety muck," Keller said.

"Uh-huh," Junior said, looking Keller up and down. "I think I better call the Sheriff and check this out."

"Okay," Castle said. "Go ahead on. We'll wait." Looking back suspiciously, Junior walked past the truck toward the office in the back.

"Let's move," Castle said. "Get the guns out of my car." Castle walked toward the MRAP.

"You know how to drive one of these?" Keller said.

"Yeah," Castle said over his shoulder, "but I'd hoped I wouldn't ever have to again."

"I know the feeling," Keller said.

The MRAP was pulling out of the garage, big engine chugging, as Keller grabbed the weapons they'd taken out of Castle's vehicle—Keller's M4, the shotgun Oscar had been carrying, and an AR-15 Castle had removed from the weapons locker at the substation. He slung the M4 on one shoulder, the AR-15 on the other, and carried the shotgun in one hand. As the armored truck passed, Keller swung up onto the broad metal running board on the passenger side and hung on with his free hand to one of the mirrors. He looked back to see Junior running out of the now-empty garage, yelling. As the truck accelerated away, he fell behind, then slowed to a walk and stopped, bending over with his hands on his knees. Castle drove the MRAP until Junior was out of sight, then stopped to let Keller climb in.

"Think Goober back there'll call to warn them we're coming?" Keller asked.

"Junior?" Castle said. "I don't think he's part of that. He ain't much of a joiner. He'll probably try to raise someone at the Sheriff's department."

"Which means they'll be coming after us."

"But they won't know where we're going. For a while, at least."

Keller nodded. "Okay. So what's the plan?"

Castle looked at him. "I was kinda hoping you had one."

"Well," Keller said, remembering Oscar's words to him, "my usual method is kick the front door in, grab who I'm after, and haul ass."

"Ordinarily," Castle said, "that's a plan I'd get behind. But on a day like today it stands a good chance of getting a lot of people killed. Including your friend. And us."

"Yeah," Keller said. He rubbed his hands over his face in frustration, then looked over at Castle. "You grew up around here, right?"

Castle looked unhappy, as if he knew where this was going. "Right."

"So do you know this farm? Know anything about it from before these people moved in?"

Castle nodded. "Yeah. Me and my daddy used to hunt on that land. Or near to it."

"So, is there a back way in?"

Castle thought. "There might be. I'm not sure. But I know who might know."

"Who?"

"My cousin Posey. Part of that farm's on his old home place. He used to farm it himself, till he got sick. Then he started selling off pieces of it, to get the money to live on. Some of it went to that church."

"He know what they're up to?"

"Don't know. But it probably wouldn't surprise him." Castle took a deep breath. "Keller, if we're going to see Posey, you need to let me do the talking. In fact, just stay in the truck."

"Why?"

"Posey hates white people. I mean, he *really* hates white people. Not really sure why, except for, you know, the usual reasons."

"The usual…" Keller said, then stopped himself. "Okay. Whatever. I'll keep my mouth shut. But hurry."

Castle muscled the MRAP into a tight turn down a narrow dirt road. "We're almost there."

CHAPTER
FIFTY

ASTLE'S COUSIN POSEY WAS THE biggest man Keller had ever seen. At nearly seven feet tall, he towered over his cousin, who was not himself a small man. He was also enormously fat. Keller figured he had to weigh at least four hundred pounds. The rickety front porch where he and Castle were standing sagged under his weight. His shaved head made him look even more menacing. Through the thick glass in the truck's windshield, Keller could see the two men talking. Posey didn't seem happy about the conversation; he was waving his arms and there was a scowl on his broad face. From time to time, he raised a hand to point at Keller in the truck, and every time, it seemed to make him angrier. Finally, he stomped down off the porch, the whole structure shivering with his footfalls, and walked over to the passenger side of the truck where Keller waited. Castle followed.

Posey stood for a moment, fists on hips, glaring up at Keller in the seat. "Get down out th' truck," he said finally. His voice was incongruously high, almost feminine.

Keller hesitated. "You hear me?" the man said. "I said get out th' truck."

Moving slowly, like a man confronting an angry elephant that might charge, Keller climbed down. Posey glared at him, not speaking. Then he said, "You tellin' me I sold my land to a buncha Klansmen?"

"No, sir," Keller said. "These people are worse."

Posey snorted. "You ever met the Klan, boy?"

"No, sir," he said, "but these people are actually putting some of their beliefs into action. They're keeping people as slaves."

"Slaves?" Posey said. "That's crazy talk. You jus' sayin' that to try an' get me to help you."

"I don't think so, Posey," Castle said. "They took a man out of the jail. A Mexican."

"Colombian," Keller corrected him automatically.

"Whatever," Castle said. "I think they mean to kill him."

"What was he, a drug dealer?" Posey said.

"No, sir," Keller said, looking the larger man in the eye. "He's a good man. A friend. He was looking for his children, and they mean to kill the children, too."

"An' the Sheriff was mixed up in alla this?" Posey turned to his cousin. Castle nodded. Posey grunted. "Told you you was a fool to trust that cracker." He turned to Keller. "No offense."

"None taken," Keller said. "But we need to get in there. Do you know a back way in? Some way though that fence?"

Posey rubbed his chin. "I reckon I do. Creek runs from their land down onta mine. Gotta be a cut somewhere. A culvert maybe."

"You know if it's guarded?" Castle said.

Posey shook his head. "Don't get down there much. Not anymore, at least."

Keller looked at Castle. "You know where the creek is?"

"Yeah," Castle said. He still didn't look happy.

"You having second thoughts?" Keller said.

Castle looked at him. "Just wondering how we're going to handle this when we do get in."

"Depends on what we find. We don't have much to go on."

"And if we run into someone who decides they don't want us

there?" Keller started to answer, but Castle cut him off. "Whatever's happened, Mr. Keller, I'm still a sworn law officer."

Posey grunted. "Law man," he said with a smile. The smile wasn't a pleasant one.

"Give it a rest, Pose," Castle snapped. "I know you don't get it. But this is who I am. I'm not going to just walk in and start shooting people."

"Neither am I, if I can help it," Keller said.

"But that's probably how this is going to end up," Castle said, "if we do it your way."

"Look," Keller said, "if you don't want to go, that's fine." He turned to Posey. "Can you show me where this creek is?"

"You gon' get yourself killed," Posey said. "And for what?"

"I can't just let a friend die," Keller said.

"You don't smarten up, boy, that's what's gon' happen, and you gon' die with him."

"You got a better idea?"

"I might," Posey said.

"This isn't your fight, Posey," Castle said.

"May be that it ain't," Posey said, "but it may be that it is, too. Those crackers tol' me they was a church. Now I find out my neighbors is some kinda Nazi motherfuckers. *Slave* owners." He spat on the ground, then looked over at the MRAP, a glint in his eye. "Keys in that thing?"

"Yeah," Castle said.

"Okay, here's what we do," Posey said. "Listen up."

CHAPTER
FIFTY-ONE

THE HEAT OF LATE SUMMER had reduced the creek to a slow trickle in a broad strip of sand. Keller could see the marks, however, where the water had risen in times past, high on the overgrown banks that rose to shoulder height on either side. He worked his way down this water-cut trench, wiping the sweat from his eyes and brushing away the gnats and mosquitoes who buzzed around him. He held the M4 at the ready, a bag of grenades dangling from his shoulder. Castle moved down the trench ahead of him gripping a shotgun. The shotgun was loaded with a magazine of nonlethal "beanbag" rounds he' ' taken from the police station, rounds designed to knock a target to the ground and stun without killing. He had a long coil of rope slung on one shoulder. His service weapon, a Beretta 9MM, rode in the holster on his hip. Posey had taken the MRAP, armed with his own sidearm, an old .45 caliber M911 that Posey claimed his father had carried on the Second World War. It looked like an antique, but Posey swore it still fired. Castle hadn't wanted his cousin involved at all, until the big man had pointed out that there was no one else he could count on for backup.

"For all you know, ever'one on that department is part o' this but you," he'd said. "Only ones you can trust right now are your own kind." He'd looked at Keller. "No offense."

"None taken," Keller had said. He just hoped the big man was up to what he was going to be asked to do. He clearly wasn't in the best of health; the effort of hauling himself up into the cab of the truck was enough to leave him wheezing, and Castle had nearly called a halt to the whole plan right there. "I'm fine," Posey had insisted. "I sure as hell ain't gettin' out o' this thing, an' as long as all I got to do is drive, I'm good to go. You just get yo' people to the truck when I come bustin' in. I ain't waitin' around too long."

"Don't worry," Keller had said. "I don't intend to be there any longer than we have to."

Castle stopped. "There it is," he whispered. Back here in the overgrown bottomland, the vegetation grew right against the fence, but they could still see the same signs: NO TRESPASSING, interspersed with the bright yellow ones warning of HIGH VOLTAGE. Where the fence and the creek intersected, a high wall, made of the same heavy timbers as the front gate, interrupted the fence. A large corrugated metal culvert ran beneath the wooden wall. At the end of the culvert, a fence made of panels of metal mesh formed a box that blocked entry.

"Shit," Keller said.

Castle walked over to the mesh box. "It's just a beaver guard," he said. "Keeps beavers from blocking the culvert to build themselves a pond." He reached out to grab it.

"Hope it's not electrified, too," Keller said.

Castle stopped, his hand in the air. He looked the cage over. "Doesn't look like it. But get ready to knock me off this thing if you see me start dancin'." He took a deep breath and grabbed the wire. Nothing happened. Castle began pulling at the fencing, rocking it back and forth to try and wrest it out of the ground. "Give me a hand here."

In a few moments, they had pulled the guard away from the end of the culvert and were looking into the darkness inside. It was barely big enough for a man to crawl through on his hands and knees. "Tell me again why this is a good idea?" Castle said.

"It isn't," Keller said. "But it's the only one we've got." He got down and looked through. The circle of light at the other end looked like it was a hundred miles away. He unslung his rifle to be able to fit inside the tube, pushing it ahead of him as he entered." The trickling creek soaked his palms and the knees of his jeans. His back brushed against the top of the culvert, causing clods of dirt and mud to cascade down around him. He had to stretch his hands out in front of him and lower his back to keep from scraping against the top. The unnatural position caused his muscles to begin cramping within a few feet. He pressed on, the sweat pouring off him even in the cool clammy darkness. About halfway down the tube, Keller saw something moving in the shadows. As he grew closer, something reared up in front of him. It was the largest rat he'd ever seen, at least a foot long from the end of its long bare tail to the tip of the pink nose that twitched at him below a pair of beady black eyes. The rat didn't seem inclined to run from the intruder. It rocked back and forth, making a soft noise in its throat, clearly trying to decide whether to spring at Keller's unprotected face. He pushed the rifle along the floor of the culvert in front to him, flattened out, and groped for the trigger. Suddenly, the rat turned and scampered at full speed in the other direction. Keller started breathing again and resumed his crawl.

There was another beaver guard at the other end of the culvert. Keller disposed of that one by getting to his knees, bowing his back and standing up, pushing the stakes holding the guard out of the earth. He sat down on the bank of the creek, shaking the water out of his rifle, and hoping it would still fire. At least there was no mud in the barrel. He looked down at himself. His jeans and the front of his white T-shirt were covered in black dirt and mud. In a few moments, Castle's head and shoulders appeared in the mouth of the culvert. "Was that a rat in there?" he said.

"Yeah," said Keller.

Castle exited the tube and sat down, resting his hands on his knees, his head hanging between them. "Jesus," he said. "That was horrible."

"Yeah," Keller replied. He stood up. "Come on, let's go."

They quickly found a trail through the woods, running along the bank next to the creek. It looked as if it wasn't used frequently; there were weeds growing up in the center and dead branches fallen across it. As they walked along it, the ground began to rise, the vegetation changing to pine and scrub oak. Soon the path turned away from the creek and the slope became steeper.

"Hold on," Castle said. "You hear that?"

They stopped. In the stillness, Keller heard the buzz of a small engine. "Someone's coming," he said.

"Get off the road," Castle said. He stepped into the trees on the right and put the trunk of a large pine tree between him and the oncoming sound. Keller did the same on the left. A few seconds later, a four-wheeled ATV came into view. The driver wore khaki pants and a black T-shirt. His eyes were hidden behind mirrored shades, and he wore a baseball cap with the familiar Odin Cross emblazoned on it. An AK-47 assault rifle protruded from a scabbard beside the driver. As he drew closer, Castle stepped out into the center of the trail and pointed his shotgun at the middle of the man's face. Keller stepped out from behind his own tree and did the same with his M4. The driver flinched backward so quickly he nearly fell off the four-wheeler. He came to a stop less than a yard away and raised his hands. Keller stepped forward and took the AK out of its scabbard before reaching past the driver and killing the engine.

In the sudden silence that followed, Castle said, "Off the four-wheeler. Hands up."

The man complied, slowly. "You two are trespassin'," he said.

"Yep," Keller said.

"We shoot trespassers around here. Especially nigger trespassers. And," he looked at Keller, "nigger lovers."

Keller stole a look at Castle to gauge his reaction to the word. There wasn't any. "Actually, Deputy Castle and I are just good friends," he said.

"Your people just brought a guy in," Castle said. "A Latino. Where is he being kept?"

"Fuck you," the man said.

Castle raised the shotgun and fired. The beanbag round caught the man in the chest and knocked him to the ground, howling in pain. Castle walked over to the man and stood over him. "Hurts, don't it?" he said mildly. "Now I asked you a question, asshole. Your buddies back there bring a guy in?" He pointed the shotgun at the man on the ground. "It hurts more at this range. A lot more."

The man on the ground tried to scuttle away, scrabbling backward on his hands. Castle followed implacably, the shotgun still trained on the man's chest. "Don't," the man said, his voice breaking.

"Talk," Castle said.

"Yeah," the man on the ground said. "Yeah, they brought some guy from the jail. Some wetback." He flinched away as Castle's finger tightened on the trigger.

Then Castle lowered the weapon. He nodded to Keller and tossed him the rope from his shoulder. "Tie him up," he said. In moments, Keller had the man bound to a tree, hands behind him. There was a key ring attached to his belt. Keller took it. "We'll send someone back to pick you up," Castle said. "Maybe."

Keller took the hat off the man's head and removed his sunglasses before turning back to Castle. "You want me to gag him, too?"

"Sure," Castle said.

Keller found a dirty bandanna in one of the man's pockets. "Open wide," he said.

"Fuck you," the man said.

Keller sighed. Moving quickly, he reached up and pinched the prisoner's nose shut. The man struggled and tried to turn away, but Keller held him still until his face began to turn red. Finally, his mouth opened and he took in a huge gasp of air. Keller jammed the bandanna in his mouth and quickly wrapped another length of rope around his head to hold it in. The man glared at Keller with raw hatred as he tied it off.

"Okay," Keller said as he walked away from the tree. "Now we have wheels and another rifle. And," he picked a black radio up from where it was secured to the ATV. "One of their radios. So far, so good."

"Yeah," Castle said. "So far, so good."

Keller noticed the expression on his face. "What?"

"Nothing," Castle said. "Just some bad memories."

Keller put the hat and sunglasses on. "Let's move," he said.

CHAPTER FIFTY-TWO

THEY CAME OUT OF THE woods into a landscape that looked like a deserted battlefield. Most of the trees were gone, leaving only stumps, dead limbs, and scrap wood behind. Weeds growing up between the stumps showed that the clear-cutting hadn't been done recently.

Castle was riding on the back of the ATV, perched awkwardly on the rear rack. He slid off and pointed ahead. "Look there." At the edge of the cut area stood a long, open-sided wooden structure. From that distance, Keller couldn't identify the machinery inside.

"Sawmill," Castle said. "Doesn't look like anyone's home."

They got off the ATV and killed the engine. They spread out and approached slowly. Before they reached the buildings, they walked into an area where the ground appeared to have been recently disturbed. Nothing grew on a small plot of ground, approximately six feet by three. The area was raised above the surrounding earth by a couple of inches.

Keller stopped and looked around. "Castle," he said.

Castle stopped and looked. There were low mounds of dirt, like the one Keller was looking at, but covered with grass. Keller counted twenty of them in two neat rows. "Are those what I think they are?" Castle said. Keller nodded and turned away, hoping that none of those mounds concealed the body of Oscar Sanchez or his sons.

As they approached the building, Keller caught the scent of cut pine. They walked under the overhang of the roof, scanning from side to side, weapons ready.

"Check this out," Castle said. He was standing by a large circular saw, fed by a conveyor. Keller walked around to where he stood and looked down where Castle was pointing.

There was a short length of chain lying on the floor next to the machine. One end was secured to a D-ring welded onto the side of the saw. The other ended in a manacle.

"They chain them to the machines," Keller said.

Castle's jaw was working in anger. "Damn it. I was having trouble believing this before. Not now."

Keller stepped to the other side of the mill. There was a fence on the other side, as high as the outer perimeter, but without the warning signs. A padlocked gate seemed to be the only entrance. On the other side of the fence, about thirty feet away from it, was another long wooden building. The sides of this one were enclosed. Castle came and stood beside him. "What do you think that is?"

"Don't know," Keller said. "Looks kind of like a barracks."

"I was thinking the same thing."

The radio they'd taken from the man on the ATV crackled with static. Keller snatched it from his belt and put it to his ear.

"All units," a voice crackled. "Assemble at the Judicial Building. Repeat, assemble at the Judicial Building. Bring your prisoners. General's orders."

"The trial," Keller said. "They said they were going to put Oscar on some kind of fake trial."

"All units acknowledge," the voice said. Other voices crackled back, affirming the order. There was brief silence before the first voice spoke again, "Loomis, acknowledge."

"You think Loomis is the guy who we left tied to a tree back there?"

Castle asked.

"I'd say it's likely," Keller said. He keyed the microphone and said, "Acknowledged." He turned to Castle. "I'll take the four-wheeler," he said, "wearing the hat and sunglasses we took off our charming friend back there. It sounds like everyone's invited to this bullshit trial in the Judicial Building. They'll all be together. I'll try to get close enough to neutralize any guards they leave outside."

"How you plan to do that, Keller?" Castle said, eyes narrowed.

"Get the drop on them if I can. Give them a chance to surrender. Look, Castle, I'm not any more eager to kill people than you are."

Castle relaxed slightly. "Okay. But then I should be the one to go."

"Have you been paying attention to who we're dealing with? These people aren't going to surrender to you."

Castle grimaced. "Okay. Point taken. So what do I do?"

"You get behind this building. Stay here with the M4 and give me overwatch. If the whole thing goes sideways, start firing grenades. All over the place. Make them think there's a whole platoon out there. Cause as much confusion as you can without killing anyone. If I take care of the outside guards, come join me. We go in, get everybody down on the ground, then grab our people, and get the hell out of Dodge. How are you at crowd control?"

"Fair to middling," Castle said. "Although around here, 'crowd control' means clearing the good old boys out of the parking lot of Duke's Bar & Grill after closing time."

"Well, let's just hope your cousin shows up, or it's going to be a long walk out of here."

AT THAT MOMENT, POSEY CARTWRIGHT sat in the driver's seat of the bright blue MRAP, arms folded across his massive chest, eyes fixed stubbornly on the road ahead. The vehicle wasn't moving. It was blocked in by two Sheriff's cars that sat nose to nose across the road in front of him and two more directly behind. A sweating, red-faced Sheriff's deputy was up on the running board, pounding on one of the thick, bulletproof windows and shouting at Posey to get his ass out of the truck. Posey pretended not to hear him. He didn't know what to do. That made him angry, and anger made him mulish. He was going to sit there until he figured out what to do. Something would come to him. He may have always been slow, but he wasn't stupid.

CHAPTER FIFTY-THREE

CASTLE OPENED THE GATE WITH the keys they'd taken from Loomis, and Keller drove through. They reached the wooden building, with Keller still astride the four-wheeler and Castle on foot. Keller got off the ATV and walked to the corner of the building. Making sure his hat and glasses were in place, he peeked around the corner.

He saw a line of similar buildings, spaced about thirty feet apart, with a path running along the space between the buildings and the fence. None of the buildings appeared to have any windows, save for a few narrow slits high up on the walls. There were no doors on this end that he could see. He faded back behind the building and spoke into Castle's ear to be heard over the rumble of the four-wheeler without having to shout.

"There's a line of these buildings," he said. "This is the back side. I'm going to head for the front, between these first two. Cover me." Castle nodded his understanding. Keller mounted the ATV and steered it slowly up the path. The sun was low in the afternoon sky behind the buildings, and the space between was cool and shadowed. There was no sound except the trilling of a bird outside the fence.

"Where the hell is everybody?" Castle said.

THERE WERE TWENTY PRISONERS LINED up in rows before the long table where the General sat, wearing his black robe. Three guards leaned against the wall on the right; another three stood guard behind the table, weapons at port arms. Oscar Sanchez stood alone before the table, in front of the group of prisoners.

"Oscar Sanchez," the General said. "You have been found guilty of violating the sacred and sovereign borders of the United States. The penalty for that is life at hard labor."

"I don't recall there being a trial," Oscar said mildly.

One of the guards started for him, but the General waved him back. "You have also been found guilty of conspiring to resist the lawful authority of this citizen's tribunal." He paused. "The penalty for that is death by hanging."

"No," a voice came from the crowd. Oscar recognized Ruben's voice.

"Silence!"

"Listen," Oscar said. "I have come for my sons. Let us go in peace," He gestured to the crowd behind him. "And these other people, and there will be no further trouble."

"Denied," the General said. "And as for your brats, they die with you."

The words hit Oscar like a blow. His knees felt weak, and his stomach roiled as if he was about to vomit. "They haven't done anything wrong," he said.

"The Lord our God is a jealous God," the General said, "visiting the iniquity of the fathers upon the children unto the third and fourth generation."

"It isn't God telling you to murder children," Oscar's voice rose as he said it. At that moment, there was a soft chime. The General reached into the folds of the robe and produced a cell phone from his shirt pocket. He looked at the screen for a moment, then Oscar saw his face go blank with shock.

"Bad news?" he said.

"Be quiet," one of the guards said, but he sounded uneasy, as if he too had noticed the look.

"Let me guess," Oscar said. "Jack Keller has escaped."

The General put the phone on the table in front of him. "And you can add conspiring to murder a law enforcement officer to the list of your crimes. Sheriff Cosgrove has been killed."

There was a moment of shocked silence, then a murmur of conversation rippled through the room. "ORDER!" the General roared.

"General," Oscar said, "if Jack Keller is out, he's coming here. For all you know, he may already be here. And if he's coming here, he's coming for you. Trust me, that is the last thing you want. Just let us go. That's all you need to do."

Walker shook his head in amazement. "You people," he said. "Too dumb to know when you're beaten." He gestured to Kinney. "Take them to the Justice Tree," he said. "And the others. But bring chairs. We will carry out this execution the old-fashioned way. You," he pointed at Bender. "Take two men. Reinforce the guard at the front gate." He looked around. "Where is Corporal Loomis?"

The other guards looked around as well. No one answered. "Give me a radio," Walker said. One of the guards handed him one. He put it to his ear, then stopped.

"Put them in position," he told Kinney, "and wait for instructions."

KELLER LOOKED AROUND THE FRONT of the building. After a moment, he pulled back.

"Goddamn it," he breathed.

"What?" Castle said.

"They've got Oscar," Keller said. "And I assume the ones with him are his sons. They're standing on chairs with their hands tied behind their backs and nooses around their necks. The ropes are hanging from a big tree."

"We need to move now," Castle said.

"Where the hell is Posey?" Keller said.

"Mr. Keller," Walker's voice came through the radio they'd taken from Loomis. "Are you out there?"

CHAPTER
FIFTY-FOUR

KELLER LOOKED AT THE RADIO for a moment, then raised it to his lips. "Yeah, Walker," he said. "I'm here."

"Why don't you come out and join us?"

"I think it might have something to do with all of those guys with guns. Why don't you tell them to put them away and maybe we can talk."

"Why should I do that?" Walker said. "You came here to kill me, did you not?"

"No," Keller said. "I came here to get my friend back. And his boys. But just so you know, I'm keeping that other option open."

"So, I'm to believe that if I give you this brown scum and his sniveling little whelps, you'll just walk away?"

"I only came here for one thing, Walker. I don't give a fuck about you or anything else you do."

"Somehow I find that hard to believe," Walker said. "Tell me, did you kill Sheriff Cosgrove? And his nigger deputy?"

Keller turned to Castle. "He's trying to keep me talking."

Castle nodded. "Yeah, I was about to bring that up."

"Which means that he's got someone out looking."

"Maybe more than one," Castle said.

"He doesn't know you're here."

"Or he's pretending like he doesn't."

Keller raised the radio. "Yeah," he said to Walker, "I hated to have to do it. But, you know, it is what it is." He lowered the radio. "He wants me to go out there."

"He'll kill you."

"He'll try," Keller said, "but he'll want to make me watch my friend die first."

"You sure?"

"Yeah. You may not have noticed, but the guy's kind of an asshole."

"I did notice that," Castle said.

"He's an egomaniac," Keller said. "He loves to hear himself talk. He's got to put on a show."

"And this helps us how?"

"I get him going. Keep him talking. Meanwhile I get in close."

"And then he kills your friend, and then his sons, and then you."

"You won't give him the chance."

Castle shook his head. "Goddamn it," he muttered. "I thought we weren't going to bust in and start killing people."

"I didn't say that," Keller said. "I said we'd try. But they're going to kill Oscar and his sons if we just sit on our asses. Come on, Castle. You're a cop. You gonna let that happen?"

Castle bristled. "Oh, do NOT play the cop card on me, Keller."

The radio crackled. "You need to show yourself, Mr. Keller," Walker said. "Before I become impatient."

"Okay," Keller said. "I'm coming out."

"Unarmed."

"Of course." He leaned the M4 against the wall of the barracks and slid the bag of grenades off his shoulder. "Don't leave me with my ass hanging out there, Castle," he said. "I'm counting on you." Without another word, he turned and walked out into the open from behind the building.

CHAPTER FIFTY-FIVE

THE OFFICERS MANNING THE IMPROMPTU roadblock were confused, and confusion made them nervous. No one had heard from the Sheriff in hours, and now a man pretty much everyone in town regarded as a crazy hermit was out here, behind the wheel of a heavily armored police vehicle. They'd radioed the Highway Patrol for help, but no one knew when they'd get here, or what they could bring that would pierce the thick armored hide of the behemoth that sat squarely and stubbornly idling in the middle of State Road 1860.

"What the hell's he up to?" A young deputy asked his older partner. The young deputy's name was Irby, and at twenty-two, he was the youngest member of the department.

"Damned if I know, son," Gillespie, the older deputy, said. "But this is the road that leads to that farm where that crazy white power church set up. Maybe Posey's got some kinda grudge."

Gillespie was sixty-two, the oldest deputy remaining on road duty. His few remaining hairs had gone to solid gray, and his bum knee was giving him fits every day. He just wanted to spend out his last few days before retirement in peace and quiet, and he did not need this shit from that nutcase Posey Cartwright.

He heard a commotion from inside one of the blocking cars, someone's voice raised. "Say again!" the voice said. "Say again!" The voice sounded panicked. He recognized the voice as belonging to Sammy Lowell, a deputy who'd been with the department about five years, maybe six. Gillespie couldn't remember exactly how much. He frowned. He'd trained Lowell himself, and the young man should have better radio discipline than that. He walked over and leaned in the car window. "What's goin' on, Sammy?"

Lowell, a hawk-faced thirty-year-old with a military buzz cut looked up at him, stricken. "The Sheriff's dead, Paul," he said. "Someone shot him."

"The hell you say," Gillespie said.

"It's true," Lowell said. "Someone found his body in the Hearken substation. Shot in the head."

Gillespie straightened up, grabbing the door to steady himself. He suddenly felt dizzy.

Irby came running over. "What's wrong, Sarge?"

Gillespie's head cleared a little. He looked over at where the MRAP sat idling. "Some asshole just shot Sheriff Cosgrove," he said, drawing his sidearm, "and I think I know which one."

THE IMPACT OF THE 9MM rounds smacking into the truck's armor clanged like stones hitting a tin roof. "Aiiight, then," Posey muttered, "that's the way you wanna play..." He gunned the engine and let off the clutch. The big truck lurched ahead, making contact with the Sheriff's car in front. There was a heavy metallic crunch as sheet metal gave way before the onslaught and a squeal of rubber on pavement as the MRAP shoved the blocking car out of the way. Its path cleared, the truck lumbered away, accelerating slowly. Posey checked the side mirrors. He could see deputies running for their cars in his wake. "Come on, then," he muttered. "Y'all just come right on ahead." The gate to the farm was a mile ahead.

CHAPTER FIFTY-SIX

KELLER COUNTED TWO GUARDS STANDING behind the group of people that stood to one side of the tree, their backs to the building. As he drew closer, he saw that one of them was the blond with the slicked back hair who'd been in the group who took Oscar. He didn't see the other one, the one with the ragged beard. Walker stood behind Oscar and his sons, his hands behind his back. He was dressed in his military style fatigues, a long knife hanging from the sheath at his belt the only visible weapon. They were facing Keller in a line at a right angle to the crowd. Oscar and the boys had their hands tied behind them and ropes around their necks. Oscar was in the center, with a thin young man who looked about seventeen or eighteen to one side, and another, smaller boy to his left. Walker stepped out from behind them as Keller approached. He was holding a long barreled black revolver down beside one leg. As Keller got closer, Walker raised it and pulled the hammer back with his thumb. "Hands up, Mr. Keller."

Keller stopped and raised his hands. "I'm unarmed."

Walker didn't answer. He walked closer, gun pointed at Keller, until he was only a few feet away. "Turn around," he said. Keller turned, slowly, until his back was to Walker. "Stop," Walker said. "Hands behind your head." Keller complied. Walker frisked him with one hand, quickly and inexpertly. "Turn back around," he ordered. "Face me." As Keller turned, Walker struck him across the face with the barrel of the gun. The blow was hard enough to stagger Keller, and he stumbled slightly to one side, pain exploding in his head. Walker hit him again, this blow laying a line of white fire across his cheek as the barrel split the skin. He almost fell, but managed to catch himself at the last minute. He felt the warmth of the blood running down his face.

"Traitor," Walker hissed. "A traitor to your race. A traitor to our country. After you've seen these three die, you'll receive a traitor's reward. Do you recall how traitors were dealt with in olden times?" His eyes were bright, like the eyes of a man with fever. He went on in the tone of one reciting a well-loved passage. "Hanged, but not unto death." He drew the long knife from the sheath on his belt. "Taken down alive, your members to be cut off and cast in the fire, your bowels burnt before you, your head smitten off, and your body quartered and divided."

"You know your problem, Walker?" Keller said, the words coming out slurred and raspy because of the pain. "You talk too goddamn much."

Walker looked as if he was about to hit Keller again, but he got himself under control. He sheathed the knife and stepped aside. "Move," he said. Keller walked in front, swaying slightly as he went. In a moment, he stood before Oscar. His friend looked down at him from atop his chair. Keller could see the sweat on his brow.

"Hey, buddy," Keller said. "How goes it?"

"I've been better, Jack," Oscar said.

"Yeah. Me, too." He looked at the other two. "These must be your boys." He turned to Walker. "Okay, Walker," he said. "This is your last chance. Let them go and nobody else has to get hurt."

Walker stared at him for a moment. Then he chuckled. "It's a pity," he said. "You could have been an asset to the cause. What was it, Keller? Where did you go wrong? Was it your upbringing?"

"See?" Keller said to Oscar. "He talks too much."

Walker stepped forward, toward the chairs. As he did, there was the sound of a loud crash in the distance, then the chatter of automatic weapons fire. He stopped. "What was that?"

"Unless I miss my guess," Keller said, "our ride's here." As he said it, he heard the bright familiar *clank* of a grenade leaving the barrel. A moment later, the ground fifty feet away erupted in an explosion of dirt and clay. People in the crowd screamed and started to scatter.

"BACK IN LINE!" the bearded guard screamed. He raised his weapon to fire at them. There was a sharp crack and he tumbled backward, the assault rifle falling from his suddenly slack hands. Keller turned to Walker. He was standing there with a look of uncomprehending shock on his face. He recovered quickly and raised the long-barreled pistol to fire at the crowd as Keller charged. Keller slammed into him as the gun discharged. The blow knocked him backward and the shot went wild as Walker stumbled. He kept hold of the gun, however, and as Keller wrapped his arms around him to drive him backward and bear him to the ground, he clouted Keller on the side of the head with the barrel. Keller's vision went red, tinged with black at the edges, and he felt himself slipping away, his grip on Walker failing. He slid to the ground, gasping. As he did, he reached out with a desperate grasp and grabbed for purchase. His hand closed on the hilt of the long blade hanging on Walker's belt, pulling it loose as he sank to his knees. He tried to slash at Walker with the blade, but the limb wouldn't respond. It felt like it belonged to someone else. He let the arm fall to his side.

Walker stepped back, a look of triumph on his face. "What is it they say?" he said. "Never bring a knife to a gunfight?" He raised the pistol to fire. As he did, the roar of an engine filled Keller's ears. He saw the bright blue MRAP strike Walker with a sickening crunch. Walker's body flew through the air, the gun flying from his hands. He landed in a heap a few feet away as the MRAP slid to a halt in a cloud of dust. Keller staggered to his feet, the knife still clutched in his hand. He stumbled over to where Oscar and his sons still stood atop the flimsy chairs. Through the haze of pain and concussion, he could hear the howling of police sirens. There was more gunfire. Some control was returning to his arms and hands, but it still seemed to take forever to saw through the ropes binding Oscar's hands behind him. When the rope parted, Oscar reached up and worked the noose away from his neck and over his head. He stepped down from the chair and gently took the knife from Keller's hand. "I'll take it from here, old friend."

"Thanks," Keller mumbled. He could still hear the sirens and the sounds of people shouting as he turned and walked back to where Walker lay on the ground. There was a brief volley of shots, he couldn't tell from who. Finally, he stood over the General. He was unconscious. Blood soaked the combat fatigues and one leg was twisted at an agonizing angle, but incredibly, the man was still breathing.

"You know what else they say, Walker?" Keller said. "Don't play in the fucking street." He heard someone walk up to stand beside him. He raised his eyes to see Castle there, holding the M4 in one hand. The other arm hung loosely by his side, the sleeve soaked with blood.

"You're wounded," Keller said.

"You should see the other guy," Castle responded.

"You got him?"

Castle shook his head. "I never got the chance. While he was drawing down on me, two of those guys from the crowd tackled him."

"He dead?"

"No, not yet. I had to threaten to drop another grenade on them to keep them from cutting his balls off. They'd gotten his pants off and everything. I think the folks here are a little bit mad at him."

"What about the other ones?"

"Sounds like they got into a firefight with some of my coworkers. Speaking of which…" He nodded in the direction the MRAP had come from. A pair of Sheriff's deputies were advancing on them, slightly crouched, pistols held out in front of them. One was older, with a fringe of gray hair around a sun-reddened scalp. The other looked barely old enough to shave. "ON THE GROUND!" the older one was yelling. "NOW!"

"Paul!" Castle called back. "Paul Gillespie! It's me! Ray Castle!"

The older one hesitated, then straightened up. "Ray?"

The younger one stayed in position. "He's Posey's cousin, Sarge," he said. "He may be in on this."

Gillespie raised the gun and crouched back down. "That true, Ray?"

"That I'm Posey's cousin? You know I am. Am I in on this? Guess that depends on what 'this' is. I could ask you guys the same question."

Gillespie stopped. "Who's that fella with you?"

"His name's Keller. The Sheriff tried to kill him. And me." He gestured around him. "He was mixed up with all this shit out here."

"You need to put the gun down," Gillespie said.

"Depends on whether or not you were in this with him, Paul," Castle said. He looked at the younger deputy. "Or you, Bobby."

"I don't want to have to shoot you, Ray," Gillespie said.

"I'd kinda hate that myself. Especially since if it looks like you guys were involved in holding people, working them against their will, and forcing some of them into prostitution, well..." he looked back, to where a group of the prisoners had reassembled. This time some of them were armed with rifles and machine guns taken from the fallen guards. They stared across the expanse of cleared ground at the deputies. "They might feel the need to shoot *you*."

Another pair of deputies walked up, guns drawn. Then another. The two groups faced each other, with Keller and Castle in the middle, standing over Walker's bleeding body.

"There doesn't have to be any more bloodshed," Keller called. "Let's all just stand down for a minute so we can talk this out. This guy needs medical attention, pronto."

There was no answer, only the sound of the MRAP's engine idling and the falling wail of a siren being turned off. Finally, Gillespie straightened up again. "Okay," he said. "We'll stand down. But you and those people have to as well."

"Okay," Castle said. He crouched down and put the M4 on the ground. The other deputies hesitated, then lowered their own weapons.

Keller glanced off to the side where Oscar was standing, with his arms around his sons. "Oscar," he said. "Can you tell those folks to put the guns down?"

Oscar started to say something in Spanish, his voice raised, when the older of the two boys tore himself out of his grasp. "NO!" he shouted. He began running to where Keller and Castle stood over Walker. "NO!" he screamed again as he bent down to scoop the pistol from where it had landed when Walker was struck.

"Ruben!" Oscar shouted. He was running toward them, his arms held out toward his son. Ruben raised the gun as he ran.

"No, kid," Keller shouted.

"He DIES!" Ruben screamed. "HE DIES!" He had almost reached them. Keller could see the tears running down his face. He looked up to see the deputies raising their weapons again. He leaped forward to grab up the boy in his arms. Ruben stopped and swung the pistol to face him. "He dies," he sobbed. "He is a monster."

"You get no argument from me, kid," Keller said. "But don't do it. You're not a killer."

Ruben began to advance again. "Don't try to stop me."

"Sorry," Keller said. "I have to." As he charged Ruben, the boy fired. Keller felt the round strike him like a hammer blow to his gut. The breath went out of him. He staggered, his knees turning to rubber beneath him, but he kept coming. Ruben raised the gun to fire again, but Keller was upon him. He wrapped the boy in his arms, pinning the gun against his own chest. He heard the deputies begin firing. *No. No.*

All other thought was slipping away from him. He used the last of his strength to spin around, putting his back between Ruben and the line of firing deputies. He felt another hammer blow to his back that knocked him forward. He fell, the boy beneath him, next to Walker's body. He heard Ruben cry out as Keller landed on top of him. The pain was all consuming, overtaking everything, filling the entire world until there was nothing else left in Keller's senses but agony. This time he welcomed the darkness as it took him all the way down.

CHAPTER FIFTY-SEVEN

HE FLOATED IN AN OCEAN of darkness, suspended between the surface and the abyss below. It was warm and comforting there, and calm. So calm. From time to time, he heard voices, muffled and sounding as if they were coming from far away. Once, he thought he heard someone calling his name. It was a female voice, one he felt he should know, but he couldn't place a name. He struggled weakly, trying to push himself toward the voice, but the dark water felt as thick as glue around him and he soon gave up, sinking a little deeper into the darkness. It would be so easy to simply let go, to sink down into the yawning warm blackness beneath, to rest at long last. He'd fought for so long, so hard, and he was so tired. He knew that above him was light, but somehow he knew there was also cold, and pain. Consciousness left him, an obliteration deeper than any sleep.

He awoke to the sound of voices, again saying his name. The ocean was brighter now, but colder. He felt himself rising up, up, and then the pain hit him and he groaned aloud. The pain and the sound of his voice shocked him awake.

He was lying in a bed, looking up at the pitted rectangles of a drop ceiling. He turned his head slightly to one side. The movement caused a spike of agony like a red-hot iron to pulse through his head from one temple to another. Everything hurt. When he tried to speak, all that came out was a dry croak.

"Easy, hon," a female voice said. "Take it slow."

He wanted to turn his head toward the voice, but he flinched away from the idea of causing himself any more pain. Eventually, after what seemed like an hour, he screwed up his courage and turned his head. The pain was still there, but there was less of it this time. He saw a set of shiny metal bed rails. He shifted his gaze slightly to look up and saw a curly-haired young woman wearing wire-rimmed glasses and dressed in a light blue pair of scrubs standing next to the bed. She was smiling at him.

"Welcome back, Mr. Keller," she said. "You gave everybody a heck of a scare for a while there." She reached down and took his wrist gently in her hands, her fingers expertly finding the pulse there. She nodded, then put the stethoscope in her ear. "Need to listen to your heart now," she said. She bent over and placed the stethoscope against his chest. She smelled wonderful, the clean scent of powder and skin bringing him the rest of the way back to awareness. She straightened up, still smiling. He wanted to take that smile home with him. He tried to say something, but his throat seemed to lock up.

"Don't talk right away," she said. "You were on a ventilator for a good long while. Your throat's going to hurt."

Swallowing proved she was right, but he needed to know. "Ruben," he said.

Her brow furrowed. "Who?"

He took a breath to try again. That hurt, too. "Ruben. Boy. Okay?"

She shook her head. "I don't know who you're talking' about, sweetie."

He sighed and took another tack. "Angela?"

"Now that, I can help you with," the nurse said. "She's been here off and on the past week. I think she just went down to get a cup of..."

"JACK!" he heard Angela's voice before he saw her. She almost knocked the nurse out of the way getting to the bedside. The nurse didn't seem to mind.

"He just woke up," she said. "Vitals are good. His throat's sore, and he's worn out, but he's making good progress."

Angela gripped the bedrails, her hands twisting on it as if she wanted to let go and embrace him but was afraid to. He didn't think he'd survive a hug, but he lifted a hand toward her. She took it as if she was afraid it would break. He gave her hand a weak squeeze.

"Hey," he croaked.

"Hey, yourself," she said. There were tears in her eyes.

"I'll leave you two alone," the nurse said. "Doctor Kensington should be along to see you in a bit."

"Jack," Angela said when she'd left. She gripped his hand as if she never wanted to let go. "I thought you were going to die."

"Ruben," Keller said. "He okay?"

She nodded. "He's fine. Oscar's fine. Edgar's fine. The boys are with me. But Oscar's in custody. Along with the rest of the people from the camp."

Keller shook his head. "Sorry."

She pulled out a handkerchief and wiped her eyes. "It's okay, Jack. The FBI's trying to figure out what to do with them."

"FBI?" Keller said. "How..."

"It's kind of a long story," she said. "And kind of weird, too. I met some very interesting people. I'll tell you more when you're feeling better."

He nodded weakly. The fatigue was beginning to overwhelm him. "Okay," he said. "Think...I'll sleep now."

"Okay," she said, and smiled. "Rest. Get well. I'm glad you're going to be okay."

"Love you," he said.

She squeezed his hand, fresh tears rolling down her face. "I love you, too," she mouthed without saying the words.

He slept.

WHEN HE AWOKE, THERE WERE two people he didn't know sitting by the bed. The male half of the duo was short, stocky, with dark hair beginning to go gray at the temples. His partner was a petite woman with a sharp, intelligent face and long jet-black hair pulled back in a ponytail that reached halfway down her back. They were dressed in dark suits that were as identical as a man's and a woman's suit could be.

The man made the introductions. "Mr. Keller," he said, "I'm Special Agent Tony Wolf, Federal Bureau of Investigation. This is my partner, Special Agent Leila Dushane."

Keller cleared his throat. "Am I under arrest?" he said. His voice felt stronger.

Wolf shook his head. "No," he said. "And there's very little chance that you're ever going to be."

The woman spoke up. "You've impressed some people, Mr. Keller. People who are kind of hard to impress."

"Glad to hear it," Keller said.

"We're here to interview you as a witness," Wolf said, "not as a potential defendant."

"Still," Keller said. "I'd like to have my lawyer present."

Wolf nodded. "Scott McCaskill, right? Fayetteville, North Carolina?"

Dushane chuckled at Keller's expression. "We did some homework, Mr. Keller. We can fly him down here, if you like."

"Let me get this straight," Keller said. "You're willing to fly my lawyer to...where the hell am I, anyway?"

"Charlotte," Wolf said. "You were choppered up here from Hearken."

"Let me put it this way, Mr. Keller," Dushane said, "if you wanted us to interview you on a beach in the Caribbean, with your lawyer present and pretty girls bringing you drinks with little umbrellas in them between questions, I get the feeling that Agent Saxon would find a way to make that happen."

"Who's Agent Saxon?" Keller asked.

"She's the one running this show," Wolf said, "and she's got some major juice from somewhere. When she says 'jump,' people go 'how high?'"

"Including the guy who's usually our boss," Dushane said, "and he's not usually one to jump any distance. At all."

"So let us know, Mr. Keller," Wolf said. "What's it going to take?"

Keller looked back and forth between the two. Then he said, "Okay. But I'd like to know a few things, too."

Wolf nodded. "I think I know what some of those may be." He held up a hand and ticked off the points on his fingers as he spoke. "The man you know as Oscar Sanchez and his sons…"

"Wait a minute," Keller said, "The 'man I know as Oscar Sanchez?' That's not his real name?"

"No," Wolf said. "His real name is Leonardo Santiago Rodriguez. Oscar Sanchez is the name on the papers he bought to get into the U.S."

Keller shook his head. "Well, I'll be damned."

"Anyway," Wolf went on, "he's in ICE detention. We're trying to make it as easy for him as we can, but he *is* illegal. The other prisoners at the Hearken camp are in custody as well. His sons are with his wife, Angela." Wolf ticked off another finger. "Deputy Ray Castle's been treated for his wounds and released. The guys from SLED—the South Carolina State police—were all over him for the killing of the Sheriff until Agent Saxon bigfooted them and got them to turn him loose, and his cousin with him. We've got agents all over that Sheriff's department, and we're turning up a gold mine of information about human trafficking, prostitution, drug-running into the States, you name it."

"The late Sheriff Cosgrove," Dushane said in a dry voice, "apparently thought that keeping meticulous records of all the nasty shit he was up to might be used as leverage against Walker someday." She shook her head. "Dumb bastard. But then, judging from some of the videos he saved on his hard drive, he was definitely one to let the little head think for the big one."

Wolf nodded. "Which brings us to Mr. Walker—also not his real name, incidentally—and his attempts to create a cracker Utopia in the South Carolina swamps. General Walker, the former Russell Samchalk, is currently in what is known as a 'persistent vegetative state' as a result of being hit by a large truck moving at high speed."

"If he ever recovers," Dushane said, "which is damned unlikely, he'll join the rest of his peckerwood militia in a Federal penitentiary."

"Does that answer your questions, Mr. Keller?" Wolf said.

"What about Auguste Mandujano?" Keller asked.

For the first time, Wolf looked troubled. "We don't know anything about what's going to happen to Mr. Mandujano."

"You're not going to just let him skate, are you?" Keller demanded. "He's the one behind all of this."

"We have reason to believe," Wolf said, "that it was one of his lieutenants, a Mr. Zavalo, who was behind the slavery operation."

"And Mr. Zavalo has mysteriously disappeared," Dushane said. "Presumed dead."

"Still," Keller said, "it's not like Mandujano has clean hands here."

"When I said we don't know what's going to happen to him," Wolf said, "I meant Agent Dushane and I."

"We're told by Agent Saxon that his fate is on a need to know basis," Dushane said, "and we need not to know. Her words."

"So," Wolf said, "now that we've satisfied your curiosity, can you satisfy ours?"

"On one condition," Keller said.

"I told you just giving him the 'where are they now' speech wouldn't be enough," Dushane said.

Wolf glared at her, then turned back to Keller. "What's your request, Mr. Keller?"

"The prisoners," he said. "The illegals. The ones you have in custody. Turn them loose. Let them stay here. Mr. Sanchez, or whatever his real name is, and the rest. They suffered to get here. Let them stay."

Wolf shook his head. "Can't do it."

"You said I could ask for anything."

"Even if we could waive all the requirements for citizenship," Wolf said, "they say they don't want to stay."

Keller remembered his earlier conversation with Oscar. *Look at this. Am I safe here? Is my family safe?*

Dushane shook her head sadly. "They've asked ICE to expedite their deportation. Including Mr. Rodriguez."

"His wife's going with him," Wolf said.

Keller went numb with shock. "What?"

Wolf nodded. "Yeah. That might take some doing. But she said she's going with her husband, and his sons. Says she wants to help raise them."

Dushane noticed the look on Keller's face. "Are you okay, Mr. Keller?"

"Yeah," Keller said. "Look, I'm worn out. I'll answer your questions. But not now. Now I just want to rest."

"We really need…" Wolf said.

Dushane interrupted him. "Boss," she said in a quiet voice. Her eyes were still on Keller's face. "We should come back another time."

Wolf looked from her to Keller, then back again. "Yeah," he said, and stood up. "We'll see you tomorrow, Mr. Keller. Rest now."

He didn't answer as they left.

CHAPTER
FIFTY-EIGHT

SHE SHOWED UP ON THE second day he was awake, as he was finally able to sit up on the edge of the bed after several attempts, all of them urged along by a steady succession of nurses. The effort left him sweating and gasping for breath. He looked up and saw her standing in the doorway. She was leaning on her cane, studying his face. "Hey," she said quietly.

"Well at least you came to say good-bye," Keller said.

She closed her eyes and sighed. "Jack, please. Don't make this any harder."

His short laugh sent jagged shards of pain through the muscles of his chest and back. It felt fitting. "Well," he said, "the last thing I want to do is make this any harder on *you*."

She opened her eyes. "I almost didn't come. I even wrote a letter. I knew you'd be angry. I knew you'd be bitter. I knew you'd say things that hurt, because I know how much this hurts you, and I didn't think I could stand it."

He picked a towel off the bed beside him and wiped the sweat from his brow. "So why did you come?"

"Because you deserve better than to hear it from someone else. You deserve more than a letter. That would make me a coward. I owe you at least the respect of saying what I have to say to your face."

He tossed the towel on the bed. "What's to say? I mean, I could have sworn you said you loved me. And I know I said it to you. And now, I guess…what? You changed your mind?"

She walked over and leaned on the back of the wooden chair that sat by the bed. "No," she said. "No, I didn't change my mind about loving you. I love you and I always will. But I made a promise. I made a promise to a good man. And he needs me."

"I need you." The words came out in a hoarse whisper before he could stop them.

"Maybe. But you need more than that. You need to run after people and kick doors in and take down the bad guys. You need to put yourself in the line of fire, like you did at that place in South Carolina. It's in your blood. You don't feel alive unless you're doing that. And I can't live like that, Jack. When they told me you'd been shot, they didn't expect you to make it. And when I heard that, I died inside. Not a little. Everything inside me turned to ashes."

"Does Oscar know that?" Keller said.

"No. He's still detained. We see each other once a week and we talk through the glass. He knows how I feel about you. But he knows I love him, too. In a different way, but I love him. He says we can learn to be happy together. We can settle down, live a quiet life, raise his sons."

"A quiet life," Keller said, in the voice of someone putting a name to a paradise he'd never see.

"Yes. A quiet life." She shook her head. "Jack, I can't go through this again. And if I stay with you, if I let myself go and love you the way you deserve, I will. Maybe not soon, but sometime, you'll find something else to chase, some bad guy that needs taking down and…" she gestured at the bed. "It'll be this all over again. I can't take it, Jack. I'm tough, I know I am, I've had to be, but I just…can't." She bowed her head. He tried to stand, to go to her, but his legs wouldn't hold him up. She saw him almost go down and rushed to him. He put his arms around her and held onto her like a drowning man. Gently, she lowered him back to a sitting position on the bed.

He looked up and saw her eyes were wet with tears. *I can change,* he wanted to say, but he knew it was a lie. He didn't want to lie to her. Not here, at the end.

There was a knock on the door. A thin, red-haired nurse in multicolored scrubs bustled in. She saw Keller sitting on the edge of the bed and beamed. "You're sitting up," she said. "Good." Then she took a closer look at his face and her smile slipped a couple of notches.

"You weren't tryin' to *stand* up, were you?"

"Yeah," Angela said, before he could answer. "He was. Sorry. My fault."

"Excuse me, hon," the nurse said, gently nudging Angela out of the way with her hip. "Lie back," she ordered. Keller complied, never taking his eyes off Angela. The nurse busied herself taking his vital signs.

"I'll let you get to work," Angela said to her, stepping away from the bed.

"Okay," the nurse said absently, not noticing the tears in Angela's eyes. "You have a good day, now."

"Are you coming back?" Keller said.

Angela shook her head. "Plane leaves tomorrow."

"Okay," Keller said, a lump welling up in his throat. "Stay safe."

"You, too." She hesitated for a moment. "Good-bye, Jack." She walked out, slowly, leaning on the cane.

"BP's up a bit," the nurse said, a line appearing between her eyes. "How's the pain?"

"Pretty bad," Keller said.

"You want something for it?"

He shook his head. "It won't help."

"It's up to you," she said. "Only thing that'll really make it better is time."

"Yeah," said Keller. "That's what I hear."

EPILOGUE

Auguste Mandujano awoke after midnight. He didn't know what had awakened him, but his hand went instinctively to the .357 Magnum revolver he kept under the pillow next to him. As his hand closed around the familiar grip, he came awake enough to recognize the scent that filled the room. It was a scent he knew well, the scent of raw meat. Meat and blood. There was something in the bed with him, a large lumped shape. When he moved, the sheets were wet and sticky.

He heard something moving in the hallway and sat up, pointing the pistol at the open door. Where the hell were his guards?

A shadow filled the doorway. The shape didn't register at first. It was the wrong height and width to be a human. Another smell assailed his nostrils, a scent that awakened a primal fear deep in the oldest part of the brain—the scent of big cat. He realized then what the lump in his bed was—a large, bloody haunch of raw meat.

The shadow drew nearer, raised a great shaggy head, and as the intruder stepped into a shaft of moonlight coming through the window, Auguste Mandujano looked into the golden eyes of a five-hundred pound African lion.

His breath caught in his throat and he froze. Then he screamed in terror, a high, shrill scream like a woman's. His scream was answered with a deep guttural roar from the lion. Mandujano pulled the trigger on the pistol, again and again.

The hammer clicked on one empty chamber after another as the lion roared again and leaped.

OUTSIDE IN THE DARKNESS, IN the shadow of the garden wall, stood two men, dressed in black combat fatigues without insignia. Their eyes were obscured by the night vision goggles they wore. One of them, a short, muscular black man with a shaved head who had recently been part of Mandujano's mercenary security detail, cocked his head to listen as the screams from within the house suddenly ceased.

"Bad kitty," he said.

"Actually," the other man said, "I feel kind of bad for the poor beast." The other man was taller, and slender. Until recently he'd been working as a "cultural attaché" at the U.S. Consulate, where everyone had known him as Mr. Huston. He'd shaved off his beard and moustache. "He'll probably be killed when they discover what he's done. But he's only following his programming. Once I saturated Mandujano's sheets with lion pheromones, and you placed that raw meat in the bed, he couldn't help himself."

"That cat was either going to fight Mandujano or fuck him, huh?" the shorter man laughed. "I guess he got the lesser of the two evils."

A voice crackled in their earpieces, a country twang that belonged to the man who'd recently been wearing the uniform of a Marine medic. "You boys about ready to haul ass?" The two men by the gate acknowledged. "Awright then. Pickup in thirty seconds. Be there or be square."

The two men slipped silently out of the gate, but not before the taller man bent down and placed their calling card in the walkway.

It was a children's toy, a small iron horse.

SIX WEEKS LATER

THE DOOR TO THE BAR swung open. "Hey, hon," the bartender said as she looked up from where she'd been reading a newspaper behind the bar. "First customer of the…" the smile on her face died as she saw who it was. "Well," she said without warmth. "Look what the cat dragged in."

Keller walked over and took a stool. He moved slowly, lowering himself onto the stool as if he were afraid it would grow spikes. Jules's eyes widened as she saw how thin and drawn he looked.

"Jesus," she said, "What the hell happened to you?" Then her face closed up again as she remembered she was angry at him.

"Long story," Keller said.

"Well, I ain't in the mood for any long stories," she said. "What do you want?"

"A beer," Keller said. "And I was wondering if there were any job openings."

Her jaw tightened. "You expect to just walk back in here, after walkin' out on me, and leavin' me high and goddamn dry, and just have everything be the way it was?"

"No," Keller said. "I'm not expecting anything. I just thought I'd ask."

"I'll think about it," she said. She pulled a Shiner Bock out of the cooler, popped the top, and set it in front of him.

"Okay," Keller said. "And by the way, I'm sorry."

"Sorriest thing I've seen in a while," she said. She looked him up and down. "You look like forty miles o' bad road."

Keller didn't answer. She started rubbing down the already immaculate bar top, not looking at Keller. He sat and drank his beer, slowly.

"Okay," she said finally. "It's only 'cause I can't find anyone else to do the job worth a damn, but you can have it back."

"Thanks."

"But don't think you're gettin' back in my bed again. I know better this time."

"All right."

"I never shoulda slept with the help, anyway. And that's all you are from now on. The help. You get it?"

"Okay," he said.

Her composure slipped a little. "You hurt me, Jack Keller."

"I know," he said. "Again, I'm sorry."

She looked at him doubtfully. "You sure you're up for the job? You don't hardly look like you can lift yourself out of bed."

"I'm getting better," he said. "Every day. It's just going to take some time."

She laughed. "Well, time's somethin' we got plenty of around here."

THE END

ACKNOWLEDGEMENTS

First and foremost, many thanks to my editor, Jason Pinter, whose response to my e-mail query "you interested in re-issuing the first three Jack Keller novels?" was "You want to write a fourth one?" You are holding the answer to that question in your hands. I hope you enjoyed it.

Second: Since 1996, I've written a weekly column for my local newspaper, the Southern Pines *Pilot*. The fact that I write a very liberal column in a very conservative area lands me on some, shall we say, interesting e-mail lists. One of my most persistent correspondents is a fellow who always signs off with the words "RACE SURVIVAL DEMANDS RACISM." He and many of the sites he sends me links to are the inspiration for the Church of Elohim. The Church itself is fictional, but those ideas and the people who espouse them actually exist. I only wish they were totally made up.